I, Never Lie

I
NEVER
LIE

JODY SABRAL

CANELO

First published in the United Kingdom in 2018 by Canelo

This edition published in 2019 by

Canelo Digital Publishing Limited
57 Shepherds Lane
Beaconsfield, Bucks HP9 2DU
United Kingdom

A CIP catalogue record for this book is available from the British Library.

Print ISBN 978 1 78863 392 5
Ebook ISBN 978 1 78863 114 3

Look for more great books at www.canelo.co

Printed and bound in Great Britain by Clays Ltd, Elcograf S.p.A.

For BD and JP

Prologue

27 February 2018

A third woman has been found dead in an east London park after being discovered by a dog walker early on Thursday morning. The victim is believed to be in her late thirties. The body was found close to the children's play area in London Fields.

The man who discovered the body refused to be named but said, 'She was lying face down in the wooded area when Hovis, my dog, found her earlier this morning. It's not something you expect to see when walking your dog. She was wearing vintage-style clothes like most people around here. It was a truly horrid sight. I've never seen anything like it. I'm not sure I'll ever be the same person again. It's an image I will never forget.'

The police are appealing for anyone who was in the London Fields area on Thursday night after nine o'clock to call the crime helpline on 0800 121 121.

More details to follow...

1

Spring 2018

There's a man in my bed. Shit. It's not what I was expecting. They have usually gone by now, but this one, well, he's different. He stayed the night, probably in the hope of securing a second shag. A mix of sweat and pine-fresh-infused sheets hovers in the hot, dry air between us. The heating came on an hour ago. It's too high but I haven't figured out how to change the settings yet. I keep meaning to, but, well, it's one of those small things I don't seem to get round to, you know what I mean? I wish I had, though. I literally feel like I'm baking in my own skin this morning.

My initial concerns about coming face to face with a stranger in the cold light of day are concealed by the darkness. The blackout blind I bought online last month to help with my poor sleep patterns was a savvy investment. There's a lot to be said for good lighting or no lighting at my age – 39 today. Shit, that's right, it's my birthday. Not that he knows. I don't give away personal details to men I shag casually or who I meet online.

His arm reaches around my waist as he snuggles up close, spooning me, which spikes my body temperature further. Moments later, his nose lightly brushes my cheek like a playful, affectionate puppy. Then comes the money move. He's running his fingers along my shoulder, down my back, around my tummy to where the sun shines. A tender kiss caresses the back of my neck at the same time, and bingo! My head is throbbing and my body aches, but this is helping to stir some energy within.

I want to reach my hand around his back to pull him closer – that's about all I can muster this morning after the big night out – but I soon realise that I can't, because it's tied to something. Tied to something? What the…? Panic starts to rise inside me and I try to vocalise it, but I can't because the fear is so real and I have no energy, not even for that. My body is spent on the booze I packed away last night. The darkness feels like my own worst enemy now. Sensing my fear, he puts a hand over my mouth and shushes me. He's got me where he wants me. I can't see what is around my wrist, but it's keeping me from any escape I might have wanted to make. I struggle for a moment, which seems to turn him on. Once he is sure I won't talk, he goes down between my legs, and I hate to say it but this scenario is turning me on. I've never been tied up before, but it is oddly erotic. I let the initial fear go and submit to the unknown. Maybe today will be the day.

It doesn't take long before he's building up to an orgasm. I must have told him last night that I was on the pill, my usual line, so he's going for it, completely oblivious to my real motives. Moments later, he's holding me down by my throat, telling me how much he wants to fuck my brains out. I was enjoying it until this bit, but now his grip is a little too tight for comfort. I struggle, but he's strong and I can't move under his weight. He is thoroughly enjoying dominating me, but I'm unsure now because he seems to have crossed a line. Is this where it goes horribly wrong and my body is found in the park? I'm finding it difficult to breathe. Is he strangling me?

To my relief, he lets out a sigh and his body shudders before relaxing into the zone of true contentment that only comes from releasing his two million swimmers into my body. His grip releases and I'm left gasping for air. That was close. I thought he was going to hurt me, but it was just a play. The things I'll put myself through to become pregnant have reached epic proportions. I can't afford fertility treatment, so I'm stuck with shagging strangers. I focus on the result, not the means, but I wonder if I really want the child of a man into domination sex.

On average, only one million sperm go the 15 centimetre distance to a woman's uterus and reach the egg, which is okay. It only takes one. He's lying on his back, as am I, staring at the ceiling with his hands behind his head, breathing like he's just run a marathon. I hope his sperm do. I feel the sweat on my chest and can only imagine what my hair looks like, but I am content that the race to my uterus is on.

'That was great, Alex. You're a real woman, you know that.'

Next thing I know, he's untying my wrists. I feel like I've crossed a line too, but am not really sure what line it is or what it means. I've got what I wanted: the possibility of conceiving my own little critter. At my age, I haven't got the time not to be doing this. Once I'm free, he stands and stretches his broad shoulders before searching on the floor for his underwear, which is a relief. I thought he might want to do breakfast.

In the dim light, an angel spreads its wings across his back. A tattoo. It's sexy. Tough, yet gentle. An indication of the qualities his offspring might have? I realise in this moment that I have little recollection about last night and how I got into such a position. I must have been completely wasted, to the point where I blacked out. That happens more often than I'd like to admit, and the scary part is I can still walk, talk and do stuff.

He pulls the blind up to look for his clothes, and I can see his reflection out of the corner of my eye in the mirrored wardrobe that runs the width of the room. He is a good-looking man, but not in a clichéd way. He has character. He runs his hands through his messy dark brown hair, attempting to tame it, but the effort is futile. He has a round face, a warm and friendly face. In fact, he's a babe. Suddenly self-conscious, I wrap the crumpled white cotton sheet around my naked body to protect myself from his gaze.

'Jesus. Did we drink this?' He has a half-empty bottle of vodka in his right hand. 'It was under the end of the bed.'

I honestly can't remember. 'I guess we might have done...'

'Wow, that was some night, Alex.'

Greg, my ex-fiancé, used to find bottles. We split up last year after he kicked me out, which was tough. He said I had a drink problem, but I don't. I like a drink, but then so do millions of people every day. I have a good job. That's not how people with drink problems live. I haven't seen Greg since I came to London nine months ago. It's been hard moving on, because I really loved him, more than I've ever loved anyone, but he was unable to get past what happened.

I'm trying my best to move forward. To heal. It's not easy. I'm sure you know how that feels.

I like this guy's style. He's wearing a black and yellow checked shirt over a white T-shirt, and has just slipped his feet into a pair of black and white striped Converse. I might not have taken so much notice of his footwear, but Greg had exactly the same ones. They came out two years ago, and I bought them for his birthday the same week. It's funny how objects can become reminders of the past and take on an almost spiritual sentimentality.

He's leaning over to kiss my forehead, which is awkward, but only for the simple reason that I really just want him to go.

'I had a great time, Alex. Here, shall I give you my number?' His phone is in his hand.

I pull myself up slowly to deliver the bad news.

'I had a great time too. It was lovely. But I'm not really looking for a relationship right now'

'Right. Yeah, of course. I mean, me neither. I just... I'd like to see you again, if only like this.'

'That's nice, but seriously, you really don't need to.'

'Right.' He's hovering by the bed awkwardly. I'm trying my best to remember his name.

'Nigel... do you have the Uber app? It's still quite early, isn't it?'

He looks away and clears his throat, then looks back and I think for a brief moment that I've got his name wrong. It wouldn't be the first time.

'Don't worry. I don't live very far. I'll get going, shall I?'

I smile softly and feel a bit guilty momentarily. But when the front door slams, I feel relieved. Free from another person's expectations, quite literally. I'm prepared to have my mind changed on this should I meet the right man, but he hasn't come along since I left Greg. I've resigned myself to the fact that he may never come along, which is why I'm just getting on with my own baby plans. I think being a mother would be the making of me. It would help me sort my shit out.

2

It's a little after eight o'clock. I spread out in bed and stretch my body like a cat, hoping to fend off the cramp in my legs. I really need to drink more water. I check my phone for any messages or news alerts. It's the first thing I do every day: check the headlines to see if there's a gem of a story out there to pitch to the editors. I work freelance at the moment because no one is giving out staff contracts in my industry, which has its own worries. But such is the world we live in now. There just isn't any security.

It's a little difficult checking the headlines on the smashed screen, which I really need to fix, and I will, soon. There is a long list of notifications awaiting my response. Most of them are from the dating site I subscribe to, COMEout. It's already buzzing.

Mr Right sent you a message at 6:34

Hey. Morning, gorgeous, sleep well?

Big Bad Ben sent you a message at 7:48

Can I be your slave?

It's crazy the number of people who are looking for love online before breakfast. The era of social media has changed the game. Mr Right can spell and punctuate properly, which is a win. When I first started using dating apps, I was surprised by just how many people are unable to string a proper sentence together. Education in this country has really slipped.

I have thought about quitting online dating, just as I do constantly about drinking, but I can't do either because I'm running out of time on the fertility scale. And even though the drinking isn't helping that side of things, it helps me in other ways that are just as important. It fulfils something in me. The void left by Greg and our unrealised plans.

I've switched the kettle on, but the vodka bottle that was in the bedroom is now in my hand. I consider the coffee option but give up just as quickly. Hair of the dog is a much quicker and easier cure. It'll help put me right for the day.

I've been in London a year now, but developing a network of friends has been challenging. There's Annabel, who worked as my producer for a few months until she had a baby. We've stayed in touch, in the hope that one day I'll have a playmate for her little ball of happiness. Then there's Charlie, my good-looking, well-meaning neighbour, who like me wants to have a child. Such is life approaching forty. I really should get out more, join some local clubs, but work is so demanding. Not that I mind. I love my job. So I reply to Mr Right because it's the simple option. Much more straightforward than meeting people in real life. It's immediate, and I like that.

His status shows him online, but a reply never materialises. Thankfully my phone rings, which stops me obsessing about it.

'Happy birthday, Alex!'

'Annabel! Thank you.'

Baby Marlow is cooing in the background.

'So how's it feel to be another year closer to middle age?'

'Not bad, considering.'

'Does that mean you're shagging someone?'

'I didn't wake up alone today.' I don't divulge the details of my initiation into the world of bondage.

'You go, girl. Did he have good genes?'

'Not bad. Bought at TK Maxx for a third of the original price.'

We both laugh at that.

'What I wouldn't give to go shopping and buy some new jeans. This little one is an economic black hole. I can't remember the last time I treated myself.'

I feel a pang of jealousy at this flippant complaint. What *I* wouldn't give to spend money on my own child. I stroke my stomach, remembering with fondness how happy I was carrying Greg's baby, a year ago. It's crazy really, how much life can change in a year. I'm okay, I'm getting over it, but I still think about him sometimes. It's a process. Letting go, that is. Of what you thought was going to be your life forever. I take another swig of vodka. It helps kill those thoughts. Living in regret is the last thing I need.

'Got any plans? Anyone else in the picture?'

'Well, actually... I have a date later.'

'No stopping you, is there? Same guy?'

Annabel and I haven't seen each other since she had the baby, but we talk as if we are next-door neighbours. Such is life since we connected on Facebook. She knows what I ate for lunch and I know how much sleep she's had.

'Someone else. Met him on a dating site. We've been chatting for a few weeks. He wants a family.'

'That's a good start, but don't you think you should be careful about meeting men on dating sites right now?'

'I am careful.'

'Yeah, I know you are. I'm just saying. There's been another murder. Have you seen the news?'

'No?'

'They found a woman in Hackney this morning. Not far from where you live. Twitter is going nuts. That's the third in the space of a month, which kind of implies it could be a serial killer, doesn't it?'

'Are they connected? Have they said that?'

'Not yet, but it's all over the news. She was found in a park, left for dead, or at least that's what people are saying on Twitter. Just like the others.'

'Where in Hackney?'

'London Fields. Switch the news on.'

Annabel is still talking, but I am only half listening. I grab my pink and green silky Chinese dressing gown off the antler-shaped hooks nailed to the wall and leg it to the lounge, stepping over piles of laundry and boxes I still haven't unpacked to reach the TV. The screen takes a moment to warm up, but when it does, I see my main competitor, Laura MacColl, standing in front of a white forensics tent. The strapline reads: BREAKING NEWS: WOMAN FOUND DEAD IN HACKNEY, LONDON. There is no more information.

'That's London Fields. It's less than half a mile from me. I walk there all the time. I probably passed that spot last night. Who is the woman? Do we know?'

'They haven't released a name yet.'

'Shit. I should probably call work.'

'Alex, it's your birthday. Today should be about you, not work.'

'A woman is dead less than half a mile from my flat and you think I'm not going to cover the story? I mean, that's lunchtime *and* teatime bulletin-worthy. It's huge.'

It's what I've been waiting for, not that Annabel can understand. She's been out of the game for a while and my career has been on the slide since my on-camera episode, so I need this more than anything.

There's a pause before she responds. 'I suppose you're right. I wouldn't be able to not do it, if it were my patch. But be careful. You know how editors are. One minute you're in favour, the next you're not. You said it yourself. I don't want you getting hurt again. How is work, by the way?'

'It's fine.'

'I haven't seen you on the bulletins much recently.'

'They've had me doing some research on an investigative report about human trafficking.'

It's a lie. I haven't been on the bulletins since I was drunk on camera. She knows it. I know it. Everyone who watched the evening bulletin that day knows it. But it's not the end of the world. Life moves on quickly in the news business. I can bounce back and this is just the story to do that. I have another swig of vodka. I'm feeling perky now, so I lean over and switch the kettle on. A coffee will put me right.

At that moment, my phone buzzes so I put Annabel on loudspeaker and swipe the screen. A message has arrived from Mr Right.

> Mr Right sent you a message at 09:35

> **Playing with myself because I can't find the right woman. Could you be she? I like it up the arse.**

It's a good job Annabel can't see my face, because I feel it contort. I block his profile with one tap of the screen. That's the advantage of online dating: you can remove people from your world as quickly as you connect with them.

'So why don't you take the initiative and call the news-room? It would be weird if you didn't. I mean, you living in London Fields and all. Just call it in.'

'I think I will.' Better than staying home. I look around me, wondering where it all went wrong. The walls are a non-descript magnolia. The place really needs painting. There are boxes littered about. No pictures on the walls, only the one of a rainforest that was here already. The flat looks like someone just moved in two weeks ago.

'Right. I really should get on.'

'Okay. Have a fab day. I know you will. Lots of love.'

The kettle has boiled, so I make a very strong coffee before I call work.

'Hello. News desk.' It's Heidi, one of the lunchtime bulletin producers. Luckily she likes me.

'Hi, Heidi. I just saw the news about the body in London Fields. You know I live less than half a mile from the crime scene? I could be there in twenty minutes.'

'Oh, really?'

'Yes. I mean, do you need someone to cover it? I know the area really well too.'

'Hang on a minute. I think we may have sent someone. Isn't it your day off?'

'Well, yes, but really I don't mind. You know us free-lancers, we'll take all the work we can get.'

She laughs. She's a freelancer too, so this strikes a chord.

'Hang on.'

She puts me on hold. I can feel the adrenalin pumping through my veins. I'm nervous, but excited too. They have to use me. It would be ridiculous not to. She's back in a matter of moments.

'Hi, Alex. I need to talk to the editors, can't seem to find them at the mo. I think we may have already put someone on the story, to be honest.'

'Look, it's literally on my doorstep. I know east London like the back of my hand. I can handle this, I definitely can.' I wonder if I sound desperate, but then who cares. I need this. Keenness goes a long way in my line of work.

'Give me five. I'll come back to you.'

She hangs up. I look down at my hands. They are shaking. The thought of being on TV again is terrifying, but I've started the ball rolling now so I've got to see it through.

In less than five minutes she calls back as promised. I'm positively buzzing now at the thought of being on air again, and although my body is aching after last night, the hangover is quickly becoming a thing of the past. The vodka really sorted me out. I've had an Alka-Seltzer too, and coffee. I'm good to go.

'Just spoke to Marysia on the lunchtime bulletin. She's happy for you to cover the story. She said she needs you down there as soon as possible.'

'Great! Thank you, Heidi. You're a real gem, you know that.'

'We can have a crew there in an hour. I'll send you an email with the details.'

'Okay. On my way.'

She hangs up. And just like that, I'm back in the game. What a coup. I haven't felt this good since I moved to London. It's like I've been given a second chance. Best get ready and make myself look super-sharp. Need to give the competition a run for *her* money. Laura MacColl may look the part, but she's young and less experienced, a bit like the reporter they had on during the previous murder: some twenty-something up-and-coming know-nothing. But now there's a third victim, they obviously want someone with better news judgement. Someone the viewers can trust.

It's a terribly sad and frightening tale, women being slain and left in parks – feels a bit Jack the Ripper – but ironically I have a sense of optimism in my step because this is exactly what I need. A lead story to sink my teeth into. The adrenalin that comes with the prospect of live broadcast is stirring in me. It's a real confidence boost.

Just then, the doorbell sounds, an annoying interruption that I choose to ignore, but whoever it is isn't going away. There's a loud knocking on the door by what I can only imagine is a giant.

'Okay. Okay. I'm coming!' I've just about managed to get my feet through some jeans without falling over when it chimes a third time.

In the hallway, Charlie's red mountain bike is covered in dried mud. I squeeze past it and glance back towards his flat. The Green Party sticker on the door looks like it's moving. Wow, I'm still pretty messed up from last night. When I finally open the front door, the courier is walking away casually. Given the effort I've just made to indulge him, I shout after him.

'Hello...?' It's a bit brisk out, but the sunshine warms my face, adding to my upbeat mood.

'Ah, sorry. I thought no one was home.' His stride is charismatic, but sadly his shoes are not. 'Name?'

'Alex South.'

'Sign here, please?' Flashing perfectly formed teeth, he holds up the electronic device in his right hand. I sign with my index finger, then he passes over the package and is gone within seconds. I wonder how many people have touched that screen this week and feel disgusted by the idea of it. Must remember to wash my hands, though that's the least of my worries.

The parcel is small and light. I guess it could be a birthday gift, but from whom? Annabel? Surely she would have told me? Intrigued, I go back inside, excited by the prospect and completely forgetting about the bad hygiene of touch-screen technology. Today isn't turning out that bad so far.

On TV, a news conference is just beginning, so I pop the parcel down for a moment and grab a notebook from my bag, hoping that I can glean something before leaving the house. According to the strapline, DI Brook is the lead detective on the investigation. I've met him at press conferences before, which is a bonus and will make reporting the story much easier. He's quite good at sharing his insights into the cases he's working on. DI Brook is a handsome man, olive-skinned and extremely well groomed, though he isn't really my type. There is, however, an attractive air of confidence about him.

'This morning a dog walker discovered a body in London Fields, Hackney. We would really appreciate the public's help. An information line has been set up that I would urge you to contact should you recognise these clothes.'

An image appears on screen of a muddied blue hoody, a navy and white striped T-shirt, a red skirt and white Converse laid out on grass in clear plastic bags. They must have removed them from the victim in order to do that. God, they must be really worried.

'We are appealing to anyone who was in the area last night to come forward so that we can gather as much information as possible. Please don't feel nervous about contacting us. It is important that we find the perpetrator as soon as possible. We believe this may be connected to two previous attacks that have taken place in east London this year.'

And there it is. Confirmation by the police that all three murders are connected. How ghastly. It chills me to think that there is some nutter out there plucking women off the face of the earth, but the upside is that this story will reignite my career. Put me at the top of the news bulletin. I see the vodka bottle on the counter as half full for a change, instead of half empty. The voice in my head is telling me to have one last swig, but the reporter in me knows I really need to not fuck up this opportunity, so I screw the lid on tight and stash the bottle somewhere I will forget.

To take my mind off the drink, I turn my sights to the surprise parcel. A blessing in disguise. There's just enough time to open it before I have to go, so I tear into the padded envelope. Under the outer layer, there's a gift-wrapped box. As I thought, a birthday present. Once I've removed the gold paper and red ribbon, I find a box of chocolates; specifically Milk Tray. I'm absolutely gobsmacked by this and check the envelope for any clue as to who sent it, although I already have a niggling feeling that I know who it's from.

There is a typed note. It reads: *Because the lady loves…*

The excitement of covering the story has suddenly drained from me and been replaced by a mix of heady hope and nervous anxiety. I am forced to sit down and take stock. Milk Tray was a joke shared by Greg and me. Every year on my birthday he would religiously buy me a box and write a card that said exactly the same thing, though the message would always end with 'me': *Because the lady loves… me.* I'm left feeling confused, propelled back to the raw emotions I thought I'd quashed by moving to London. Staring at the card, I realise those feelings are still there, simmering under the surface as if we spoke yesterday.

I find the bottle I've just stashed and take one more swig of vodka, knowing this time it's not hair of the dog. It's to numb the anxiety. The past is never that far away.

3

Dear Diary,

It's funny, isn't it, how one person can bring about so much change in your life. Of course I guess deep down it depends on whether you truly desire to change. That's what they say, don't they? That it's down to your personality. Maybe I was ripe for change even though I wasn't aware when it happened. Meeting Alex was the key. I guess I might have gone on drinking myself to death had we never met, but we did, and the world looks very different now. Life is better than it has ever been and that's because for the first time in my life I have a genuine friend. Someone who gets it. Who gets me.

I met Alex a week ago in the park in town and I suddenly have a new sense of direction in my life. I want to stop drinking. To get sober. I've never spoken about my addiction before. Not to anyone. In fact, up until now I didn't even know I had a problem because it has had its hold on me since I was really young and that's a complex thing. When the only thing you know is drinking, it takes over. Becomes your reality. Becomes the norm. It took Alex to point out that it isn't the norm. And from that moment on, it's like a light went on, because we made a connection. I now know that I have absolutely no confidence in myself. And honestly, I guess I never have. It's why I've never done anything with my life.

Alex is inspiring. She knows lots of things about everything. She's so full of life and so worldly. I, on the other hand, am too embarrassed to admit that I've never left Manchester. Not even for one night. But then my days just roll into one, because I drink them away. Time is unaccountable in my life. The first thing I'm going to do when I get sober is travel. Get out of here, see somewhere new. Maybe the capital. Who knows?

It was funny how we met, almost as if it was meant to be, if you believe in that sort of thing. I was due to start my shift at the pub, but that day I was running late. I'd had another argument with Mum and felt really low, so I went to the park in town to chill before work. It takes about an hour to walk there, which always sorts me out. So I was sitting in my quiet place, a bench next to the railway track with the loving inscription 'To my darling wife Lydia who loved to sit here and think. Forever yours, George' carved on it. It's so touching that someone would make such a public declaration of love and commit to it in this way.

It's nothing like my family, who show zero affection towards each other. It's almost as if we are allergic to it. Perhaps for that reason this bench has always been my favourite place to sit and think about life. Not that I do all that much thinking, to be honest. I come here to watch the trains rumble past and wonder what kind of people Lydia and George were. Even in the middle of winter I sit here with my bottle of gin. It's much easier to think about their lives than look at my own. It's become a habit. Like a stuck record. A way of coping.

Anyway, it was a bitterly cold morning, the day we met. I could see my breath, that's how cold it was. But the bottle of gin wrapped in a paper bag in my hands was helping to keep me warm. I'd seen her before, walking through the park, but we'd never said hello. She always seemed in a hurry, on her way from one place to another. And always dressed in cool clothes. She looked like the kind of woman I might like to be, if I'd had a different life. She never lingered in the park like me, which was how, on that day, I knew something had changed. And I was right.

On that day, she sat down on the bench beside me wearing a scruffy leather jacket and asked for a light. Her lips were blue from the cold and her posture was different. She looked defeated, like me. I recognised myself in her that day, and that was strange. Maybe she'd seen me before, I don't really know. I like to think she had. That she had noticed me just as I had her. I could see from her face that she had worries too, but I didn't want to pry so I didn't say anything. What was I going to say anyway to someone like her?

So I sat in her company until her cigarette was almost done. And that's when she started crying. A silent cry. The kind that displays a hidden sadness. I thought I could cheer her up and offered her some gin. She took it, but instead of drinking it, she emptied the bottle onto the frosted ground, saying nothing. My first reaction was disbelief: she had just taken my lifeline away, not long before I had to go to work. I wanted to say something but I didn't, I just froze like the ground beneath our feet. Then she got up and walked away.

The act took me aback because it was such a confident statement: to take something that belonged to someone else and destroy it. I've never seen anyone do that before, take charge of a moment so definitively. In fact, it changed something in me. I felt respect, respect for her and her conviction. I even wished I had that kind of confidence myself. That I could take control of my life the way she just had. I think that was the moment that changed everything.

In the days that followed, I returned to my bench, waiting to see if she would turn up, but she didn't. She didn't come back.

21

After that, my thoughts of Lydia and George were replaced by thoughts of her. Who was she? Why had she thrown away my gin? In fact, I thought about it so much I even started to believe it wasn't real, that I'd imagined it. But today, on the seventh day after we met, she appeared again, holding out her hand. 'I'm Alex,' she said, and she asked me to go somewhere with her. I went willingly, to a room beneath a church where there were other people like me. Alcoholics. And I knew when I got home tonight that things would never be the same.

4

'Watch it!'

An angry voice alerts me to the reflective Lycra strip that has just whizzed by within inches of me, forcing me to jump back on the wet pavement. I'm left shaken, adding to the already self-perpetuating state of anxiety I find myself in thanks to my pending appearance on national television and the birthday surprise from Greg. My past has manifested itself in my present after I spent a year trying really hard to stop it from doing so. I eventually float across the road as if having an out-of-body experience. I'm still not quite right after last night. I will be, though. Just need to make it through the lunchtime bulletin.

The sun has graced Hackney this morning, casting ghostly shadows from stark leafless trees across the damp streets. It's still chilly out. I pull my tweed blazer tight around my black silk chiffon blouse, wishing I'd worn something warmer. It's definitely not the kind of day to spend lingering in a park. A thought that brings me back to the story. I must get back to that, my career, and push the thoughts of Greg aside.

As I turn down Navarino Road, my hands reach for the warmth of my pockets. The left one finds a couple of dusty aspirin. I neck them, which isn't all that easy without water, but it's not the first time I've done this. There's also a piece of sugar-free gum, which I shove in my mouth hoping it'll help with the anxiety. I realise I haven't done a top story for months now, not since I fucked up on air.

I need to get myself together before I get to the Fields. Can't let the crew see me bent out of shape. This really is a second chance and I need to not screw it up. I guess I could blame my mood on the weather, which fooled me into thinking spring had arrived.

On this stretch, the three-storey houses set back behind their large front gardens seem much less welcoming than they did just twenty-four hours ago. The trees that hang over the street, which I once viewed as protectors, feel complicit in a murder, which is utterly nonsensical. Trees and buildings can't kill, can they? They can't drag someone out into the middle of a park and leave them for dead.

It's almost eleven o'clock. The crew should be here by now. The walk and the fresh air have helped, but I'll need to get some drink in me after the bulletin or I'll tank and that won't be good. I know what I need to do. I need to make sure I've got just enough alcohol in my blood that I'm neither pissed nor hung-over. It's quite a challenge on days like this, but I'll manage it. I'm not going to make the same mistake twice. The episode that halted my rising career was down to me not paying attention to this small but critical detail. The day it happened, I'd reached my tipping point too early. Had a lunchtime drink with some colleagues, which on top of my daily intake led to a painful exposé on air of my inebriation. It was a total failure on my part. Since then, I've implemented a strict rule never to drink socially with people at work.

As I turn the corner towards the park, there are two police cars, two ambulances and a TV satellite truck parked by the entrance to the Fields. It's not like I haven't seen a crime scene before – I've been to plenty in my line of work – but to see it on your own doorstep, well, it's unsettling. There's a deeply unpleasant ring to it all.

In what now feels like an episode of *Black Mirror*, a silver Range Rover playing Radiohead's *Karma Police* excessively loudly stops at the zebra crossing. The tattoo-covered driver smiles to let me cross and I manage a polite nod to say thanks. I'm still puzzled by the chocolates. Truly puzzled. I mean, why now?

Once through the park gates, I follow the asphalt path past the tennis courts, up a small incline and around a bend to the left, where I'm met by a frail-looking woman slumped on a bench sipping from a can of Special Brew. She's wearing a Rolling Stones T-shirt. Even the drunks in this neighbourhood have a hint of hipster about them. She probably found it at the clothes bank on the opposite side of the park. That's where I dump my old clothes. Dropped off a bag end of last summer. In fact, the closer I get to her, the more I think she's wearing *my* old T-shirt. It had a tear in the neckline and hers has the same. It was a gift from Greg, the last reminder of him I'd kept since moving south. On today of all days, I see my past once again staring me in the face.

'Terrible business, that woman dying here. I saw it, you know.'

She speaks to me with boozy breath. Her accent isn't local. It's Brummie. She's drunk, but maybe she really did see something. Maybe she sleeps in the park.

'What did you see?'

'Saw her with my own eyes.'

'Have you told the police?'

'Fuck the police.'

Flinging the now obviously empty can of Special Brew onto the path, she stands next to me readying to leave. Her face has changed. She looks like she might swing for me, so I take a step back.

'It's you. You. Leave me alone. Get away... I'll call the police. See, they're coming... they are coming.' She sets off in the opposite direction on unsteady feet.

The interaction hasn't helped with my nervous disposition. A couple walking towards me with their dog are amused by the scene and smile in that knowing way at me. The smile that says she's crazy and we're not, but I can't smile because she's wearing one of my once most prized possessions. I feel like I'm being tested, but by whom I don't know.

From this vantage point I can see a number of hipster-looking folk with frustrated children being questioned by uniformed police officers on the other side of the park. Behind them, a white forensics tent stands to the right of the children's play area. A chill runs through me, as if I'm not already chilly enough. It's an extremely grim picture of a place usually filled with sweetness and laughter. It feels bleak. I wonder how long before the children will return, if they ever do. I'm not sure I'd bring my child here, to the site of a murder. If I had one. If only I had one.

I turn off the path. Within a few metres the long grass has soaked my leather shoes, and I regret having worn them. Sometimes I'm amazed at my absolute lack of judgement when it comes to such things. I'd be useless hiking or camping in the wild.

Police tape and a media huddle greet me as I come closer to the crime scene. There are already plenty of people commenting on Twitter about the murders terrorising east London. The second case, in Homerton, of a woman found drugged and left for dead, was quickly connected to online dating. People who knew her came forward to say they believed she may have met her killer online, possibly a date gone wrong, although the police never elaborated on it. They might have to now that a third victim has turned up.

To my right, a gathering of dog walkers in their trendy parkas and wellies are whispering amongst themselves. I wish I had warm clothes on. Their duck-down jackets look so cosy. All the dogs are on their leads, gunning to be free. Poor doggies. I'd love to have a dog, but my work life doesn't permit it.

'Morning, Alex. You all right?' Jack, a cameraman I have worked with before, is already here.

'You just got here?'

He nods slowly. Jack isn't easily spooked, but even he looks bothered by the scene we are confronted with. He also looks snug in his waterproof jacket and outdoor boots.

'Can't really believe it. We had a BBQ over there last summer.' He points to the south side of the park. 'I come here all the time.'

Behind the police tape that marks out the crime scene, a tall man in a black mac is talking to a woman with red lips and equally red hair in white forensics overalls. DI Brook is a solid-looking man, a man who can handle himself. The woman looks enamoured with him. He is just about within shouting distance; not that I want to holler, but I do need to talk to him, and the sooner the better, so I take the few dreaded steps towards the tape to see if I can get his attention. My heart is doing somersaults. I open

27

my mouth, but staring at the tent, I find myself unable to produce a sound. Then someone taps me on the shoulder, making me jump.

'Sorry! Didn't mean to scare you! I'm Audrey. Your producer.' An extremely petite hand covered in silver rings and a four-leaf-clover tattoo reaches out for mine. She has a firm handshake, thankfully. And she is gorgeous; multiracial in appearance, although I'm not quite sure where from.

'Hi. Sorry. I'm just having one of those days. Bit creepy, this.'

'Me too.' She winks. 'I know what you mean.'

'I live a couple of streets away, so it's a bit daunting having all this on my doorstep.'

'I can imagine. Well, I'm glad to be working with you if that's any help. Big story, this one. Should keep us busy, which is good.' She does look genuinely pleased.

Jack pipes up. 'Oh yes, should keep us very busy.'

I'm used to his silly quips and ignore it. He leaves us alone and goes to set up.

A second forensic officer exits the tent and joins the detective's now animated conversation. The group look in the direction of the Pub on the Park, which stands close to the outer boundary of the crime tape. The pub where I met Nigel last night. I wonder if they think she met her killer there.

'Audrey, right?'

She gives me a smiley nod.

'I'm sorry...' I'm looking in the direction of the tent, 'but I really need to talk to DI Brook.'

'Right. Of course. The body is still here, just so you know.'

'Ah, okay.' That sends a shiver along my already chilly arms. 'Who found it?'

'A dog walker apparently. You okay? You look a bit pale.'

'Fine, just cold, that's all. Haven't got the full studio make-up on today either.'

She laughs at that. 'Got ya. What would we girls do without make-up, hey?'

'Exactly.' I wipe my runny nose with an old tissue I find in my pocket. 'They aren't giving much away, are they? I mean, about the victim.'

'No. Don't think they've ID'ed her yet, but what's-her-face...' Audrey is pointing at the competition.

'Laura?'

'Yeah, her. She says they found something at the scene.'

'Like what?'

Her green eyes, heavily made up like a fifties movie star, blink back at me. 'I'm not sure. That's all she said. Really helpful, that one.'

I nod at Laura, who is a few metres away interviewing a member of the public with her cameraman. She smiles back in recognition.

'Can you run me through what we know so far, Audrey?'

Audrey gives me the update, then turns away to answer her phone, which rings with the theme tune of *Newsnight*. I think we'll get along.

When I turn around, Laura MacColl is right behind me, grinning, which seems inappropriate given the circumstances. She's been here since early this morning, not that you'd ever guess. She positively sparkles. Her shiny long, dark hair is well styled, as is her make-up. She's wearing a crisp navy suit, unlike my crumpled, eclectically put together ensemble. She's probably fifteen years younger than me and always looks smug about that fact, but today I'm one up on her, as UKBC has a much larger audience, being the public broadcaster.

'Bit nasty, this, another murdered woman in the borough of Hackney.' Her Scottish purr only adds to her attractiveness. 'Feels a bit close to home, doesn't it? I mean, I have friends who work and live around here.'

'Do we know any more about how she died?'

'No, we don't.' She returns the pronoun, albeit in a slightly sarcastic tone. 'I've been here a couple of hours already and can't get much out of them. It's similar to the Homerton case and the Victoria Park one by the looks of it. Thirty-something woman left for dead in a park.'

'You spoken to DI Brook?'

'Good eye candy but not particularly helpful, that one.'

'My producer said you got a tip from the Met?'

She pushes her hair off her face and makes me wait for a moment.

'Well, they found a gym card at the crime scene. The dog walker found it, actually, but he's been told to keep shtum. I'm guessing it belongs to the victim.'

'Right. Have you seen this card?'

'No. No one has. My source won't say any more than that. Lots of lost items get found in London parks every day.' Laura's eyebrows lift as she says it.

5

Dear Diary,

Today has been really rough. I feel physically sick: all I want to do is throw up. My brain isn't working. My body has the shakes and is behaving in ways I've never known it to before. The optimism I felt about kicking the drink has all but vanished. I don't know if I'm doing the right thing by stopping. My body hurts. My brain is like jelly. I feel like I'm about to die any minute. I can't get out of bed, but I can't sleep. I can't do anything. I can't function. Detoxing is so hard.

It's been two weeks since I went to my first AA meeting with Alex. I thought it would get easier, but it's not getting easier, it's getting harder. Alex told me she went to a walk-in clinic recommended by her GP before she tried AA. She is trying to cut down because her partner is really fed up with it. She says we exist in a state of oblivion to escape real life. A woman at AA asked me why I drink, and honestly, I don't know. I've just been doing it for so long that I don't know how to do anything else.

God, I feel terrible today. My stomach aches, my joints ache, everything aches. My body isn't reacting well to the withdrawal. It's shaking. A woman in the AA group, Lorraine, recounted how she went through violent shakes when she quit and how it's actually quite dangerous for you to just stop drinking. She said it can kill a person, said that it's better to cut down slowly, wean yourself off it, which I hadn't even thought of before. Even so, I decided to go cold turkey. It's as if I have something to prove to myself. Although now I'm not sure it was such a good idea.

I can't really imagine my life without drink. It's like trying to take the roots from a tree, I just don't see how it will work, but I'm up for giving it a try. My mum isn't helping. On the contrary, she is being moody and aggressive as usual. She was really angry last night because she doesn't like me talking about it. I told her about the meeting in the church, but she just thinks I've joined some crazy cult. She doesn't get it. She's in denial, like I was until Alex saved me.

I don't know why I expect my mum to behave any differently really. For as long as I can remember, she's said I was a mistake. That I ruined her life. That she was going places until I came along. She says I bring her down. She blames me for everything. Nothing is ever her fault, always someone else's. She was so moody last night, I had to leave the room after she threw a plate across the kitchen. I'm used to her blaming me for her failed life, that's nothing new, but the difference now is I'm starting to feel it isn't about me at all, because AA is helping me to see things differently. The group tells me not to believe my mum. That it is her own frustrations that make her angry. That I'm not responsible for my mother's life. That people are responsible for themselves. I'd never thought about it this way before.

In a way, I feel sorry for my mum, because I am a bit of a burden if truth be told. I still live at home and I don't pay rent. I wanted to be a writer when I left school but I haven't written anything since I was sixteen. After I got back from the last AA meeting, that's when I decided to stop drinking altogether and write this diary. Maybe one day it'll mean something. Maybe I have a book in me after all.

I have accepted that I am an alcoholic and I want to get better. I really want to get sober so I can have a successful life like Alex. It's tough, though, I won't lie. All I can think about today is having a drink.

It's probably a good thing that I can't get out of bed because there is a lot of alcohol downstairs in the lounge. We always have lots of booze in the house. It's quite normal for my mum to drink before lunchtime. In fact, I'm starting to think it's my mother who taught me to drink the way I do and that's a good reason to stop, because if I don't, I may end up like her. I repeat: I may end up like my mother. She bitches at me all the time yet needs me at the same time. I'm starting to think about our relationship differently. It's something I need to change, and I need to get sober to do that. I must not drink today.

6

The pressing need to talk to DI Brook takes over. When I turn around, I spot him lingering behind the tent, so I fill my lungs with air and shout his name as loudly as I can, but to no avail. He has clearly decided not to hear me.

'They not listening to you, love?'

An elderly woman dressed in black with silvery blue hair and a lively red setter has suddenly appeared beside me. Her face is half hidden behind what look like very expensive sunglasses. 'Such terrible news to wake up to this morning.'

I nod silently, unsure of what to say. The last thing I need right now is a member of the public asking me silly questions. I have a job to do and sometimes they just get in the way.

'I've seen you before, haven't I? You live around here?'

'Yes.'

She pulls her glasses forward, resting them on the end of her nose, to reveal watery grey eyes. 'I know you, you're on the news. Although I haven't seen you on for a while. Not since that...'

She stops herself. I know what she's going to say. Not since that time you were pissed on air ranting about how the system had failed us all.

'I've been busy doing research for a new investigative report I'm working on.'

'So you got lucky today because you live around here? That it? I know how it goes, the pecking order. Worked in broadcasting when I was younger. Couldn't take the cynicism and got out after a few years.'

'Right.' I really don't need this now. It's only midday and my nerves are shot. She's not going away, though.

'I love watching the news and talking about politics. You really must come for tea. I don't get many visitors these days. I live on Navarino. Right on the corner of the park.'

'That's very kind of you, but I imagine I'm going to be quite busy with this story.'

'Of course. I didn't mean today, silly. Number three, the red door. Just knock.'

Audrey is back, looking purposeful, her eyes willing the pensioner to move on.

'Sorry to interrupt, but they want a two-minute hit into the lunchtime bulletin. What we know now.'

'Goodbye then, Alex. Please make sure you come and see me.' The woman pushes her glasses back up her nose and shuffles off with her dog.

'Who was that?' Audrey nods towards her. 'A neighbourhood pal?'

'Just a dog walker.'

'Not *the* dog walker?'

'No. No.'

'Oh. Okay. So, the report?'

'It's fine. Have you spoken to the police? I can't seem to attract their attention.'

'Managed to grab DI Brook at the press conference earlier, but only to get his business card.' She hands it to me. *DI John Brook, Serious Crime Division*. There's a mobile number on it. I already have it in my phone from dealing with him on previous cases, but I decide not to mention it. Best to let Audrey think she's on it, which she is. In fact, I don't know why I didn't just call him before, rather than shout at him like a complete loser. I'm embarrassed to say my memory fails me more often than not, especially after a big night out.

'Thanks, Audrey, you're a star.'

'No worries. I don't think he's going to talk to the media again today – at least that's what he said – but give him a call. I did mention you might.'

'Okay.'

'It'll be the first live report from the scene for us, so the editors say just keep it simple. They're leading on it.'

'I have done this before, Audrey.'

'Yes, of course, sorry.'

She looks a bit hurt by my reaction, which happens when I'm not fully in my right mind. Greg used to get on me for that all the time. Snapping at people. I should say something nice.

'Sorry. Didn't mean to sound short with you. It's my first live for a while and I suppose I'm a little nervous.'

'You'll knock 'em dead, Alex. You're great at this job.'

'That's very kind. Thank you.'

'We all have bad days. We're only human after all.'

She is being very sweet and understanding. Buttering me up. That's nice even if she doesn't mean it, because it's exactly what I need today.

'Thanks, Audrey, but today is going to be a good day.'

With the business card in my hand, I put my headphones on and pull up DI Brook's number from my contact list, then hit dial. While it's ringing, I check my Facebook page. Two thousand and fifty-three people have wished me happy birthday. Wow. I guess many people feel like Audrey does, ready to give me a second chance. I mean, it wasn't so bad what I did, bitching about the government live on air. There were a lot of people who wrote to me afterwards saying well done for speaking honestly. Didn't help me with the editors, though. Anyway, that's behind me now.

DI Brook isn't answering, and I hang up. Just then my phone buzzes. It's a message from Richie, the chap I'm planning to meet later. I met him on a dating site, just like I met Nigel.

> Hey, sorry to do this to you, Alex, but something's come up at work. Afraid I can't make it tonight. Can we reschedule?

It's annoying, but I don't bother to respond; there's really no point. That's how online dates go sometimes. They don't always materialise, and if I'm honest, I can't be bothered anyway, not now that I have a huge breaking news story to contend with. This is much more important.

I try Brook again, and this time he answers after the third ring.

'DI Brook.'

'Alex South. Need a quick line on this item that was found by the body.'

'Up to your old tactics, Ms South?'

I take a deep breath and let it slide.

'Thought I'd help you with some questions.'

'Was that a question?'

'A source says a gym card was found at the location. Can you confirm this?'

'What source is that?'

The question lingers unanswered between us. I am asking for a lot, I know.

'Look, I can help, you know. I want you to catch the bastard who did this. We're on the same side, you and I. I live around here and I'm female, for Christ's sake.'

Another pause before he finally gives in.

'Off the record?'

'Of course.'

'Yes, a gym card was found by the body. It probably belongs to the dead woman. We are still trying to ID her.'

'Okay. Not the murder weapon, then…' My humour isn't something he can appreciate right now, so I push on with the questions. 'Do you think these women met their killer on a dating app? You know there were hints that the second victim, Maggie Horrocks, met her killer that way.'

'No comment.'

'You mean yes?'

'I mean no comment.'

'You do realise that this is a public safety issue?'

'I'm fully aware of the dangers, Ms South, but thanks for pointing them out to me.'

'So how was this latest victim killed?'

'We think strangled, possibly drugged.'

I put my hands to my throat and remember my sexual encounter this morning. It's time to wrap this up. I'm not feeling well at all.

'I'm assuming it was a Hackney gym?'

But he's already gone.

Six minutes later, I'm readying to go live on air, impatient for my next drink, when a message from DI Brook pings on my phone. There's an attachment; it's a photo of a gym card belonging to Hackney council leisure centres. The name and picture have been blurred. I think Laura is right. I'm guessing someone dropped it in the park, probably on their way to the public lido, but it's the only lead we have, so I need to pay attention to it.

7

Dear Diary,

I feel better today. The shakes come then go, usually after I've had a drink. This time I've made it through two full weeks with only a few bottles of white wine and I'm feeling so much better about myself for doing that. The first step was admitting I have a problem, and that feels good. I have also, to a certain degree, admitted I'm powerless over alcohol, encouraged by the group at AA, and that has changed my relationship with it. It feels like progress. I thought I'd celebrate with Alex and bought two tickets to see the new Bond film, but I hadn't realised it's her birthday tomorrow and she has to spend the day with her fiancé and his family. I was disappointed, but I understand, especially in her condition. She told me she's pregnant, which is amazing. It's why she started going to AA. Neither of us are completely dry yet, but we will be.

I wish I could just cut back and moderate my drinking like her, but I know myself. I can't. She says that perhaps I have an addictive personality, so I read up on it online. I think she might be right, because I'm becoming addicted to her in a way. Sometimes when I'm alone I replay the voicemail she left on my phone after our first AA meeting, in which she tells me to believe in myself. I like the sound of her voice. It's very comforting.

I found it upsetting to not be invited to her birthday party, but I am trying to understand. She has to do the family thing too. I get that. I gave her a gift anyway, a bracelet with our initials on it. She looked like she was totally blown away by it. It wasn't expensive but it was real silver. Maybe it was a bit over the top, but I just wanted to show her how much she means to me. How grateful I am that I met her. She has changed my life forever and I owe her so much. I can't imagine life without her in it now.

8

It has been a long day and it's not quite over yet, such is the life chasing a big story. It's okay, though; it's a buzz and helps distract me from the voice in my head that wants another drink.

I left Audrey and Jack gathering interviews with locals and went to King's Hall pool and gym to see if I could find out anything further on the membership card. It also gave me a much-needed breather from the crew, as my head is still pounding. I need to drink some serious amounts of water today.

Visiting the gym turned out to be pointless. The receptionist was really nice but I felt like a bit of an idiot if truth be told, because she couldn't tell me if anyone had reported their card lost. She said that even if she could, it would be inconclusive. Many people lose their cards and replace them apparently. Without the name she said she really wouldn't know where to start. It could be an old card for all she knew.

So I find myself sitting in a pub with a glass of wine on the table. I really didn't mean to do it, but here I am. I don't drink all the time. I have periods when I'm more prone to it than others. And it just so happens that this story broke while I was in the middle of one of my drinking weeks.

I can control it, though. I can detox, then get dry again. That's what I do. I can wean myself off it by reducing the amount I consume. It's just a physical addiction, you see. But that will have to wait until tomorrow, because it'll totally wipe me out and I can't afford for that to happen while I've got a top story to report on. It's really important that I get this right, which means that for now, I just need to have enough alcohol in my blood to keep me going. Tomorrow the story will die down and I'll be able to nip this in the bud once and for all. This time I'm going to make it stick. Being on the lunchtime bulletin was a wake-up call and I do really want to be someone in my career. I have another chance and I'm not going to blow it this time round.

Audrey has just texted me to say she's had a tip from her source at the Met that they might name the victim soon, so we should be prepared. UKBC's rolling news channel will be keen to have us live as soon as that breaks. The lunchtime and evening bulletins are the flagship programmes that every reporter wants to be on, but the channel never stops, which means there will be no let-up if the story continues to develop. I need to get my head straight, so I finish the wine and go and buy some chewing gum to disguise what I've been up to.

As I'm leaving the shop, I get another text from Audrey to say they are about to name the victim and I should get back to the park so we can go live with it. Shit. Right. I shouldn't have sat down, really, because it's made me feel tired. My body is hurting; muscles I didn't even know existed aching. I really need to get back to the gym once I'm dry this time around. I mean, if a one-night stand can make me feel this achy, what would happen if I got pregnant? I need to be stronger.

Audrey is calling.

'Alex, where are you? We need to be live in twenty minutes. Can you make it?'

'Hi, Audrey. Don't panic. I'm only five minutes away. I'll be there in a mo.'

I hang up and pick up the pace. She has been listening to gossip in the news centre, I suppose, and is worried that I'm unreliable. It's not fair that I'm still living in the shadow of what happened. I mean, am I ever going to live that down? It was one incident. I'm going to have to prove them all wrong. I'm good at what I do. People make mistakes, don't they? I am only human after all.

When I get to the park, Jack wires me up while Audrey paces up and down nervously with her headphones on.

'I'm listening to a press conference from the Met. DI Brook left here shortly after you went to check out your lead. He's going to make the announcement outside the police station.'

'What?' This makes me a bit angry, as that's where I've just come from. Hackney. 'Why aren't we there?' I'm looking at both Jack and Audrey now. 'I mean, why are we in the park when he's making the statement at the station? It's only a ten-minute walk from here.'

'We weren't sure where you were, Alex. Anyway, it's too late now. Plus I'm set up for here. We know the signal works. There's still a crime scene behind you. I think it'll be fine. The agencies are there covering his statement.'

'Okay.'

I'm feeling a bit ratty now, but Audrey has given me one of her headphones so I can listen to the presser. She has cleverly got the news centre to play it down the line from the gallery. I like Audrey. She's resourceful. DI Brook has just started talking.

'We are appealing to Sarah Wilcox, a woman who we believe probably lives in the local area, to come forward to the police. A gym card belonging to her was found near the body and we'd like to rule her out of our enquiries, so I ask you, Miss Wilcox, to get in touch by calling the helpline on the screen. That's all the information we have at this moment. Thank you.'

I'm a bit thrown, as we thought the police would announce the name of the victim, but instead they have issued the name of someone wanted in connection. I feel like I could throw up, and I'm not sure whether it's my hangover or the fact that I'm not properly prepared, having been given the wrong information by my producer.

Embarrassed, Audrey pulls the headphone away from me while Jack stares down his viewfinder. A voice in my earpiece asks if I'm ready, which I am, I guess. It's now or never. I don't have a lot to go on and I feel really ill. I can hear the presenter explaining to our viewers that the police have released the name of someone potentially connected to the crime, before asking me for an update from the scene.

'Yes, that's right, Jane, the police have just given us the name of someone who they believe may be potentially connected to the crime, a Sarah Wilcox. They say they got this name from a gym card found near the body. They haven't gone as far as to say they believe she is a suspect, but it would seem they think she might know something that could help the investigation. We don't have much more information than that at this point. They were quick to release this name, though, so they must think it's important.'

'Indeed, Alex. Let's hope it does help their investigation, as you say, I imagine it's very worrying for the residents of east London. Alex South, thank you.'

The news bulletin has moved on.

'Nice work, Alex!'

Audrey is buzzing with the excitement of live TV. I'm having a bit of an adrenalin rush myself, which is helping my tired body stay upright.

'So what now?' I look at Jack, who looks at Audrey.

'We find out who this Sarah Wilcox is and locate her family. We need to get ahead of the story. I'm on it, don't you worry. I'll talk to the news centre.'

Audrey looks like a woman on a mission. She has already left us, phone in hand, looking purposeful. Moments later, she's back with a big grin on her face.

'We're going to Manchester.'

'What? Why?' A feeling of dread washes over me.

'Tip-off from James Pastor, the security correspondent. His missus works in the Met's Serious Crime Division. Says the Wilcox girl is from Manchester.'

'Is he sure?'

'That's what he says. Anyway, it's a gift, Alex, we can get ahead of the pack on this one. Find the Wilcox family, interview them and get a scoop.'

I'm not sure how I feel about this development. I haven't been back to Manchester since I left a year ago, since my life fell apart there, since the miscarriage, but it's stellar work by Audrey, I'll give her that. The news gods have deemed it a credible lead, so we're going. The last train leaves at eleven o'clock and we're booked on it. They've told us to go home and pack, while the on-shift reporter in the newsroom picks up the slack. Our focus has shifted now, to finding the Wilcox family and getting an exclusive with the mother or father. It's the part of the job I don't like so much, because it feels intrusive, but such is the business we're in. Audrey and I agree to meet at the train station later. She reckons by then she'll have the Wilcox address nailed down. I really do like her, although I am nervous about returning, given my past there. I lost a lot and I'm not sure if I'm ready to face that yet.

–

Back home, the box of Milk Tray greets me when I enter the kitchen. Another reminder of the past. God, what if I run into Greg? Perhaps the opportunity to head north is a sign that I should look him up. Not that I'd know where to start; I don't even know if he's still in Manchester. I can't believe how fast this year has passed really. It feels like only yesterday I was living and working there, presenting my radio show.

I'm starving, so I cast off my initial reservations about who sent the chocolates and get stuck in. The sugar rush hits moments after my first kill. Praline. It sticks to my teeth. The second I eat in stages, sucking out the soft centre first. Greg's favourite, caramel, which makes me feel oddly close to him for the first time in a year. They say you know when you know, don't they? About potential partners. That's how it felt with Greg. I knew the day I met him we were destined to be together. I didn't know then that we were also destined to be apart.

47

After my fourth chocolate – or is it my fifth? – tears begin to trickle down my cheeks. It's the longing for true love again rearing its ugly head, I suppose. I have spent the best part of the last year telling myself I don't need it, that I'm better off without it, but the truth is I miss that bond that comes with connecting through silly objects like Milk Tray. I put the kettle on and tell myself not to give into these feelings, because wallowing in regret is no way to live. I'm actually doing really well. I'm becoming a success story. Northern lass making it big in the capital. Better to wipe the tears away and toast my new life. To this story. A story that got me on air today, back in the game where I can truly shine.

I open the fridge to get the milk out, but staring back at me is half a bottle of white wine. I don't even bother with a glass; it'll only slow me down. A large swig turns into the rest of the bottle. I actually feel quite pissed now. Thank God I don't need to be on air until tomorrow. A stroke of luck really: the whole return-to-Manchester scenario has helped me get through the day in a way, because I got to come home in the midst of a binge. I should be grateful for it, not resentful. Small miracles and all that.

As I'm stuffing another chocolate in my mouth, I notice a Post-it note stuck curiously to my teapot.

> Hey, Alex, I really enjoyed last night, so if you do change your mind and want to hang out again, my number is 07825 467768.
> Nigel x

Maybe I should take a risk for a change and give this guy another chance. I'm doing so much better than I was.

But then I feel my neck and decide against it. Just as I'm thinking this, there's a loud crash above my head, followed by the sound of breaking glass.

9

When Charlie opens the door, his hand is wrapped in bloody paper towels.

'What happened?'

'Was hanging a mirror.' He shrugs. 'The hook broke off.'

'Your DIY skills are appalling.'

'Thanks. So, have you got a minute to help sort this out?'

He ushers me through the door and up the narrow wooden stairs to the kitchen.

'Have you been drinking, Alex?'

I guess he can smell the wine.

'Do you want me to sort this out or not?'

He shuts up.

'Have you got plasters?' I ask.

'In that drawer over there.'

I run his hand under cold water while he winces, then bandage him up.

'There. All done. Shall I put the kettle on?' I don't want tea, but I'm trying to prove to him that I can *do* normal. Charlie knows more about my drinking habits than he likes to let on.

'You've done a good job. Thanks, Alex.'

'Couldn't do that if I'd been drinking, could I?'

He smirks.

'Anyway, I've been in the park all day. Working.'

'Oh shit, yeah. I saw, sorry. You been busy with this news about these women? All sounds a bit mental. Big story for you.'

'Yeah. Watched a body bag being taken away a bit earlier.'

'Shit. Whereabouts on the Fields?'

'Close to Pub on the Park. Our end.'

'That's rough. You all right?'

'Can't really get my head around it. Feels a bit surreal, you know.'

'Could happen anywhere, I suppose.'

He has his back to me. His broad shoulders tense as he opens the overly stuffed cupboard to find a couple of clean mugs. We've had our moments, but it's never come to anything serious.

'Yeah, but it didn't. It happened here.'

'How did she die?'

'The police haven't confirmed it yet, but my source says she was strangled.' I rub my neck again.

'Don't they think it's linked to online dating? I hope you're being careful on your dates.'

'Not officially, but Twitter thinks so. The greatest news source these days. But I am being careful, don't worry.'

'You go out with strangers all the time.' Charlie's blazing blue eyes sparkle at me.

'Do I detect a hint of jealousy?'

'Don't be ridiculous. I have no claim on you, but I do worry about you.'

'Well, that's very sweet, but I'll be fine. My editors want me to go to Manchester.'

'Why?'

'That woman they're looking for, that's where she's from, apparently.'

'Oh, right. So you're going home.'

The thought of it leaves me cold.

'Yep, looks like it. Career opportunity, you know.'

'Will you have time to visit friends and family?'

'Maybe. Depends on the story, I guess.'

Charlie doesn't know much about my life before London, and I prefer it that way. Some things are better left in the past because they can taint the present and ruin the future. Although I realise that my philosophy on this is quickly falling apart having eaten half the box of Milk Tray.

'When are you going?'

'Later tonight.'

'That soon? What about your birthday date?'

'He cancelled.'

'He what?'

'In a text message.'

'What a plonker. Did he know it was your birthday?'

'Yep.'

'Find another. Isn't that what the Internet is for? You can't stay home alone on your birthday. Work, work, work makes for a dull life, Alex.'

I can hear Annabel's voice in my head. They're both always saying this to me. They are probably right, but my personal life is shit, so it's easier to just avoid it, especially when there's a meaningful story to report on.

'If you're so bothered about me being alone on my birthday, why don't *you* take me out?'

'I'd love to, but I can't tonight. I have a date.'

'You have a date? Are you serious?'

'Yep. I'll tell you more after the fact.'

'Fair enough.'

'What about you? Did you have someone here last night? Thought I saw someone leaving early this morning.'

'You spying on me, Charlie?'

'Why don't you ask him out for your birthday?'

'Hmm, let's see. Because I don't plan on seeing him again?'

'You and your no-second-date policy...' He hands me a cup of tea. 'You okay, Alex? You seem a bit...'

'A bit what?'

'I don't know. Like something is bothering you. You seem restless.'

'Just tired, that's all.' I take a sip of tea, although it's still too hot.

'Shall we adjourn to the salon?'

I nod silently and follow him into the lounge. He's carrying a packet of biscuits. We sit in our usual places, like an old married couple. Me cross-legged on the worn, stained pale green carpet and Charlie on his curvy 1960s blue velour sofa, which he rescued from the street. He turns on the TV.

'Let's see what's going on, shall we?'

There's a photo on screen that almost makes me choke on my tea.

'You all right?'

'Yeah, just went down the wrong way.'

'So that's the woman they're looking for, is it? This Sarah Wilcox?'

'I guess so.'

'She looks familiar.' He's scratching his chin while concentrating on the image. 'They think she's a suspect, then?'

I'm trying my best to act as if I don't recognise the woman staring back at us, but I do, though I can't remember why. God, my memory is so shot these days.

'You sure you're okay, Alex?'

'Yeah, why?'

'You look like you've seen a ghost, pardon the cliché.'

'You and your clichés.'

I need to move this conversation on. The photo disappears from the TV screen, which is a relief. I'm not going to admit to Charlie that I think I've met Sarah Wilcox; in fact, I'm not going to mention it to anyone unless I really have to. I need to remember first.

'I forgot the sugar. I'll be right back.'

Charlie darts out of the lounge, and when he returns, he's holding a cupcake with a candle on it and singing a really bad rendition of 'Happy Birthday'.

'Happy Birthday to you... happy birthday to you... you look like a monkey and you smell like one too.'

'You've got a terrible voice.' Mine is starting to wobble. As I stare at the flickering flame planted in the pink icing, my emotions get the better of me and I suddenly and without warning become a blubbering idiot. Just to top it off, my cheeks are quickly turning crimson.

'Hey, hey. I didn't mean to make you cry.'

He puts the cake down in front of me and I manage a slight puff, enough to blow out the candle. I try to compose myself, but it's useless. I've got mascara on my hands. 'I'm sorry. It's idiotic really, isn't it? I mean, it's just a cake, but it's so nice of you to do that.'

'Come here, silly.'

He gives me a warm, healing hug. It feels safe. It feels comforting. I secretly admit in the darkest part of me that I do need comfort in my life. I know I do.

The cake makes me feel better. It is deliciously moist and sweet, exactly how a birthday cake should be. Charlie is rolling a cigarette.

'Thought you were going to quit?'

He just shrugs.

'Can I have one?'

'Are you kidding? You don't smoke. What's going on?'

'It's a birthday cigarette… you know. I think the story today has really shaken me up.'

'Yeah, right.'

He passes me his roll-up and starts to make another.

The tobacco tastes disgusting, but it packs a powerful punch, quelling my anxiety, and I start to relax. In contrast to my flat, which has nothing in it, Charlie's lounge is cluttered with all kinds of trinkets collected over the years. He has an affection for wind-up toys, music memorabilia and cacti. On the far wall are shelves literally about to collapse under the weight of too many books. He's an avid reader of non-fiction, mostly history, when he's not running his online clothing store.

'So what do you want to listen to, birthday girl?' He's on the other side of the room now, thumbing through his extensive collection of vinyl.

'Anything by Stone Roses or New Order.'

'What time you off?'

'Eleven.'

'Okay, well it's getting on for six o'clock, so why don't you text the guy back from last night. See if he's available for a birthday drink before you go. What was his name?'

'Nigel.' I can see Charlie isn't going to leave it.

'It's your birthday. Seriously, what have you got to lose?'

'My reliable love affair with low expectations?'

He laughs. 'Just bloody text the guy. It's not a declaration of love, is it?'

'Here, you write the message if you're so keen to fix my personal life.'

He takes my phone and crafts a somewhat generic message that doesn't have any personality or improper suggestions, while I pop downstairs to grab Nigel's number.

Together we wait for an answer, and within moments a message arrives.

> **Sounds great! See you at the Pub on the Park again at 7.30? Nigel xox**

'He's totally into you!' Charlie is grinning; a dimple has appeared in his right cheek, a detail I have never noticed before. 'Wait, do you think he could be the murderer? Did you meet him online?'

I haven't told him about being tied up by Nigel, and I won't.

'Well seeing as he was with me last night, I doubt it. He has the perfect alibi!'

Charlie laughs. 'Make sure you wear a low-cut top. Want to send the right message, don't ya?'

My head is in a happy place now thanks to the cake and Charlie.

'Shit, it's almost six thirty. I'd better get going.'

'What's new! Have a good time tonight, and enjoy Manchester.'

'Thanks. If I'm not back in two days, can you water my plants? You've still got the spare key, right?'

'Yep, no problem. Hey, I just remembered. I've seen that Sarah Wilcox at the lido.'

'At the lido? How can you remember that?'

'She's really pretty and I've got a good memory for faces. Plus it was winter and the steam was coming off the water. I remember talking to her, she'd just moved here from up north somewhere, bit like you did.'

I don't follow up on what's he said and instead start downstairs. It won't do any good. Plus I need a drink. Today's developments have been upsetting in all kinds of ways, some of which I've yet to quite put my finger on. As I open the door to my flat, a flash of memory comes back to me and I know why Sarah Wilcox looked familiar. We met just before I left Manchester. Bloody hell. This isn't great. In fact, it's downright terrifying.

10

May 2017

Dear Diary,

Since her birthday, Alex hasn't been to an AA meeting. It's like she just fell off the face of the earth. When I called her phone, someone called Greg answered. I didn't like his tone. He told me to stop bothering them. Said that Alex wasn't well and that she didn't need more stress, whatever that means. Said I should leave her alone. I really don't understand what has happened. I'm hurt. I don't know how you can share so much with someone and then suddenly be cut out of their lives just like that. I read an article in the paper about it a few weeks ago. They call it ghosting someone, apparently. It's when you completely eradicate a person from your life so that you can forget them. It's a way of getting over a friendship or an intimate relationship.

I'm really sad that Greg won't let me talk to her. For the first time in a long while, I don't want to get out of bed. The only thing I really want to do today is drink so I can blot out what happened. It's terrible, the not knowing what is going on and why Greg answered her phone. I want to forget today. There's really only one way to achieve this: the stash of alcohol downstairs and my faithful park bench. I think they call this a relapse.

Sarah's face is all over social media. A collection of photos from her Facebook page. One of her on holiday holding hands with someone they have cut out. I didn't know she had a boyfriend, but then why would I? We weren't friends; we hardly knew each other. Audrey has called to say that she has the address and we are all set.

After polishing off another half-bottle of wine I found under the sink, I finally manage to pack my bag with clean clothing suitable for telly. Tomorrow could turn into a busy day depending on whether the Wilcox family agree to talk to us. I can't believe I'm actually going to her family home, but that's exactly what we're doing. Before that, though, it's time to celebrate my birthday at the pub with Nigel. Not that I really feel like going. I can't remember the last time I went on a second date, and I'm not sure how I feel about that.

Nigel seemed nice until he almost strangled me. I wonder if I should bring that up and prod him about it. The other two women left in parks were strangled; they haven't confirmed what happened to the latest victim yet, but it's alleged they all met their killer online. I guess I'm confused more than anything.

En route to the pub, I buy some extra-strong mints and munch my way through a handful to cover up my boozy breath. I feel embarrassed pulling a small suitcase. I wonder why I didn't just put stuff in a shoulder bag, but it's too late now. I'm so bad at organising anything, let alone myself.

The Fields is still a crime scene, with police stationed at carefully selected points around the cordon. In fact, there are more people milling about in the park now than earlier. The after-work crowd have descended to have a good look. I don't blame them. It's the first thing I wanted to do when I heard the news. Stick my nose in.

The pub is busy when I arrive. Packed with handsome people dressed in muted tones, sporting vintage styles and sipping locally crafted beers. It's noisy even without music. The acoustics of the room enhance the volume of conversations, forcing people to talk louder in a bid to be heard. There are old radios and ghetto blasters displayed on rustic wooden shelves above the bar. People who live in Hackney ooze cool, which propagates more coolness, or so I like to believe. I like this pub and claimed it as my local not long after moving here. Not that I know any of the people who drink here. Even the bar staff remain aloof to any familiar interaction, which suits me most days given my drinking habits. The less scrutiny the better.

Scanning the room, I assume he's not here yet. Either that or he's watching me from afar, and I'm awkwardly hoping it's the latter because I don't think I can take the wait. My heart is pounding with worry that I won't recognise him, such is the unfamiliar territory of the second date. There's a man standing to my left with an AC/DC T-shirt on and numerous body piercings, including a nose ring. The T-shirt makes me smile, but the piercings are terrifying. He keeps looking at me as if I have food on my face, so I turn away and lean on the bar. I'm fiddling with my hands because they feel awkward. Watching the door, I see a man enter the pub, and our eyes meet. Is it him? It could be. He has dark tousled hair, is casually dressed. He's smiling, flashing perfectly white teeth, I smile back but he walks clean past me towards a girl standing behind Mr AC/DC.

My body twitches. Perhaps he's not coming? Then across the room I spot him, sitting at a table for two. He looks skinnier than I remember. He's spotted me too and is waving frantically. I wave back and make a gesture with my hand that says 'Would you like a drink?' He shakes his head and stands up to join me at the bar, but I make another gesture: 'Stay where you are, I'll just get a drink and join you.' He smiles and sits back down. At least I know that if we lost our voices we'd still be able to communicate with each other.

I have the opportunity to bolt, but I don't. I buy myself a drink before awkwardly navigating the pub with my suitcase to reach his table. His aftershave is strong, but not in a good way. There are scratches on his neck. God, did I do that? I don't remember.

'Hi, Alex.' He half stands and leans across the small wooden table ready to plant a kiss on my cheek, but as he does so, the drink in front of him tips over and the surface becomes a puddle of orange juice.

'Oh God, sorry!'

Frantically he attempts to wipe up the mess with a napkin that is lying on the table, but he can't stop the stream running towards me. I take a step back.

'I'll go and get something better to clean this up.' He heads for the bar. He's nervous, which is highly unattractive. In my game, confidence is everything. Within moments, he's back.

'I'm so sorry. I'm not usually this clumsy.' After he's finished clearing up, he plops himself down behind a defensive mound of wet napkins.

'No harm done.' I pick up my glass to say cheers in a joking manner. My heart is racing because I'm weirdly also nervous. 'Would you like another drink?'

'I'll wait for the next round.'

'It might be a while.' I gesture to my full glass.

'It was just juice anyway. Having a day off. We got through quite a lot last night, didn't we? You can really hold your drink, Alex.' He grins nervously. His teeth are pearly white and straight, which is a relief. I once went on a date with someone who had rotten teeth. There are many details you can miss online, because people are very good at hiding details in photos.

His side of the table looks kind of wrong without a drink, because having a drink sets a time reference. It's like saying you'll give this person an hour to make an impression. If he is stone-cold sober, which I assume he is, I'm not sure what kind of impression I am going to make given that I've had a few already.

'Are you sure you don't want a drink?'

'Quite sure, thanks.'

'Okay.' I suddenly feel acutely aware that I'm already quite pissed. Not that I'll openly admit it.

'I'm actually on some medication at the moment, so taking it easy today,' he says.

'Oh.'

'I'm not a manic-depressive or anything. Don't worry. I've just been through a rough spot lately.'

'Oh.' This isn't going how I was expecting it to go.

'Do you say anything but oh?' He smiles. He does have a nice smile. It's warm, inviting.

'When I feel like it. I didn't think we'd run through addictions and mental health quite so early on.'

We laugh together, which breaks the ice. His is a genuine belly laugh. He thinks I'm funny, which is good. But his smile soon gives way to a more serious face.

'I'll be honest with you, Alex. I broke up with my girlfriend of five years a few months ago and it hit me quite hard. I'm not wishing I was back with her. It was definitely over. We'd grown apart. Wanted different things. It's just been a bit tough, that's all. My therapist says it's a temporary phase and it will pass.'

'Okay.' I wonder if I'll ever be this honest with anyone, ever.

'I feel like I can talk to you, and that's nice.'

He reaches across the table and takes my hand. A tingle runs up my arm and caresses my heart. I do like his style. He's wearing a scruffy tour T-shirt, grey jeans and an electric-blue plastic watch. His large, dreamy dark brown eyes glisten in the evening light. He is sexy in a mellow rock-star kind of way, but I need to keep a level head. He almost tried to strangle me this morning.

'You look nice. That colour really suits you.'

My clothes are varying shades of grey.

'That was me trying to be funny.'

'Ah.' I laugh, but it's a little too late.

The evening goes on much the same. The conversation keeps starting and stopping. It never finds a natural rhythm. But it's nicely awkward. The kind of awkward where we have time to check each other out. He definitely fancies me.

'Hey, did you hear about that girl who was murdered on the Fields? It was only a few hundred metres from where we're sitting now. What was her name, Sarah Wilcox?'

I suddenly feel quite sober.

'I don't think that's the dead girl. They're looking for Sarah Wilcox in connection to it.'

'Yeah, right. Do you think we should contact the police?'

'And say what?'

'Well, we were in the area last night.'

'There must have been hundreds of people around. Do you think they are all contacting the police?'

'I would hope so.' He's staring at me, unsure what to make of my ambivalence. 'Are you okay? You seem a bit...'

'A bit what?'

'A bit... I don't know. A bit stressed?'

Like he knows me. I *am* stressed. I don't want to talk about work on a date, or Sarah Wilcox. I need to redirect the conversation.

'It's been a really long day and it's not over yet. I have to get on a train to Manchester tonight, and frankly I'd really rather not talk about work. It's my birthday. Can we lighten up the conversation?'

'Oh, were you reporting on this story today?'

'I was.'

'Wow. So that's what the suitcase is for? Bloody hell, doing that on your birthday is rough.'

'Yep.'

'Why didn't you tell me it was your birthday last night?'

'I don't know. Sounds a bit sad, doesn't it. "Hi, I'm Alex, it's my birthday and I have no friends to share it with. Would you like to fill that hole in my life?"'

He laughs. 'I understand. I spent mine on my own last year. All my mates were working.'

I like his reaction to the news that it's my birthday. It's comforting.

The pub is rocking now, bursting at the seams. Nigel offers to buy me a Prosecco and says he'll get himself half a lager seeing as it's my birthday. I'm trying to keep it together, but my drunken, paranoid self is starting to surface. I can't help but wonder if his story about his ex is just that, a sob story he wheels out to gain sympathy and make girls lower their guard. You never know when meeting people online what their real agenda is. I realise I'm being ridiculous, because he's presented me with no reason to mistrust him, but my mind gets like this when I'm in the midst of a binge. That's why I need to stop, and I will. I just have to get through this story. Fortunately for him, my paranoia is quashed by what happens next.

As he is making his way back to our table, a woman stands up, blocking his path. Next thing I know, she's emptying a glass of wine over his head. The pub suddenly goes quiet, punctured only by a collective gasp. All eyes are on Nigel's wet face and the woman storming out into the night. He looks around and takes a bow – a few people cheer and applaud good-humouredly – then shrugs before sitting back down. The pub returns to being its noisy self again. His T-shirt has a big wet patch on it that stinks of wine, though that's better than the aftershave.

'Lucky it was white, not red.'

He puts the drinks down and attempts to dry his face with his wet T-shirt. The Prosecco glass is almost empty – he spilled most of it during the confrontation.

'What was that?'

'That's her.'

'The ex?'

'Yes.'

'So she lives around here?'

'Yes.'

'You could have said. Could she be waiting for me outside? Is she psycho?'

'What?'

'Is she insanely jealous?' My imagination is running away with me. The paranoia is back and it's being brutal.

'She's not the jealous type, Alex, trust me.'

'You could have fooled me.'

He sips his lager as if nothing happened, offering no further explanation.

'She looks a bit like me, doesn't she? Slim. Short blonde hair. Is that your type?'

'What do you mean?'

'I mean, do you have a type?'

'What, a type that throws drinks over me?'

I'm not sure what to say. On the table, his phone is buzzing. The name Fiona is flashing, along with a photo of her, the girl who threw the drink over him. And within moments he has gone, exiting through the door, into the night, running away from this awkward moment and me, perhaps chasing after his ex. I put down my unfinished drink and stumble out of the pub shortly afterwards. No one notices.

Great. What a birthday. There's a reason you shouldn't meet a one-night stand a second time, and tonight is it.

12

May 2017

Dear Diary,

Alex rang me today. She sounded very cold. She asked me to stop calling. Said that she couldn't see me again. Told me that even after Greg had asked me to stop contacting her, she was still receiving text messages from me and that those had to stop too. That she was sorry she couldn't help me and that I had to leave her alone. I asked her about going to an AA meeting together, thinking that might work to get her out, but she said she was done with AA. That she didn't need it. That she was in control. That she didn't need help from me. That we weren't friends. That she hoped I could move on and heal myself.

I think this is worse than when my mum told me to fuck off out of her life. It feels so much worse. I don't want to live. I don't want to do anything. All I want to do is forget who I am. There's one thing that will help me do that: a bottle of gin. I don't expect I will hear from Alex again, but the worst thing about it is that I have absolutely no idea why. Why she just cut me out. I hate my life and I hate being me. I wish I'd never met her now. People can be so cruel. They shouldn't be allowed to get away with it. They really shouldn't. Karma will prevail. It always does.

13

The hotel alarm wakes me up. My head is really sore. I only got to sleep about an hour ago, and I feel terrible, like I've been hit by a ten-ton truck. Every muscle in my body aches. I've got cramp in my legs. Coming back to Manchester has bothered me more than I thought it would. The air tastes different here. Bitter. The minibar has been demolished. It's not the kind of homecoming anyone would wish for. There is tension in my stomach that won't shift, and my head is pounding like my brain wants out of my body. I don't know if I can even lift my head off the pillow, that's how much pain I'm in.

Staring at the ceiling, I recall why I left this city. It was because my life was falling apart here. *Had* fallen apart. I wanted to escape. Run away. Go somewhere new. To form new memories and discover new places. A fresh start. But now that I am back in the place I ran from, surrounded by empty bottles, I realise the idea was futile. You can run from a place, but not from yourself. That doesn't go away just because you change your postcode, your city. That follows you wherever you go.

We are staying in the revamped northern quarter, the cool part of town, which is close to the Manchester news bureau. Later, though, we will go to Didsbury, where the

Wilcox family live. Where I lived with Greg for six years. It's an uncanny coincidence, but not in a good way.

Fortunately, I have one last Alka-Seltzer in my bag, so I knock that back. The caffeine in it gives me a perk and tames the headache. A can of Coke helps too. Audrey is sipping black coffee when I enter the hotel restaurant, which looks a bit like the set of a bad nineties sitcom. Chrome everywhere. Not to mention the red and black faux-leather seats. I feel unsteady on my feet this morning, but I'm hiding it well. I'm good at hiding it. It's what I do. Amid the harsh decor, Audrey's youthful skin glows in the soft morning sunlight, and it makes me wonder what happened to my own youth.

'Morning, Alex. Sleep well?'

'Not really. You?'

'Not too bad, thanks. Had a really weird dream about an ex-boyfriend, though. He was from Manchester.'

She's wearing a red silk blouse that matches the red of the blinds. Her hair is styled the same as yesterday, with hair clips separating her fringe from the rest of it. She reminds me of myself at twenty. Full of energy and ambition and a bit on the kitsch side. We don't know each other at all, but her enthusiasm at being here is endearing and I appreciate that in her, I really do. Someone needs some enthusiasm, and I'm finding it quite difficult given the circumstances. She's a girl after my own heart, munching her way through a piece of heavily coated Nutella toast.

'I don't usually eat breakfast, but I figure we'll be camped out all day so I might as well.'

'It's the...'

'... most important meal of the day, I know. You sound like my mother.'

'Gets the metabolism going, which will help your waistline when you're my age.'

I do sound a bit maternal, and as if on cue, my phone buzzes to inform me there are five days left in my fertile window. The need for a male orgasm is looming again. My sex life seems to revolve around 'the window' these days, which is a bit tiresome, but there's nothing I can do about it. I am biologically predisposed to run out of eggs very, very soon.

'Where's the waiter when you need one?'

'Coffee?' Audrey wants to please me, which is really sweet.

'Thank you.'

A waitress appears moments later, but Audrey is already up and striding towards the coffee machine so I order a sensible vegetable omelette, hoping it will counterbalance the abuse I've inflicted on my body in the past twenty-four hours, then check my messages. Nigel has sent a text to say sorry for last night. He has also expressed a desire to meet up again to make up for it. Not sure how I feel about that yet. The crazy ex-girlfriend thing has put me off, let alone the depression treated with meds. He's got way too many issues. Charlie has texted too to ask if he can borrow my iron. His is broken and he has a posh dinner later. I reply with a thumbs-up emoticon because I can't be bothered to type anything.

'Got you a latte. Will that do?'

'I prefer black.'

'Shit, sorry, I should have asked.'

'Might have been a good idea.'

I'm being a bit snappy. It's the hangover. She's only trying to be helpful.

'I'll change it.'

'Thanks, Audrey. Sorry, just milk doesn't sit well with me.'

The breakfast room is empty. We are the only people in it besides the waitress, who looks how I feel. The place is bright and airy, a little too bright for my liking.

My omelette arrives. The smell makes me heave, but I make an effort to eat it under Audrey's watchful eye. She has her notebook and pen at the ready, like a novelist collecting material to use against me, and insists on filling me in on what she knows. I'm too hung-over to argue, so I listen and try to be nice, although I don't feel very nice this morning.

'Mr and Mrs Wilcox live about five miles from here. UKBC Manchester is sending a cameraman from the bureau to work with us for the day. He should have a car, so we can drive over to Didsbury together. See if we can get them to talk to us.'

'Sounds like the obvious plan.' I don't know why I'm being so sarcastic, but hangovers do that to me. Thankfully Audrey is ignoring it.

'I'm hoping the police will release something new on her today. It would help, wouldn't it? If we can get her mother asking for her to come forward, they can then run it on the lunchtime bulletin.'

'Seems like a bit of a stretch right now, but let's see.' Thankfully, the omelette is helping soak up some of the booze in my bloodstream. It tastes better than expected. 'Where are we meeting the cameraman?'

'He's on his way here. I just got a text.'

'Where's he coming from?'

'Should I know that?'

'Don't panic. I thought they might have said, that's all.'

'Okay.'

With nothing more to say to each other, we both check the morning headlines on our smartphones. Sarah's face is all over the Internet. A smiley, carefree, attractive woman. Twitter has gone nuts. There's a new line posted on most news' sites that says: *The police are also seeking a man who they believe may have been in the area at the same time.* Audrey has already read it.

'Did you see this?' Her face has lit up.

'Well, that's something at least. Gives the story a fresh angle.'

'Our exclusive will give the story a new angle.'

'That it will. That it will. Well done, Audrey. Really great work.'

She positively beams at the praise and I make a note to myself that I should offer more of it to offset my snappiness, because I'm sure there'll be more of that given that I'm in the eye of an emotional hurricane.

The papers have mixed opinions on Sarah Wilcox and her role in the crime. They range from her being the main suspect to being an accessory. The official line is that they are seeking to rule her out. The man the police say they are looking for is six foot, brown hair, stubble, wearing casual clothes and seen leaving London Fields train station around seven o'clock. The description sounds a lot like Nigel, but then it could be anyone in east London really.

'Did you read that new comment on Twitter by a bloke who said he'd been on a date with the Homerton victim? He said he met her on a dating site called COMEout. Do you know it?'

Do I know it? That's the website I met Nigel on.

'Heard of it, yeah. It matches people when they pass each other in the street, I think.'

'God, that's terrifying. So someone who means harm to another could literally have them within their sights.' Audrey physically shudders.

'I guess so, yes.'

'Look. Here it is.'

> @Davetherave: She was a bit odd, but charming when we met.

'Is that it?'

'What if the murderer really is an online dater using this site? It was alluded to in the Homerton case, although the police didn't confirm it.' Audrey is scrolling on her screen.

'I asked DI Brook about it yesterday. He didn't want to confirm or deny it.'

'Looks like a pattern is emerging, though, doesn't it? I mean, after the second victim... what was her name?'

'Maggie Horrocks.'

'Yes, that's it, Maggie Horrocks, and now this one. Maybe Dave the Rave came forward because he thinks it's important, now there's been a third victim, you know. Maybe he's a good guy who just wants to help. Maybe he's worried about Sarah Wilcox.'

'Maybe, but we can't report that. We can't use the name of the site unless the police release it.'

'Are we going to wait for the police to tell us everything?'

'That's not what I'm saying, Audrey, but we can't just go claiming that a dating app is being used by a serial killer. Where's our proof? We'll be sued.'

'Right.' She's not particularly listening now. Her face has come alive with the possibility that all three deaths are tied to a dating site. 'God, can you imagine if there is an online serial dater who kills women in east London by using an app where he can literally have them in his sights? I mean, a serial dater who has become a serial killer. It's terrifying. A modern-day Jack the Ripper.' She's reading from her phone. '"The UK has the highest Internet dating turnover of any European country. Last year more than nine million Britons logged on to dating sites."' She scratches her nose.

'Let's just stick to the facts, shall we? Don't go getting ahead of yourself. It will do no good.'

She looks deflated but accepts my comments.

'Okay. Looks like our cameraman has arrived.' She nods towards reception, where a stocky man wearing the usual garb – casual sports clothes and good walking shoes – is standing.

The receptionist points him in our direction, and as he gets closer, I realise I know him and that he knows Greg. We all went to school together. How is this happening to me?

'Alex South? Is that really you?'

Stephen Holland, aka Dutch. Last I knew, he was living in Europe. He looks just the same, although with less hair. He throws his huge arms around me in a bear hug. Dutch is a big bloke. He always was taller and broader than the other boys in the class. No one ever messed with him, so he was a good person to know.

'You look great, Alex. You've kept yourself well. Shot up in the world, I see, working in London now, huh?'

'Thanks. Life brings its just rewards, you know.'

'As cocky as ever, I see.' His grin is wide and his eyes light up as he looks at me.

'I'm Audrey, the producer.' Audrey asserts herself by extending her hand.

'Nice to meet you, Audrey. I'm Stephen, but people call me Dutch.'

Before long, we are on our way to Didsbury. I let Audrey sit in the front of Dutch's dog-hair-covered estate car. I don't want to get into personal questions about my life or relationship status. I'm not sure how much he knows about me and Greg, and whether he's been back in touch with Greg since moving back. It's not a subject I want to get into before the interview.

It takes about half an hour to get to Didsbury from the city centre. Driving through the village is torturous. Every time we slow down, I get butterflies in my stomach imagining I'm going to see Greg walking towards us. Stupid, I know, but I have no idea what he's doing these days: I can't see his Facebook page any more since we blocked each other.

Number 22 Mill Avenue is a semi-detached two-storey red-brick house with a well-kept front garden and a gravel driveway made of white Cotswold stones. The downstairs bay window is dressed with a display of fresh exotic purple flowers. This is a wealthy neighbourhood, although the street Greg and I lived on was modest. We made our home in a two-bed terraced house at the other end of the postcode.

'What do you suggest, Alex?' Audrey has her notebook in hand as ever. Now that the moment is here, she looks quite nervous.

'That we knock on the door and see if anyone's in?'

Dutch smiles, recognising that Audrey is wet behind the ears.

'I should probably go on my own first,' I say. 'We don't want to scare them.'

'Yes, of course. What if they won't talk?'

'Then they won't talk.' I shrug. 'We just wait and try again.'

'Okay.'

There is no gate to the driveway, which is good. Fiddling with a latch is the last thing I need right now. This part of the job never gets any easier, and today is exceptionally hard given the circumstances. I really need to get through it quickly, as my need for a drink is looming. Without it, I'm going to crash. I need to keep my blood alcohol content topped up so that I can function for one more day. My headache is back, and it isn't helping my mood, which is utterly depressed and shitty.

I step across the border that separates public from private property, crack my knuckles and take a deep breath. There's a bell and a knocker. I choose the bell. Moments later, the door opens, and standing in the doorway is a very handsome older woman dressed in racing green from head to toe. I assume this is Sarah's mother. She's clutching a pack of cigarettes. I guess the police have already contacted her. Not that it would matter: her daughter's face is plastered over every front page in the country. She invites me in silently with her body language, as if we've met before. Not quite the welcome I was expecting.

14

May 2017

Dear Diary,

I don't think I've ever felt this bad, ever. It's a mixture of what I'm going through physically and what happened with Alex. I thought I'd found a friend, someone who got me, but she just left me high and dry.

I went to the pub yesterday to tell them that I couldn't work there any more. There was a guy there. He was wasted. He fell over and the manager had to call a taxi to send him home. Apparently his missus had just left him. He was in such a state. He looked really broken. A bit like me. It's terrible how people treat each other, it really is.

Amy, the girl I work with, said he'd been plastered in the pub every day this week. I wondered if I could help, seeing as I know a thing or two about drinking, but then I didn't want Amy to know about that. Funny that his name was Greg, though. The only Greg I've come across recently is Alex's fiancé, the man who answered her phone and told me to stop calling. I wondered if it might be the same guy. I thought if I spoke to him, I might be able to recognise the voice, but I still don't have the confidence to do things like that, approach complete strangers, so I didn't bother.

Work were sorry to see me go, but they understood. They've known about my drinking for years, apparently, and are glad I'm finally doing something about it.

15

The Wilcox home is orderly. Everything has its place. A hint of furniture polish wafts through the tidy hallway. The coat stand has a box for umbrellas and a separate rack for hats. It's the kind of house I dreamed of raising a family in with Greg.

We haven't said a word yet. I follow Mrs Wilcox over terracotta tiles so well polished they glint in the morning sun. The hallway walls are covered in framed photos of a teenage girl, a younger Sarah. She's an only child, by the looks of it. We enter the kitchen at the back of the house – a well-designed room with shiny surfaces. It's so clean it looks like it has never been cooked in. A handful of newspapers are spread on the kitchen counter. Sarah's smiling face stares back at us. Haunting as it is, it's a find, too. Work will be pleased.

Mrs Wilcox leads me out of the house to a beautifully groomed garden, where we sit on painted metal chairs by a matching table on a spotless stone patio. I can't get over how composed she is. Not a hint of emotion. It feels strange, but then you never know how people will react to these types of events.

She takes a cigarette from the pack and lights up. She offers me the box and pushes the lighter across the table in a suggestive manner. I join her. I know I shouldn't –

it doesn't go well with trying to get pregnant, or with a hangover for that matter – but I'm so messed up today I don't think it will make much difference, and there's a bond formed in sharing a cigarette. I'll just have one. Maybe it'll encourage her to open up to me.

'Don't feel guilty… Haven't done it for years myself, but today… well, today is today.' She has a Manchester accent. It feels friendly, soothing and familiar.

I smile and nod empathetically, then light my cigarette, take a long drag and watch the smoke melt into the morning sunlight.

'Have you ever lost someone you love?' She's looking at me curiously.

'Yes.'

'A family member?'

I shake my head. My life fell apart a year ago, but it's not really the same. A speckled bird lands on a feeder at the end of the garden. The ashtray on the table contains three cigarette ends.

'We lost Sarah a long time ago.' She pauses. 'I haven't cried yet. I can't. It's strange that, isn't it?'

'It's the shock,' I say.

I take another drag on my cigarette. It's so quiet I can hear the tobacco smoulder, and wonder what it's doing to my lungs and possibly my ovaries. Mrs Wilcox has been drinking; I can smell it. I don't blame her. I know how that goes. Every parent assumes they can keep their child safe.

'Have the police been in touch?' I ask.

She nods.

'I see.' I wonder what she knows that we don't. It still feels odd to be here reporting on this.

'So you're after a headline like everyone else, are you, Ms South?'

I'm not sure how to respond, so I nod. We sit in silence, smoking, watching the bird on the feeder as another one joins it. My body is crying out for a drink. The cigarette is helping with the need to put something in my mouth, but my legs are starting to cramp.

'The police said they'd send a family liaison officer, but they haven't. We don't know what's going on.' She takes in a lungful of smoke. 'All we know is that they want to talk to her.'

She seems angry.

'She hasn't been in London long.'

I'm in the middle of taking a drag on my cigarette and I realise in this moment that securing the interview is going to be harder than I thought. My phone is buzzing in my pocket but I can't look at it now. It's probably Audrey asking what's going on. I try to move the conversation on from what I know to what Mrs Wilcox knows.

'Does she like London?'

'I don't know. We haven't spoken since she moved. Don't even know where she lives. After she moved, she stopped telling me anything. Just cut me out.'

'Oh, I am sorry to hear that. Do you know why?'

'She hates me. She has good reason.'

I'm not sure how to respond to this, so I don't. I try another approach and talk about something less charged.

'Your garden is really beautiful.'

'Sarah used to help sometimes. She loved it out here.'

'I can see why, it's so peaceful. I'm sure there will be a logical explanation for all this.'

She exhales, letting the smoke stream out of her nostrils this time like a real smoker.

'Logical explanation?' She's standing now. 'Would you like some tea?'

'If it's not too much bother. Sure. Why not.' I follow her lead. I do need to drink something, and at this point anything will do.

'Why don't we go into the house? It's a bit chilly, isn't it?'

'Okay.' I stub my cigarette out next to hers in the ashtray and follow her back indoors.

'Can I use your toilet?'

'In the hallway.'

I lock myself in the downstairs loo and text Audrey. She replies immediately. She's getting impatient. There's only a few hours before the lunchtime bulletin; more than likely she's feeling the pressure from London.

In the kitchen, Mrs Wilcox makes the tea and plates up some shortbread biscuits, then suggests we sit in the lounge. There's something very cold about her, something I can't put my finger on. She's so composed for a mother who has had this kind of news. I would have expected her to be more distraught.

'Sarah loves shortbread. It's her absolute favourite.'

I follow her into the lounge and perch on the edge of the firm velvet chesterfield, which is the same colour as Mrs Wilcox's outfit. There are more family photos in here. Happy images, it seems. But photographs can lie, can't they?

'So you want to interview me? That's why you're here, isn't it?'

'Only if you feel comfortable, yes.'

'How did you find me?'

'My producer, Audrey. She's very good at tracking people down.'

That doesn't sound quite right, but it's too late to take it back. Mrs Wilcox stares out of the window for a moment, lost in her own thoughts, before speaking again.

'Sarah's dream was to be a writer. It seems she may have finally got her story.'

Her gigantic diamond engagement ring sparkles as she rubs her neck with her left hand. I can see some marks on her wrist. Telltale signs of attempted suicide. This is a troubled home.

'I wish she'd never gone to London. We should have helped her buy a flat here. She'd met a nice man, Greg I think his name was. They were quite smitten with each other, or so she said.'

The name hits me like a cold, hard slap across the face. Not my Greg? Surely. Mrs Wilcox continues talking.

'I'll give you your interview, but only if you promise to keep me informed of any developments in the case. It seems you're a better bet than some family liaison officer. The police are only talking to me to help the investigation. They don't actually care about our feelings.'

I'm still trying to work out what she just said about her daughter and a man called Greg.

'So is that a deal?'

'Yes, of course. Anything I can do to help.'

Be rational, Alex, I tell myself. Keep it together. Hearing his name has kind of knocked me sideways, and right now I'm desperate for a drink. 'Do you know where he lives? This Greg? Perhaps he could help with finding her?'

A telephone rings somewhere in the house, stopping her from answering my question. She excuses herself and leaves the room.

I let out a huge breath of anxiety and shake myself down. I need to keep my cool and get the interview done; my career depends on it. I can see a bottle of gin on the shelf and wonder if there's time for me to have a quick swig to perk me up. Almost at once, Mrs Wilcox reappears right behind me.

'Sorry, that was my sister checking up on me.'

She's standing next to a very well-stocked drinks cabinet.

'Will you join me for one? I know it's early, but it's been quite a morning.'

'I don't usually drink when I'm working.'

'Go on. Won't hurt, will it. Just a quickie. I'm sure you have the capacity for it as a journalist.'

Thank God for small miracles. I was starting to get twitchy. This will level me out until after the interview.

'Is Mr Wilcox around? Maybe it's better that you're not on your own.'

She hands me a heavy crystal tumbler. I take it, pretending to be reluctant. I desperately want to knock it back in one go, but instead, I sip at it cautiously. Better to make it last anyway, because I'd only be ready for a second. She puts the bottle on the coffee table within reach of a refill, which is tempting.

'He's at work. Always working. Always worried about money. I don't know why, we have plenty of it.'

She's knocked back her own drink and is pouring a second, this time without tonic.

'Shall I call my cameraman in? He's sitting in the car.'

'Yes. Let's get this over and done with. I'll go fix my make-up.'

I nod with a half-smile. After she's left the room, I have a second quick shot of gin and find a stick of gum in my bag before calling Audrey, who appears almost immediately, like a guard dog. We set up in the garden. Mrs Wilcox is as good as her word and gives a great interview, after which we exchange telephone numbers and promise to keep in touch.

On the street afterwards, Audrey is euphoric about what we've just pulled off.

'Well done, Alex.'

'I'm not sure you can really congratulate me on flogging the emotions of a middle-aged woman who is obviously lonely, confused and guilty about something, but I'll take the compliment.'

'The editors are going to be really pleased with this. It's an exclusive.'

'Yes, it is.' There is nothing else I can say.

'I suggest we drive back to town and send it from the bureau.' Dutch lights up a ciggie. 'It'll be faster than trying to do it remotely.'

The craving for another fag is niggling at me. 'Can I have one?'

'I didn't know you smoked.' Audrey looks on disapprovingly.

'I don't. It's just...'

'It's just that you've spent an hour with a mother who is extremely upset because her child is missing and wanted in connection with a murder.' Dutch finishes my sentence and looks at Audrey before he hands me a cigarette.

She doesn't reply, but gets in the car, leaving us to smoke.

'You okay, Alex?'

'That was tough.' I don't mention the details.

'Yeah. Must have been.'

'She said they haven't spoken in months.'

'I wonder why. Says something about her parenting, if you ask me. You got kids?'

'No.' I say it a bit too curtly.

'I didn't mean to pry.'

'Don't worry about it. I'm just feeling precious. It happens.'

'Sure.' Dutch is swiping his smartphone. 'Looks like Sarah was a troubled person. This article says she went to rehab just six months ago. People can discover bad things in rehab. I wonder if that has anything to do with it. Something definitely felt a bit off with the mother, don't you think?'

16

May 2017

Dear Diary,

I went round to Amy's house today to see if I could find out anything on that bloke who was in the pub, Greg. I couldn't get it out of my head that he might be Alex's Greg and therefore he might be able to tell me how I could contact her. Amy didn't really want to help, but in the end she did, after I begged her. She called a mate who knows him and got his address. It's less than half a mile from the pub, so I walked over there. When I knocked on the door, I was so nervous, but I knew I was there for the right reason so I stood my ground and waited. When he answered the door, I recognised him from the pub, but he didn't recognise me. He must have been so drunk that day.

I asked if I could come in, but he told me to piss off, so I explained that I was looking for Alex and wondered if he knew where she was. It was a shot in the dark, but it worked. He got really angry. Told me how he never wanted to see her again. That she was his fiancée but she had just got up and left. Walked out without a word. Left him high and dry. He was drunk again. After his ranting, painful monologue, he slammed the door in my face.

I tried to call her, but the number was dead. I tried to find her on Facebook, but I think she's blocked me. It's really bad. How can she just get up and leave like that? It makes no sense. No sense at all. I considered that Greg might have done something to her. Something terrible that made her leave.

On my way home, I passed three off licences where I was tempted to buy wine, but I didn't have any money on me so I couldn't put those thoughts into action. It's a trick I've started doing to stay sober – not carrying money. They suggested this at the meetings as a way of stopping yourself from buying booze. Now I just have to figure out how not to touch the stash at home. There's always plenty there.

At the meeting there was a woman who hasn't had a drink for six years. It was inspiring. I cried when I listened to her story, it was so touching. I wonder if I will ever be like that. I hope so. I want to be. I want to be sober and live a healthy life. I'm powerless over alcohol. I have to remember that.

I feel quite lost since Alex upped and left. Just disappeared without any explanation. Cut me out. I thought we were friends. Best friends. That we would always be together no matter what. That's what she said. We made a pact to always look out for each other. That we would always be there for each other so that we could stay dry, but now I don't know where she is.

Drinking or not drinking consumes my every thought, but I'm not going to let that get the better of me. I went to a meeting today, which helped. It's the third one I've been to this week. At the meeting, I discovered there are others like me who feel very lonely. I feel hurt, abandoned and rejected all at the same time. I don't know why she would treat me this way. I just don't get it.

It is good to have AA, though. The connection I experience in that room is profound and life-changing. I can listen to others. Just listen. I recognise myself in them. I'm starting to feel that there is a way through this darkness. They all talk about their higher self, but it's my lower self I need to get a handle on. That *part of me that caves in to the addiction. That part of me that gets annoyed and frustrated with life, with people like Alex. I shouldn't let it affect me so much.*

17

The Manchester bureau is much bigger than I expected. There are at least fifteen members of staff all eager to meet me. Such is life being a local success story. I'm in no mood to talk to anyone after the morning I've had. Audrey, bless her, can see my fatigue and reminds them we have a pressing lunchtime deadline, asking politely that they leave us alone until later in the day. They adhere to her request and shuffle off.

I let Audrey take the lead on this as she's gunning to do it and I'm not feeling particularly well. I've made an excuse about a migraine and she's taken it upon herself to sort the sound bite and let me rest. So while she finds an edit suite, I take refuge in one of the meeting rooms. I close the venetian blinds to create some privacy, then sink into the worn leather sofa.

My muscles hurt as much as my brain but less than my heart. Greg's name is still whirling around in my head. The opportunity to ask Mrs Wilcox for clarification didn't really present itself after we'd done the interview, but I do need to follow that up. Perhaps I'll text her this afternoon, casually, to thank her for talking to us. For lack of knowing what else to do, I resort to my go-to distractions, Facebook and Twitter. That's one thing social media is great for, filling time.

There's plenty of public outrage about the police not having released the name of the dating app and instead dishing out advice on how to date safely.

I have a friend request from Nigel. The dilemma of the second date continues. Thankfully a message alert from my fertility app interrupts that thought.

> TRYING TO CONCEIVE (TTC) TIP: Staying well hydrated helps you produce plump eggs and follicles, and will make your cervical fluid more fertile, helping the sperm travel to the egg.

I look in my bag for water, which I really need more of anyway, but instead I find a shot-size bottle of vodka hiding in the bottom. I probably bought it on the train on the way up or swiped it from the hotel minibar. For a brief moment I wonder if I'm slipping back into my old habits, the ones that drove me and Greg apart, but I dismiss this thought as soon as I've had it. I'm so much better than I used to be. I'm about to be featured on the lunchtime news for two days running. I'm a success story, not a failure.

I return to Facebook and take the plunge by accepting Nigel's friend request. Perhaps it's time for new beginnings. And at least this way I can get an insight into his world should I need to. Browsing his page, it all looks quite normal. There are still plenty of pictures of Fiona, the ex. I wonder what went wrong with them, because they actually look quite sweet together. After I'm done snooping on his life, I launch the dating app to see what the talent looks like in Manchester. Yet another distraction from the pain I'm in. At least I've got a vodka stash to knock back before the bulletin. If it lasts that long.

The first image appears on my screen: Peter, 36. Blonde, good bone structure. Moody-looking. Long hair and very skinny. Pictured on a fairground ride. I swipe left for no. Darren, 42. Black. Holding a glass of champagne in a sports car, sunglasses perched on head, smiling. I swipe left for no. Samin, 38. Bald, bearded, wearing sunglasses in an alpine setting. Overweight. Looks old enough to be my father. Left. Niku, 41. Stocky, clean-shaven, thick black hair, chubby cheeks. The camera angle is weird. He's next to a tiger. Left swipe. Carl, 41. Clean-shaven, wearing a black vest, full arm tattoos, sunglasses so I can't see his eyes. Left. I keep at it for a while and am about to close the app, having decided that the talent pool is much better in London, when a photo appears that sends my nerves into a state of emergency. Greg, 39. Hazel eyes, chiselled jaw, lumberjack shirt, morning stubble, half-grin. It's a photo I have never seen before. His hair is really short. He looks different; good, actually.

I can't actually believe it's him. On a dating app. Is this what's become of us? Lonely and looking for love online? His face stares back at me innocently, as if nothing ever happened between us. The scars of our break-up are hidden by his charming good looks. I remember how much I loved him and how happy he made me. Maybe leaving him was the biggest mistake of my life. I feel so confused. Before I know it, the vodka bottle in my bag is empty. That didn't take long.

I swipe back and forth. There are three photos. Images taken after me. One on a ferry at sea. One in a café. One at night somewhere. He looks happy, but then he always was the life and soul of the party, and he loved me. He really loved me, like no one ever has. He got me completely. We shared the same dreams. Loved the same bullshit. Life was fun in his arms. My heart fills with hope remembering the love, then quickly fades into pain. There were so many arguments, really bad arguments, but maybe now enough time has passed. Maybe the Milk Tray was him reaching out to say sorry.

There's a knock on the wall and Audrey pops her head around the open doorway.

'We've cut the clip. Do you want to come and have a listen?'

My phone clutched in my hand, I get up and brush myself down. 'Sure.'

'Are you all right? You look a bit pale, like you've seen a ghost.'

I tuck my phone in my bag and shove some gum in my mouth.

'I'm fine. I wish everyone would stop asking me if I'm all right, though.'

I follow Audrey across the newsroom to the edit suite.

'Take a seat, my lady.' Dutch turns the chair to face me. 'There were a few clips that worked, but I guess this one is the best. She talks about Sarah being a person who loves life, someone who wouldn't hurt a fly, which could be interpreted as guilt about something.'

'Okay. Let me hear it.'

Audrey leans against the wall, looking nervous. The first shot is of Mrs Wilcox and me.

'You can talk into this bit. It's around thirty seconds.'

I nod approvingly. Then Mrs Wilcox's voice comes in.

'Sarah is a loving person. She wouldn't hurt a fly. She loves life. She went to London to find a new opportunity. She wanted to be a writer. We love her so very much and hope she comes home.' Then she breaks down in tears.

Watching the clip makes me shiver, not only because it's good TV but because there's something quite surreal about it. Mrs Wilcox looks like she's giving the performance of a lifetime. It's real-life drama; perfect TV, in fact. And as Audrey said, it's an exclusive the nation will be fascinated by, earning us some professional kudos and probably a fair few more Facebook and Twitter followers, which equates to power and success in my game. Editors are obsessed with how many followers we have. It's as if our entire career is judged on a statistic.

'Good. Very good.'

Audrey is glowing with excitement. The time is 12.15 pm.

'I've spoken to London. They're happy to run with it seeing as Mrs Wilcox has agreed and now that Sarah's identity has been confirmed with the image published by the police, but they also really want us live from outside the family home.' She is fiddling with her pen as she says it, scribbling in her notebook.

'Seriously? We need to go back out there?'

I feel like I could cry. Every inch of me is about to collapse. The voice in my head is desperate for another drink.

'Yep, afraid so.'

'What do you think, Dutch? This is your area. Can we make it?'

'The weather is good. I think it's better to be on location.'

I was hoping he'd advise against it as he's the driver, but no.

'What time are we in the line-up?'

'It's not the lead because of the vote in Parliament. So third story, probably like ten past one?'

'Third story? This should be leading. Oh well, it'll buy us some time. Have you sent the clip already?'

'Doing it now.' Dutch is busy on the computer. 'Done.'

'So we have fifty minutes to get back and set up?' I nod towards the clock.

'Yep.' Audrey looks really nervous now.

'Better get a move on then.'

There is traffic on the way. I'm watching the clock, as is Audrey. This is quite a scoop. We are silenced by the urgency of the task we have set ourselves. My phone is in my bag. I haven't looked at it since I discovered my ex-fiancé searching for love online. These thoughts fill my mind for the rest of the journey. Maybe he's been unsuccessful, which is why he's contacted me. Maybe he's realised his mistake letting me go.

When we get there, Dutch and Audrey begin a mad rush to set up, leaving me to think about what I am going to say. The editor has called and talked me through the report. He likes the clip, so that's a relief. My deployment has already been justified in their eyes, which takes the pressure off.

Dutch cables me up and Audrey dials into the news centre. We do a sound check with the gallery, and within three minutes we are live on air. Jane, the presenter, cues me in. I can feel my hands starting to shake. It's the booze blues. I just need to hold it together for a bit longer.

'Now to Manchester, where our crime reporter Alex South is live for us with an exclusive from outside the family home of Sarah Wilcox, the woman wanted in connection with the investigation involving three women murdered in east London parks. Alex?'

Without warning, I have a flashback to Sarah sitting on a park bench in Manchester, looking at me, and the gravitas of the moment hits me so hard that for the first time in my broadcasting career I find myself unable to utter a word.

'Alex? Can you hear me?'

I am paralysed. My big moment is here, and what do I do? Freeze, that's what I do. My fucking brain needs to get sober.

'Alex? I believe you are outside the home of Sarah Wilcox?'

Jane pauses again to allow me to speak, but I can't, I can't speak because I'm having what I think is a panic attack and the only thing I want to do is not let it show on air to millions of people. So I stand as still as I can and act as if I can't hear her.

Jane's voice travels down the wire from London explaining to our viewers that we are experiencing technical problems with the line. She follows that up by ad-libbing about Sarah Wilcox, and while Mrs Wilcox's interview is being played out, a voice from the gallery, the news editor or his assistant, starts swearing at me asking what the fuck is going on. I stay still, silent, as if I can't hear them either. Jane gave me my get-out-of-jail card. Dutch stares at me from behind his lens. He knows there's no technical failure.

18

June 2017

Dear Diary,

Today has been hard. I went to a birthday party with Amy, thinking that getting out of the house would be helpful. Keep me busy. I promised myself I wasn't going to touch a drop, because I've been doing so well lately, but what do you know, I broke my promise. Amy's friend kept bugging me to have one, wouldn't leave me alone, and I didn't want to explain that I'm an alcoholic. I didn't drink a lot, though, just one glass of wine.

There's so much pressure when I go out socially to have a drink that it's actually really hard not to. People don't want to hear it when I say no. I didn't really enjoy the wine, to be honest, because I was nervous about drinking too much, but I sipped it and made it last all night. There would have been a time when I downed it and went back for another. So even though I broke my promise, I feel like I am in control. Although that is a slippery slope. As an alcoholic, I must remember I'm powerless against alcohol.

I will go to a meeting tomorrow to talk about that pressure. It's been difficult this week because I'm still really hurt by Alex's disappearance from my life. I can't really believe she's gone. I keep playing it over and over in my mind, but I can't understand what happened. I went to church yesterday morning. I don't really know why. I'm not religious or anything, but I wanted to go. I found it comforting. At the meetings they talk about handing yourself over to a higher power, and it makes sense to me because I can't handle my addiction on my own. I need something bigger than me to believe in. I've learned a prayer that really helps when I feel low, which goes like this… 'God, give me the serenity to accept the things I cannot change, the courage to change the things I can and the wisdom to know the difference.' It is life-changing to say this when I'm feeling low.

I prayed that Alex would get in touch. I'm afraid something bad has happened to her. I hope that writing these thoughts down in my diary will help me process them. That's why I write. I love her and hope she is somewhere safe. Amen.

19

Dutch and I didn't make it back to the office. Audrey called from the bureau to say she was ready to return to the hotel. I told her to go on without me. That was hours ago. We're now in some dive rock bar surrounded by scallies, knocking back our fifth… or is it our sixth round? It could even be our seventh, I don't really know. I lost count when we started. It's been a while since I went drinking like this, socially, because the alcohol levels in my blood don't really permit it. You see, I get outwardly wasted really quickly compared to the person I'm drinking with because I'm already way ahead of them. That's what happened when I had my incident on camera. Since then, I've become painfully aware of this and have learned how to manage it.

I tried to close the gap by buying Dutch two shots of tequila when we first arrived, under the guise of thanking him for covering up my on-air freeze. I'm hoping it might make him less likely to notice my much more inebriated state. We haven't discussed what happened on air yet, but it's bound to come up.

The bar is a real blast from the past. It reminds me of the kind of place Greg and I used to hang out in when we first met, when I was a radio DJ. There's a jukebox and a snooker table. It's shabby and smells of spilt beer and stale cigarettes.

'Let's have some music.' Dutch has just put the drinks on the table. I've switched to whisky. The beer was making me run to the loo every ten minutes, which was becoming embarrassing, plus I'm better on spirits. Vodka is my favoured choice, but drinking straight vodka isn't quite as acceptable as drinking straight whisky. Straight vodka is my secret.

Together we teeter over to the jukebox. He has his arm around my waist to prop me up. I can't remember how much I told him about why I left Manchester, but I don't really care. The time on the wall clock reads 9.45 pm. We started drinking around five. I feel a pang of guilt that I'm not diligently watching the ten o'clock news from my hotel bed to see if they rerun the clip with Mrs Wilcox, but that feeling passes quickly. Alcohol really does help.

At the jukebox, Dutch flicks through the choices. There is a definite theme. Eighties rock. I feel a bit senti-mental about my Manchester days and half expect to see Greg sauntering in through the door. It feels reassuring to be with someone who knows where I'm from for a change. Someone I can just be next to. Don't get me wrong, I don't regret moving to London, but there is something comforting about being here in the north with Dutch. It's a good end to what has been a very rough two days.

'Whitesnake?' Dutch's grin is as wide as his shoulders. 'Jon Bon Jovi? I can see the lady is not impressed. Okay, Fleetwood Mac it is.'

Before I know it, we're dancing, singing along to 'Go Your Own Way' like a couple of teenagers. I lose myself in the music and let go for the first time in a very long time. Dutch is playing the greatest air-guitar solo performance ever seen. As the record comes to an end, we stumble back to the table and land on the sofa next to each other, utterly elated and out of breath.

'You always did have to push the boat out.' He's teasing me.

Our legs lean against each other. It feels nice.

'Like that was all me!'

He sips his whisky and we sit there for a moment enjoying the buzz. Then his expression changes to one of concern.

'So what happened today, Alex?'

'What do you mean?'

'The freeze on air. That wasn't a technical issue.'

It had to come up before the night was out. He's good at his job.

'I don't know. Stress?'

'Was it nerves? The pressure? I know the lunchtime bulletin is a big deal for your career, make-or-break territory, but you were on it yesterday, so what happened?'

'Honestly, I don't know what happened, Dutch. Maybe it's coming back here.'

He changes his posture so his shoulders are turned towards me and his arm slides across the back of the sofa. 'Go on.'

'I used to live in Didsbury, so maybe it brought up some emotions, you know.'

'I see. What happened to you and Greg?'

The expression on my face must have changed, as he quickly corrects his question.

'You don't have to tell me, I just thought you guys were set.'

'I don't want to talk about it.'

And that's when he leans towards me and whispers, 'Do you want to get out of here?'

'Yes please.'

His large hand brushes my face and he leans forward to kiss me. I don't resist. I need this. He's saying something sweet about how much he always fancied me and that he's going to take advantage of me now that I'm single. It doesn't really matter what he's saying, because I'd rather be listening to anything other than thinking about what happened on air today. This is my second chance to prove myself and I just hope I haven't fucked it up for good with this stunt. My colleagues all tell me I'm good at my job; I guess I just need to believe it a bit more. I take his hand and follow him out of the bar.

Before I know it, we are knocking back a bottle of wine from the restocked minibar in my hotel room and making out on the queen-size bed. He is a really good kisser. His hands fumble with my bra strap, but they eventually find the clip. It doesn't take long before we are having sex, drunken sex, which is fine by me. In the heat of the moment I whisper in his ear that I'm on the pill and he can relax on that score. Moments later, his body shudders before he lets out a soft groan. Bingo. He rolls off me and wraps his strong arms around me before we descend into a deep sleep.

–

When I wake, my alarm is beeping. Dutch has gone, leaving the imprint of his head behind on the pillow. It's eight o'clock. He must have only just left. There are three empty wine bottles by the minibar. Ouch. My head really hurts this morning. My mouth is parched. I need water. I pull myself out of bed and stumble towards the bathroom. I don't normally do this, sleep with people I work with, and I'm not sure how I feel about it. Unusually for me, I kind of wish I'd seen him this morning, if only to make sure we're on the same page.

I wonder how much I told him about anything last night, as I can't recall much of it. It's going to be one of those nights that comes back to me in dribs and drabs and I only hope I didn't embarrass myself. Then I remember yesterday's on-air freeze. Shit. God, I feel awful. I look for the Alka-Seltzer but it's not there in my bag and I guess I must have run out. I search my case frantically for some other form of painkiller, and fortunately I find one ibuprofen in a small pocket. It'll have to do.

Audrey is already eating breakfast when I surface. I don't really know how I'm going to hold a conversation with her. I wonder if I shouldn't have skipped breakfast altogether, but I need to eat. I wish I had my shades on, though. This room is way too bright. Make-up is a godsend at times like this. I don't know how men live without it.

'Morning, Alex.'

'Morning.' I take the seat opposite and order a coffee from the waitress.

'Did you have a good night?'

'Wasn't too bad. Feeling it this morning, though.' At least I can justify my hangover with a white lie. 'Saw some old school friends, drank too much. You know the story.'

'Yeah, right. I guess they all wanted to buy you a drink now that you're on telly.'

'Exactly.'

She leaves me alone and puts her head down to check the headlines on her phone. My coffee arrives and I order the vegetable omelette again out of sheer lack of imagination.

'Our interview with Mrs Wilcox is all over the papers this morning, which is good. Well done us!'

'Yes, that's very good.'

'Yesterday was unfortunate, wasn't it? The technical issue, I mean. Are you pissed off about that?'

'A bit, but it happens. You win some and lose some. That's the nature of the news business.'

'Right.'

'You have to learn not to take it personally. Grow a second skin. We made the front page of almost every newspaper today, that's quite a coup.'

'Yes, of course, you're right, Alex. It's so good working with you, you know. I'm really learning a lot.'

'Good.'

My omelette arrives, and although I really don't feel like eating, I force myself.

'The police have released a few more details on the investigation this morning.'

'Like what?'

'Don't know if you remember, but the previous victims were drugged with GHB, a drug that is used a lot in the gay scene. Bit like a date-rape drug, can be fatal when taken in the wrong dosage along with alcohol. They suspect it was used here too.' She puts her hand on her neck as she says it. 'Gives me the chills just thinking about it. God, it's grim.'

'Have the police reacted to our interview?'

'In a roundabout way. They say they still want to speak to Sarah Wilcox.'

I polish off the dregs of my coffee and down a pint of water.

'We should try and track her down next,' Audrey says. 'Wouldn't that be a scoop?'

'Indeed.' Not sure I like the sound of that, though. As I think this, our phones beep in unison.

Audrey has already launched her Reuters app and her face responds to the news flash. 'Flipping heck. Car bomb at Glasgow airport.'

I open the browser on my phone and see the headline: THREE DEAD IN TERROR ATTACK.

'You know what this means, Audrey. It means that London probably won't care about us today.'

She looks disappointed. 'We need to find Sarah or get a reaction from the police to our interview.'

'It's a terror attack. That's the only story that will get on today.'

The concern on Audrey's face creeps into a smile. 'So I can go shopping?'

'Effectively. Yes.'

'Shall we head downtown then before we catch a lunchtime train?'

'Sounds good.'

'Let's meet by reception in an hour.' She's readying to leave the breakfast room.

I give her the thumbs-up and she heads back to her room. Moments later, my phone buzzes. It's a text from Dutch.

> Hey, Alex! I had so much fun last night. We really should do that again. I'm sorry I crept out without waking you, but I needed to change my clothes (Audrey may have figured it out :-)), and if your head felt the way mine did I was sure you would need some more sleep. You're the powerhouse here! You are a gorgeous lady, for the record. Dutch x

It's a really lovely text that makes me feel warm and fuzzy inside. A feeling that has evaded me for a long time. He's such a darling and was just what I needed. I wonder if his sperm might go the distance. I check my fertility app: today could be my lucky day.

20

July 2017

Dear Diary,

I thought life would get easier when I stopped drinking, but actually it's getting much harder. I have to face myself now. I have to get up every day and think about my life. What I'm doing with it. What I plan to do with it. Now everything revolves around abstaining from drink. I literally calculate the hours until I can go to sleep and wake up another day sober. I don't know how this is going to go on.

Today I called the debt-collecting agency and spoke to a woman about my credit card bill that I haven't paid in eight years. How is that even possible? When I was drinking I really had no sense of time passing at all. I mean, eight years! But now I am sober, I am getting on top of these things. That feels good. I'm taking control of my life. Doing the things I should have done a long time ago and getting my affairs in order.

21

We have a few hours to kill before the train. I don't know why, but I have an overwhelming urge to visit the house I used to live in with Greg. Maybe it's because of what Mrs Wilcox said; I don't know. It's one of those things I probably shouldn't do, but I'm going to do it anyway.

The taxi drops me at the end of the street lined with two-storey terraces that lean towards the pavement's edge. There are no trees in sight. It looks so much bleaker than I remember. The only greenery that exists here is a wheelie bin outside each house, making it a challenge to walk along the narrow pavement.

Now that I'm here, it feels like a terrible idea. I'm not sure what I was thinking, but since the Milk Tray arrived I can't seem to get him out of my head. I feel out of place on this modest street now. I have outwardly changed to such an extent that there is nothing left of the girl I was when I lived here. Scruffy trainers and hoodies were my signature then. Such is life on the radio, but TV, well TV is TV. It demands more.

The window of number three displays the same tired sign it always did: TORIES OUT. BRING BACK FREE EDUCATION. It makes me smile. A reminder of where I came from.

A black cat shoots out from behind a bin, crossing my path. I can't remember if it's lucky or unlucky; either way, my stomach is in knots. I haven't had a drink this morning for the sheer lack of anything in my minibar. I wonder how long I can go without one. I'm going to try my best. It's a good day to detox; what with the terror attack, the news centre won't be bothered about the London murders. I need to make the most of the opportunity to wean myself off this binge. I feel sick, exacerbated by fear pulsing through every cell in my body. I'm afraid to see Greg and I'm afraid not to see him. I'm just a mess and am having serious doubts about what it is I want to achieve by coming here, but then retreat is not an option.

Outside number 11, I have a flash of fondness remembering our very first day here. We had fun, Greg and I. He really got me for a while, more than anyone ever has. The day we moved in, he carried me across the threshold as though we were some loved-up married couple. Wouldn't let me put my foot through the door on my own, like we'd bought the place, when in fact we were only renting. But then that was Greg, a man of outdated romance and traditions. The thought makes me smile, but it's soon replaced with anxiety. I have no idea what I'm going to say if he is here.

There's no bell where there used to be one, so I hammer on the door with my fist. After a minute or so, I try again, but there's still no answer. The net curtains look like they've seen better days. I don't remember there being net curtains. Someone else must have moved in. Maybe he has a new lover? I try again, but no one comes.

Across the street, a petite girl comes out of number 14, struggling to carry an art case. I wave to get her attention but it's a futile attempt: she's off at a pace, most likely late for class. Then an elderly man exits the house next door. He must be in his seventies. I've never seen him before.

'Hiya. Sorry to bother you, but I wonder if you know who lives here?'

'Sorry, love. My hearing isn't what it used to be. Can you speak up?' He's pointing to a pair of hearing aids.

I repeat the question and he smiles in understanding.

'Only been here a few months, me. The place has been empty since then. Think the bloke who used to live there moved, not sure.'

I fish out my phone to show him the photo of Greg on my dating app, but it's crashed and I can't retrieve it. I beg him to wait a moment so I can restart it. He locks his door and waits politely for me to find the image. When the app finally opens, the photo has gone and a new profile is in its place.

–

In the taxi on the way back to town, I feel deflated by my morning. I'm not sure what I was thinking. It was strange to stand outside our old house and yet see nothing familiar in it, not even the neighbour. Like our lives never existed there. I really need to talk to someone. I need to get my head straight and my drinking on the right track. I wonder whether I should open up to Charlie when I get back to London, but then my phone buzzes and my thoughts of good intentions come to an end.

The taxi crawls through traffic slowed by a torrential downpour. That's one thing I don't miss about the north, the rain. There's a woman about my age standing at a bus stop who has been completely caught out by it. I almost want to offer her a lift, but I don't. Instead I ask the driver to head in a different direction, because she looks like someone I used to know and reminds me of how and why I met Sarah Wilcox.

Twenty minutes later, we pull up outside a church and I wonder if this is an even worse idea than visiting the house I lived in with Greg. It's where I attended my first AA meeting, one of a handful. It didn't really work for me, all that talk of a higher self, of God, but I'm trying to figure out what happened, I suppose. Looking for remnants of the past, something that might help explain how I got to where I am. I ask the driver to wait and he agrees for a cash deposit.

Fortunately, the rain has stopped. I walk slowly through the church gates, taking a moment to remember why I came here in the first place. I was a mess. My life was spinning out of control. It had become unmanageable. Greg had threatened to leave unless I did something about my drinking. He blamed it for our failure to conceive, and then for the miscarriage, which really hurt. I'm not sure that's what happened, though. People get pregnant all the time while drinking too much.

Maybe he was just tired of me. Tired of not being able to make plans. Tired of my mental instability, as he put it. Tired of being provoked into arguments. Tired of my bullshit basically. Tired of my lies. He was desperate to be a father, as I was to be a mother; as I still am.

Standing here in the rain, I ask myself whether I'm really fit to be a mum. I mean, I say I won't do it again, but then I do. I binge-drink to the point where life blurs into one long messy corridor and the only way forward is to have another drink. I don't mean to do it. I truly don't. I've been doing so well lately. But then the voice in my head reappears and tells me it needs it. So I give in and the voice wins.

The place looks exactly the same. I make my way around the back of the building and down the ramp towards the green door. A door that held so much hope for me then. It made Greg so happy when I decided to come here. It held our relationship together. It supplied us with hope that things could be different. It convinced Greg that we were on the same page, but we weren't.

He seemed to think I couldn't control my drinking, but that's where he was wrong. I've always been able to control my drinking. If I couldn't, I wouldn't be able to hold down this job, would I? I mean, people who can't control it, well, they end up on a park bench, doing nothing with their lives, just like Sarah Wilcox. Yes, I remember now how we met. She's a real alcoholic, not someone like me. Not a news reporter.

As I approach the door, I see the letters on the bottom bell: AA.

The door is locked. Of course. The group meet on Thursdays, and today is Wednesday, or at least I think it is. There's a groove in the door where someone tried to break in once; I remember that from when I used to come here. I run my finger over it, wondering what happened to all that hope Greg and I had, but my thoughts are brought to an abrupt end by a woman who appears behind me.

'Hello. Can I help you?'

'Oh, no. No. I'm just, um…'

I was so lost in my own thoughts, I didn't hear her sneak up on me. I feel like I've been discovered, but doing what I'm not sure. My hand pulls back from the door and takes cover in my protective pocket. Then I realise, as does she, that we've met before.

'Alex? Is that really you?'

It's Jessica. One of the women in the group.

'Shit, it is. It's you. How the bloody hell are you?'

'I'm okay. Was just passing and thought I'd… you know…'

She smiles. It's a genuine smile born of a profound sense of empathy nurtured in AA. 'It's good to see you.' Then her expression changes and she looks at me differently. 'Oh gosh. I just realised. I've seen you on the news, haven't I?'

'Yes.'

She repeats my sign-off: 'Alex South, UKBC.'

'Yes. I…' I don't know why I came here.

'It's okay, Alex, don't worry. I won't tell anyone. You know we practise confidentiality. What stays in the room and all that.'

'Yes.' I can't seem to say anything else.

She's nodding. 'So you've made it big in the south? Did you see what I just did there?'

'I did.'

'Well done. Really, well done.'

'Thank you.'

'So you're doing okay?'

'Yes, I suppose I am.'

My head is pounding and I can just about stand up right. I need something to drink, but I'm doing okay, better than Sarah Wilcox.

'You do know Sarah Wilcox used to come here?'

'Yes. I know.'

'Is that why you're here?'

'Yes. I suppose it is.'

'Well, she hasn't been here for a long time. Heard she'd gone to rehab. You look great, by the way. Really great.'

'Thanks. Look, I really must get back to work, but do you know which rehab?'

'I don't, I'm afraid. Somewhere near Manchester, though. Possibly Wilmslow, out that way. We'll pray for her at the weekly meeting. Shall I call you if I hear anything? Stranger things have happened.'

I don't want to give her my details, so I take hers instead and leave, relieved as the taxi carries me away from the past back to the present. I shouldn't have gone there. Rehab. That's hardcore. I'm not a hopeless alcoholic like that. I'm a success story. I've moved on. Done well for myself. Achieved a lot.

I stop and buy some ibuprofen to stave off the pain. I also buy a healthy drink, a fruit juice, aimed at keeping my oral fixation at bay. I have to detox today if it's the last thing I do. I need to get myself straightened out. I rub my tummy and recall Dutch's message. An offspring with his sweetness would be grand.

Audrey is in the bureau when I arrive and beckons me over.

'Have you seen the news?'

'Have they caught the Glasgow bomber?'

'Not that. The police have just named the victim from yesterday as Alice Fessy.'

'What?'

My phone is ringing. It's Mrs Wilcox.

'Shit.'

'Who is it?'

'No one. Look, we need to get back to London. This will make the evening news bulletin now.'

'But the terror attack…?'

'They can't really ignore this, though.'

'I think DI Brook is about to give a press conference on one of the agency feeds.' Audrey has the remote in her hand. 'Yep, here we go.'

DI Brook is readying himself to speak to the press.

'We have been able to identify the woman in the park yesterday as Alice Fessy, a French citizen. Aged thirty-eight. Actress. We have notified her family, who live in Paris.'

A journalist out of shot shouts: 'What about the online dating angle? Is it possible the killer met her on the site COMEout?'

Brook hesitates, then clears his throat. 'We will release that information when we feel the time is right, but until then, I would ask the women of east London to remain vigilant.'

The journalist pushes him for a proper answer. 'What does that mean, vigilant?'

It's a good question and it's the right question.

'My advice would be to refrain from using all dating sites until we have caught the person responsible for the deaths of three women. Thank you.'

'So you are connecting all the deaths?'

He ignores the question and disappears inside the police station once more. My phone is ringing. It's the London newsroom.

'I take it you've seen the latest developments?'

'Yes, we're on the next train.'

'Good. Please come to the news centre when you get back. We need you on the ten o'clock bulletin tonight. And look into this online dating theory. That's serious. See if you can firm up which site, something official from the police. If there is a guy out there plucking women from dating sites, then that's terrifying. Jesus.' Marysia hangs up.

Ten minutes later, we are in a taxi heading to the train station and I'm thinking about the drink I need to get my hands on to get myself through the ten o'clock bulletin. Today is not a day for detox after all. I had good intentions; it's just a question of life getting in the way.

'This is crazy. We need to find Dave the Rave and interview him.' Audrey is on her smartphone, scrolling through various news feeds.

'Dave who?'

'That guy on Twitter who Laura what's-her-name spoke to. He said he met Maggie Horrocks on COMEout. It's a lead. It might be what we're looking for to move the story on.'

'I thought you wanted to find Sarah Wilcox?'

'I do, and I'm going to make every effort to do that, but this is what we've got for now and I think the online dating angle is huge.'

I'm relieved that Audrey's focus has shifted. The information I got about Sarah going to rehab could be a start, but I'm not going to go there. I need to push away thoughts of Greg, Sarah and the past, if I can, and concentrate on the present. Audrey is right. The online dating angle is huge. So I'll support her on that.

The first thing I do once we are safely on the train is call DI Brook, but the reception is terrible and I can't get a stable connection. Somewhere around Birmingham my phone starts vibrating and doesn't stop until we reach Rugby. It's Mrs Wilcox. I have no idea what she wants, but I can't deal with it right now. My head is such a mess. It feels like it's about to explode into a million tiny pieces. I need a drink and I can't have one until we're off the train because I don't have any on me and I can't let Audrey see. I really thought the Glasgow terror attack would give me a breather, let me detox, but it hasn't panned out that way. This story is still developing. I just need it to die down for a day. I lean my head on my jacket rolled up against the window and try to get some sleep, if only to stop me thinking about booze.

At Euston station, I manage to grab a small bottle of vodka while Audrey goes off to use the loo, which perks me up. We jump in a cab and head for the news centre.

'Alex. Good to see you.' The editor on shift, Marysia, has risen from her perch to greet us when we arrive. 'How was it?'

'Sad. Mrs Wilcox was a wreck. She didn't know what to think, you know?'

'I bet she still doesn't. Poor woman. The police have handled this really badly. They should have, at the very least sent a family liaison officer with some compassion talk to her. Listen, we need you to be back at the scene for the ten o'clock bulletin. I know you've had a long day, but you did a really great job securing the interview with Mrs Wilcox and I think you should stay on the story. It won't be forgotten.' She winks. And there it is, the respect I deserve. I'm back in the game. A success story. That's what I am.

'Of course.'

22

August 2017

Dear Diary,

I was doing so well, two solid months off the drink and I felt like it was coming together, until my mum said yesterday that if I don't get a job she is going to throw me out. I've thought about talking to my dad, asking for his support for me getting sober, but he's never around. He's always working, which helps him to avoid having to deal with what's going on at home. The changing relationship between me and my mum. I've decided that I need to stand on my own two feet, and she doesn't like that. She's always goading me.

The other mad thing that happened last night is that I saw Alex on the news and she looks amazing. She was reporting from Hull on a murder case. I didn't know she was a journalist. It's been ages since I thought about her, so it was quite a surprise. The story was grim. A toddler was found dead in the attic of his family home. They've arrested the mother's boyfriend. That must have been a really difficult story for her to cover. I miss her. I miss our friendship. I want to know how she is and how her journey to sobriety is going. Mine is really rough, mostly because I find it difficult to be anywhere near a pub, which rules out any socialising with Amy because she works in a pub and hangs out in pubs. And to be around my mum, makes being at home tough too.

I decided to revisit Greg and see if Alex has been in touch, but he was super-moody with me. He hasn't heard from her. He actually blamed me for her leaving, which is really unfair. Going by his attitude, I'm not surprised she left. He was really rude and said that if I didn't leave him alone he'd call the police and tell them I was stalking him, which was spiteful, so I decided never to go there again. I don't need negativity in my life.

23

Dear Diary,

Being blamed by Greg for Alex's disappearance really got to me. More than it should have done. I don't know why. She obviously had her own reasons for going. The fact that she is now on telly shows it was probably more a case of her ambition and a failed relationship, which has nothing to do with me. I really had no idea she was a journalist. I just thought she worked in an office somewhere. It's very impressive what she does. He probably didn't appreciate her, but what he said kept niggling at me, so I went back to see him. To my surprise, this time he let me in. He'd been drinking. He was in a right mess. The house was a state. Dirty clothes everywhere. Dirty plates. It looked like he hadn't cleaned up in over a month. The place was disgusting, actually. He'd lost so much weight too because he hadn't been eating properly, if at all.

I'm not sure why he let me in. Perhaps it was because being near me made him feel he was close to Alex? We do look quite similar since I had a haircut like hers. I gave him a hug and he wept in my arms for a long time. After that, I went to the shop and bought some vegetables with money he gave me and made some soup. While that was on the stove I told him to have a shower and then I cleaned the place up.

There were still reminders of Alex everywhere. The house was almost like a shrine to her. Books she used to read. Her hand cream. A pair of shoes, some clothes. Piles of post addressed to her. Electricity and gas bills. Everything here was in her name by the looks of it. I put it all together thinking that I might forward it to her when I figure out where she lives, which I plan to do. I'm not going to give up on finding her now I know who she works for. She has a problem and she needs help. I'm going to save her just like she did me. I owe her. She changed my life and I want her to know that she can change hers too.

After Greg was out of the shower we ate the soup and he thanked me for coming round. I explained properly how I knew Alex and how she had changed my life. I think he found it comforting. He opened up about her drinking and said he was pleased to hear I had decided to go dry. It made him feel hopeful that Alex could get to the same place too, but even though he still loves her, he said he needs to move on and that packing up her things would help, so we put all her stuff in bin bags and stacked them in the spare room.

As I was leaving, Greg gave me a big hug and apologised for being such a dick on my previous visits. He was glad I'd come back, he said, because no one understood how he felt. He gave me a box of Milk Tray that was in the house to say thanks. Said he used to give them to Alex on her birthday as a joke. He asked me to come back and visit again. I don't know if I will, but I'm glad we've been able to have a proper talk. He doesn't seem that bad, actually. He just seems like a man who's had his heart broken.

After that, I went to a meeting because I was worried that something in the house might trigger a relapse. I told Clive, my sponsor in the group, about what had happened and he was very supportive. He thinks I should try rehab if I can afford it. He thinks I'm ready. He says it will help me find out what sets off my drinking, which could help me quit for good. He says I need to deconstruct who I think I am and find out who I really am. I'm going to seriously consider it because I want to get better, but it is expensive and I have no idea where I would get the money.

It's mental how expensive it is to get help when you're an alcoholic. I can't afford rehab on my own without my parents' help, and I can see why many people wouldn't be able to tell their parents. It hasn't been easy.

The only thing I do know is that I need to take my recovery to the next level because I like being sober and I want to keep it this way. I wish I could tell Alex about it all. I really wish I could.

24

We are still working out what to do on the ten o'clock news. We don't have much to go on other than the victim's name and nationality. Audrey has been stalking Alice's online presence hoping to come up with something.

'So what are you after? A straight-up live? An interview with a local? Or...'

Marysia talks with her hands, as if words are not sufficient. 'I think a straight-down-the-line. A couple of questions from the presenter. We could play a clip if you find a good interview, possibly with someone connected? Needs to be meaty, though. Emotional, you know.' As she finishes her sentence, she pushes her trendy black-framed glasses back up her nose.

Audrey looks like she has a plan already. I know that face. I saw it in the park when she'd hatched the idea to go to Manchester and interview Mrs Wilcox.

'My sources tell me Alice Fessy worked at an advertising company in Brick Lane part-time, while looking for acting jobs. Maybe we can talk to her boss? They love the publicity, don't they, ad agencies.' She is looking down at her notepad as she says it.

Audrey is good. She's made for this job. Marysia looks impressed too. I can see it in her eyes. The way she's watching her, silently admiring her commitment and determination.

Marysia's hands sink into her pockets and she visibly relaxes. 'Alex, can you give your friends at the Met a call and follow up on the dating angle that seems to be gaining traction on social media? That's a matter of public interest.'

'Sure.'

'I need to make a call too.' Audrey doesn't wait for a response. She leaves without looking up, focused on her phone.

'So, how was it? Going back to Manchester? Isn't that where you're from?'

I nod. 'Was nice to be back although it would have been better under different circumstances.'

'I bet. Not sure how I would react if my daughter was wanted in connection to a murder. You have children?'

'No.'

There are twelve editors who run the news bulletin and I realise in this moment that I hardly know anything about their personal lives; about as much as they know about mine, which is probably a good thing.

'You want kids?' she continues.

'Yes. It just hasn't happened yet.'

'My friend missed the boat last year. Doctor told her she can't now.'

'Oh no.'

'She's thinking of adopting.'

'Right.' The thought of adoption hadn't crossed my mind, but perhaps it should.

'I'd better get on, Alex. Make sure you're cued up in good time for the live.' She doesn't even ask about my frozen moment on air yesterday, which is a relief. But then such is the nature of the newsroom and shift work. People move on. The pressure to deliver today is what consumes us. It was a technical fault in her mind and it will stay that way.

I smile. 'Will do.'

'Good. Talk later.'

Looking around the newsroom for someone familiar, I spot Ayla, one of the output producers. We became quite close for a while until she got a four-month attachment to Jerusalem. She's already up from her seat and striding towards me, her long curls tumbling around her shoulders.

'Alex! How the hell are you?' She leans forward to kiss me on both cheeks.

'You're back! When did that happen?' It's genuinely lovely to see her.

'Last weekend. Just getting into the swing of things, you know. Bloody cold here in London.'

'Tell me about it. Was even colder up north!'

'Oh shit, yeah. What happened yesterday with the live?'

'Lost the connection, couldn't hear a thing.'

'Christ. You'd think we could get a line to Manchester sorted, wouldn't ya? Still, amazing work with the interview. Really well done. What a scoop.'

Her hand reaches for my shoulder affectionately. People want to touch success. It makes them feel important. It reaffirms their own sense of professional progress. I don't tell her it was Audrey who secured the interview.

'So how was it? Jerusalem?'

'It was great. I'll have to tell you about it some time. So what are you up to today?' she asks.

'We're doing the ten o'clock bulletin tonight on Alice Fessy.'

'Oh Christ, yeah. What a fuck-up by the police. It's a horrible story. Reminds me of one in Ireland a few years back. The girl met her killer online. In fact, he groomed her before he killed her. Tell you what, I feel like I've seen Sarah Wilcox before, you know. Didn't she go to that yoga class you took me to in London Fields, the one under the arches?'

'The hot yoga class?'

'Yeah. I'm pretty sure I spoke to her there. Jesus, the thought of it gives me the shivers.'

'I know. Well, if she does live in London Fields, I suppose you could have met her.'

'You know this drug they reckon was used, GHB? It's used by the gay community all the time, known as "G" on the scene.'

'Are you saying you think these women were gay?'

'It's a possibility.' Ayla thinks every woman she encounters has the potential to be attracted to her.

'Well, we don't know how relevant that is yet, do we?'

'I guess not.'

'Have you told the editors your thoughts on the gay angle?'

'No, and I'm not going to. I'm just sharing it with you because I trust you and your journalism.'

Audrey is back and ready to roll.

'I've secured an interview with Alice's boss, but we need to leave now.'

'Look. I'll let you get on.' Ayla smiles at Audrey. I know that look. It's the one I got when we first met. The pair introduce themselves to each other before Audrey hustles me out the door.

–

Jack greets us polishing his lens outside the building on Brick Lane. Audrey takes the lead and with her short legs strides through the giant sliding door that seems to extend to the heavens.

'This way Jack.'

He puckers his lips behind her back. He doesn't like being told what to do by women, especially those younger than him. I ignore him. I am on her side. It makes my life easier not having to worry about the production part of what we're doing. Ambition can be a beautiful thing when harnessed for the right purpose.

In reception, every available surface is bright white, which doesn't help my state of mind. I need a darkened room where no one can see how absolutely fucked I am. I feel the urge to put my sunglasses on. Jack looks at me in sheer panic. I know what he's thinking: this is a terrible space to conduct an interview in. Moments later, however, we are ushered through another sliding door into a large open-plan office where the materials aren't quite so abrasive. There are at least twelve workstations that are vacant. Everyone must have already left for the day.

From the back of the room a painfully handsome man glides towards us. I almost missed him because his grey shirt matches the walls. His jet-black hair is swept up in a quiff and his glasses remind me of Marysia's.

'Thanks for agreeing to talk to us, Mr O'Riley.'

'Cathal, please.' He extends his hand to greet me. 'Alice was a gentle soul. We are all absolutely devastated.' He has obviously spoken to the media before, judging by his composure.

'How long had she worked for you?' Audrey starts with the questions.

'A few months.'

'Did you ever see a boyfriend pick her up from work?' She says it so casually that it doesn't sound intrusive.

'I don't know much about her personal life. She only worked here one day a week. I was doing a friend a favour really.'

Jack is struggling with where to set up, so Audrey goes to his aid.

'A friend, you say?' I ask.

'Yes. Well, my wife's friend actually. She goes to a local writing group and I think they met there. Alice wanted to be an actor but was finding it difficult in London, so I gave her a job to help her pay the rent really.'

'Would it be possible to get the address of this friend?'

He looks uncomfortable with this question. I have already spotted a bottle of Jack Daniel's on a desk at the back of the room. The voice in my head is telling me to go get it, but I know I can't. I need something, though, so I find a piece of gum in my bag and shove it in my mouth, hoping that it'll create the kind of distraction my mind needs.

'To be honest, I...'

'I know what you're thinking, but it'll only be a matter of time before the media find her, and UKBC will treat the story with dignity. We are much better placed to take the lead on this story.'

He nods in a serious manner. 'Yes, I see what you mean.'

'Shall we?' Audrey is back, ushering him towards the camera, where she and Jack do a sound check.

'If you could first state your name and your relationship to Alice Fessy, that would be really helpful. Then tell us what kind of person she was and how you felt on hearing the news of her death.'

He clears his throat and starts to talk.

'My name is Cathal O'Riley, Alice was my employee. She worked on reception and was always very polite to people. It's a tragic loss. None of us could believe it when we heard the news. She will be missed terribly. I hope the police catch whoever did this.'

'Perfect! Thank you very much.' Audrey expresses her gratitude with a beaming smile, which feels slightly inappropriate.

'Thank you.'

We shake hands and say our goodbyes. As we leave the building, Audrey gets busy on her phone. Jack suggests grabbing a bagel from the Brick Lane Bakery, so we head north on foot. It gives me time to gather my thoughts and check my messages. There's a new one from Nigel asking if I'm okay. I reply to say I'm fine but busy with work and that I'll be in touch later. There's also a message from Mrs Wilcox. She sounds distraught, and desperate to talk to me. I press delete and hang up on my voicemail service.

When we reach the Shoreditch end of Brick Lane, Jack goes to get the food while Audrey and I hang about outside surfing on our phones. She's rambling on about whether she should delete the Tinder app or not. Not that I have an opinion. I'm tired physically and emotionally, drained on both fronts, but we've still got work to do. The voice in my head is back, telling me to find a bar as soon as possible.

As Jacks exits the bakery laden with food and Audrey announces that she is going to delete the app, I spot my neighbour Charlie further along Bethnal Green Road, walking away from us with a woman. They look like they are definitely more than friends. Jack is pointing out that the bag has broken, but all I can do is focus on Charlie holding hands with someone new. I've never seen him display such affection in public. He's generally so opposed to it. I surmise that he must really like her, and while I'm happy for him, I feel a pang of jealousy.

'Come on, Alex. We've got to get going!' Audrey shouts at me from a taxi they have summoned. Moments later, we're driving along Bethnal Green Road past Charlie and the woman he looks so smitten with. I feel betrayed, yet I don't know why. My hand finds a half-bottle of wine in my bag. I must have picked it up when I went into the small Turkish shop to buy some water. My mind is playing tricks on me, as are my emotions.

25

August 2017

Dear Diary,

I woke up today and knocked back a half-bottle of vodka. That was just so I could get out of bed. After that, I called the rehab centre to see if there was a space because I hate what I'm doing to myself. They said yes. I booked myself in. I had a long chat with my dad and he agreed to help me. He has given me the five thousand pounds I need. That's how much it costs. It's insane. How can anyone afford it? Especially if you have to tell your parents. The cost of that is immeasurable.

It has taken months of meetings for me to get to this point. Dad hasn't told Mum and he asked me not to. Said she wouldn't be able to cope with it. He said that when I come back he would tell me stuff that he hasn't been able to say before about when I was really young, when I was a baby. I asked him to tell me now, but he said no, that I would be better prepared to hear it after rehab. He's glad I'm going. I have mixed feelings about it. I'm really nervous, but pleased with myself at the same time. I hope it will help me sort myself out. I hope it will cure my addiction, if that's even possible. It's taken me six months — well, much longer really — to get to this point.

I wonder if Alex has gone dry now that she's on TV or whether she still believes she's in control. I need professional prescribed help, which is why I'm choosing rehab. I want to have a life. I thought going to the meetings would do it, but it hasn't been enough to make me stop. I need to get to the bottom of why I drink so that I don't do it again. To find out which came first: the drinking or the depression. It's a chicken-and-egg scenario.

The place looks nice in the brochure. Peaceful. The building is surrounded by a forest and it's all very green, not unlike Didsbury. I like being close to nature. I have to take the train to Wilmslow and from there get a bus. I'm going to be there for at least three weeks. They recommended I stay for a month, but I can't afford that so I'm just going to do what I can. I'm working on the principle that three weeks is better than no weeks.

I went to a meeting last night and spoke to Clive. He's pleased that I'm going. He thinks it will be good for me. There are a few people in the group who have been to rehab; they told me the best way to approach it is with an open mind and to submit to the process. They also say it's going to be hard and I have to try my best to be as honest with myself as I can be. I'm afraid of what I might discover about myself, because I don't have many childhood memories thanks to the booze, and my dad's face looked sad when he spoke to me. He looked guilty, as if he had a confession to make.

At the same time, I'm looking forward to being proactive about my addiction. I really wish I could talk to Alex about it. Clive said he'd met her at a meeting once but didn't believe she was ready to fully admit the extent of her addiction. He said he felt like she was going to AA because she had to, not because she wanted to, but he also said it can take some alcoholics a few goes to really enter a twelve-step recovery programme, and this might happen over the course of several years.

When I asked why he hadn't expressed these thoughts before, he said that he didn't want to hurt me because he knew how much she meant to me, but he now felt I could listen to his opinion. Plus the twelve-step programme does not encourage passing judgement on others, although he had been worried about how much importance I'd put on Alex being in my life. On reflection, it surprised me to hear this, because she was the one who took me to a meeting in the first place. She started this journey for me. I really thought she wanted to get better herself, but I'm starting to think maybe she wasn't quite as altruistic as I originally believed.

I don't want to judge her because whatever her motivation was it got me on the right track, and for that I'm very grateful. But it does change things a bit if she was using me for her own gain. I'm starting to question whether she was really ever my friend at all.

26

The crime scene in London Fields is still cordoned off, with police dotted around the perimeter. The white tent has gone, though. It's dark and the park is empty. I'm miserable. I'm in pain and it's cold. Being a lead story on the evening news isn't always the most glamorous job, that's for sure. It's the buzz I enjoy, that feeling of adrenalin just before you go on air that lingers with you for a while after. There's nothing like it. It's what I live for these days – well, that and my next shot of vodka, which I am going to cut out. I just need one day off to detox. Just one day so I can shut the world out and face the demon in myself.

Jack has set up with a policeman standing behind us. I am cabled up with a few minutes to spare when Audrey runs over and hands me her phone.

'What?'

'Just listen.'

There's a press statement being made live from the Serious Crime Division. Audrey is up to her old tricks again and has got the news centre to play it down the line so I can listen in. She really is a great producer. I can hear DI Brook's voice talking to the media stationed outside the police station. Moments later, he confirms what we've all been waiting for: that all three women were members of the dating site COMEout. He also confirms that all three were drugged and strangled: the first victim, Jade Soron, on 27 January; the second, Maggie Horrocks, on 9 February; and Alice Fessy on the 27th. The Met is appealing for women in east London, and in particular Hackney, not to use online dating apps until the case is solved, because they believe this could be how the killer is choosing victims.

We have a new line on the story, which has pushed the report up to second place, just below the Glasgow attack.

'What did they say, Alex?'

'We have one minute till air.' Jack is counting down. 'Audrey, can you get out of the shot, please.'

'Alex?'

'Audrey, please.' Jack looks like he's about to swing for her.

Then a voice from the gallery speaks through my earpiece.

'Ready, Alex? Can you give us a sound check?'

I count down the line. 'One, two, three, four, five, six, seven...' The light on the camera is blinding. It blots out everything. I feel completely disorientated. I try as hard as I can not to squint, but it's difficult. My head hurts.

The producer in the gallery is still talking. 'Sound is great. Picture is great. Are you up on the latest coming out of the Met? We haven't got time to turn a clip around.'

'Yes. I can talk about that.'

'Great. In thirty... You're right at the top, Alex, lead story.'

And just like that, we are pushed to the top of the bulletin. Caroline, tonight's presenter, introduces me and I'm cued in.

'Yes, Caroline, that's quite right. The Metropolitan Police have just announced that they strongly recommend that anyone subscribing to the dating site COMEout should not use it for the foreseeable future, because, and I quote, this could potentially be an evolving pattern. Three deaths in the borough of Hackney within the space of a month, and the police are clearly worried this could be the start of something sinister. Earlier this evening, we were able to speak to the employer of Alice Fessy, the latest victim in this terrifying story that could potentially involve an online date killer. He described her as a gentle soul.'

The gallery plays the clip and we are cleared.

'Nice work, Alex.' Audrey's adrenalin has her pumped. 'That was amazing. The way you turned around that information. Well done.'

'Thanks.'

The need to get some alcohol in my blood is intense. I feel like I'm crashing and I can't, not yet. Not until they've packed up and we've said our goodbyes. I'm doing my best to keep it together, but it's not easy. It takes all my energy. At least my shakes can be put down to the fact that it's absolutely freezing, which weirdly I don't mind as it's masking the pain I feel in every inch of me. Thankfully it doesn't take Jack too long to pack up, and we all go our separate ways. I'm going to start my detox tonight, after I've had my last fix.

–

On the way home, I have this dreadful sense that someone is following me, but when I turn back, there's no one there. I put it down to the paranoia that comes with day

138

four of a binge, although when I start walking again, I swear there are footsteps somewhere along the road behind me, and every time I stop, they stop too.

As I turn onto my street, my phone is buzzing. Mrs Wilcox is calling again. She's probably just watched the report and wants to talk to me about it, so I pick up.

'It's all my fault. I didn't take care of her.'

She sounds hysterical. I try to comfort her, but she's not listening. She sounds really drunk. I know how that goes.

'I did love her. I did. I just have problems. I'm not fit to be a mother.'

I let her talk until she stops, until the sobs drown out her thoughts. When all is quiet, I ask her where her husband is.

'He didn't come home today. He's probably done with me too.'

Then she says something that worries me.

'She talked about you all the time, you know.'

'About me?'

'Yes. She wanted to be like you.'

'Excuse me?'

'She never wanted to be like me.'

'I'm really sorry, Mrs Wilcox, but I don't quite understand. You know I hosted a radio show in Manchester. Do you mean Sarah listened to the show?'

The line cuts off and I'm left confused, not sure what to make of what just happened. I need to find out if Mrs Wilcox is aware that I knew her daughter. I can't afford for that to come out. I mean, I only met her a few times. The first time on a park bench when I was a mess, and later at an AA meeting, which admittedly I introduced her to. I hardly knew her, though. She was just another drunk going to AA. I had no idea she was from such a good home.

It's around 10.45 pm by the time I get home. I am craving a drink like no one's business, but there's no booze in the flat, so I go to the corner shop to get something to keep me in check. I need to detox slowly. I'm hoping that this binge won't go on past tonight.

On the way, I pass the local pub and glance through its large windows. It's quieter than usual. The shop is quiet too, so I don't have to wait too long to get my hands on a half-bottle of vodka, which I open as soon as I'm back on the pavement.

As I'm walking back towards my street, there's a couple walking ahead of me, laughing, flirting and having a good time. I cross the road and go on my way thinking nothing of it, until I hear a voice carried by the wind from across the street. It's a voice I recognise. It's Nigel, and he's with a woman who isn't his ex-girlfriend.

It's closing time at the pub, I imagine they must be coming from there. Shit. I suddenly feel quite exposed and hang back, then seek shelter under the huge weeping willow tree that marks the halfway point between the shop and my flat. Thank God for big trees. My heart is pounding and I feel physically sick, because they look quite fond of each other. Not that I have dibs on him or anything, but still.

I lean back against the wall and contemplate what to do. I'm tired, and my nerves are probably getting the better of me. It has been a long day, and a gruelling one at that. My body is in free fall about my drinking and I'm rapidly in need of detox so my head can straighten itself out. After a few deep breaths and a couple of large swigs, I've calmed down, but my journalistic curiosity gets the better of me, so I follow them. If he's a bullshitter, I want to know about it.

Moments later, I'm crouched behind a parked car like a police officer on a stakeout. My shopping bag rustles in the breeze, making me panic for a moment because it's quiet on the street, but the wind carries their voices in another direction, so I feel I'm safe. I can't get a hint of their conversation, though, which just riles me further.

Next thing I know, they turn down Navarino Road, and by the time I reach the corner, they have disappeared from sight. Shit. I'm not entirely sure what to do next. More people are filtering out of the pub and coming my way, so I turn down Navarino after them, because the journalist in me isn't ready to go home yet, and neither is the drunk. I owe it to myself to take a walk up and down the street. The voice in my head is telling me to do it. So I do.

It's dark and cold, but I keep walking, and before I know it, I've reached the park. I can't go into the park at this time of night, not on my own, not after what happened here. That would just be plain stupid. And stupid is one thing I am not. I get a grip on myself and stop to think. And while I'm preoccupied with what is happening, I totally fail to notice someone approaching me. It's the woman with the red setter who invited me round for tea on the day Alice Fessy's body was found. That's when I realise I'm actually standing in front of her house.

'Alex? Is that you? Are you okay?'

She almost caught me swigging from a bottle in a plastic bag, but thankfully not.

'It's quite late to be wandering around.'

'I'm just on my way home. Working late, you know.'

'Yes, of course. I saw you reporting from Manchester.' She comes closer. 'Look, why don't you come in and have a cup of tea? I'm just back from a walk and would love the company. I find it difficult to sleep at the best of times.'

'It's been a long day, you know. I'm not feeling great.'

'All the more reason to have some company, no?'

I'm now in such a state that I'm finding it hard to gather my thoughts.

'Come on, you look like you need a good hot drink. I'm Mary, by the way.'

She links her arm through mine – I'm too weak to protest – and we walk up the path towards her house. It's huge. Grandiose. We mount the wide stone steps leading to a glossy black door dressed with a brass knocker as large as my fist. Everything seems oversized, and I feel very small.

Whiskey, her dog, is being very affectionate. I guess he can pick up on how I feel. Once the door is opened, he runs off towards the back of the house. Mary follows and her voice disappears into the darkness, leaving me in the hallway on my own.

'Make yourself at home, won't you. I'll just open the back door for Whiskey.'

The house is overwhelmingly large. High ceilings. Walls covered in art. The staircase curves its way upwards to the heavens. I enter the lounge, which is furnished with items that shout the Orient. From the front bay window there is a clear view of the street, and directly opposite, a red-brick mansion block divided into flats. Moments later, Mary is back, pushing a trolley holding a silver teapot and two porcelain cups.

'You live on this street, don't you?' she asks.

'Me? No. I live on the Grove.'

'Oh. Silly me. I suppose my eyesight isn't what it used to be.'

The trolley is quite spectacular in appearance.

'That's a very posh cup of tea.'

'There are some traditions I like to uphold. Please… take a seat.' She taps the edge of the red velvet sofa.

'Thank you. You have a lovely place.'

'I lived here with my family for many years. Now there's just me left.'

'Oh, I'm sorry.'

'Don't be. That's what happens in the end. None of us are getting out of this alive, you know.' She chuckles to herself.

I offer to pour the tea.

'That would be very kind of you.'

My hands are shaking. I'm doing my best to keep it together. To push aside the pain. The pot is well polished. Mary obviously takes care of her things, and can afford to.

'You have so much going for you, Alex. Tell me, why do you drink so much?'

'Sorry?' I'm a bit stunned by what she's just said.

'I'm at the end of my life and done with being polite. What you do from here will determine the next twenty years of yours.' She looks older now, frailer. 'None of this matters, you know.' She glances around the room. 'My treasures. They are beautiful, but I can't take any of it with

143

me. My mother was a drinker. It tore the family apart, you know.'

'I'm not sure I do know.' This is bullshit. I'm not going to sit here and listen to it, so I stand up.

'I've seen you buying wine at all hours of the day in Costcutter. That's where you're just coming from, isn't it?' She looks down at my carrier bag. 'Chewing gum to hide the smell is a dead giveaway too. The irony is that vodka doesn't smell so you don't really need to chew it. Your cheeks are always a little rosy. I grew up around it, I can read the signs.'

There are two bottles of wine in the carrier bag by my feet, along with the vodka. I swore I only bought one bottle.

'Your head will be much clearer once you stop, you know.'

'Work can be quite stressful, and I like a drink in the evening to wind down, that's all.'

'The two aren't mutually exclusive, you know. Your career isn't how one measures a life in the end.'

Suddenly I feel extremely vulnerable, and before I know it, the tears are streaming down my cheeks. She says nothing, but places her hand on my arm. She has an energy that feels healing. Maternal. It's not like anything I've ever experienced before. When I eventually stop crying, I feel like a weight has lifted from me, but I still need another drink.

'I'm sorry. I don't know what came over me. I really should be going before it gets too late.'

The time on the brass wall clock reads almost midnight.

'Of course. I hope you come back. We all have our crosses to bear, Alex. Perhaps it's time to accept yours before it destroys you.'

27

September 2017

Dear Diary,

I almost turned back when I got off the train because I couldn't really get my head around what I was doing. How was I going to go to a strange place alone and tell more people I was an alcoholic? The thought of it scared me. I mean, it's not like I haven't told people before – the group at AA, for example – but a new group of complete strangers, well, it's quite a challenge is all I'll say. Self-doubt had set in and I wondered whether Clive and the guys at the meeting had talked me into it.

I bought a bottle of gin for the journey, my last ever drink. I toasted myself for taking this step, going to rehab. I don't think I've had a celebratory drink ever. I drink to suppress my insecurities, and boy, am I filled with those. I was scared, but then I remembered Alex's words about getting sober. She believed I had the potential to do something special with my life. I know now she wasn't completely honest with me about why she took me to the AA meeting, but at least it has helped me start to sort out my life, so I must focus on that. I have forgiven her for lying to me. I'm sure she had her reasons. I'm not sure whether that's an indication of who she is. We all lie as alcoholics. Mostly to ourselves.

When I arrived at rehab, a woman greeted me and took me to my room. She seemed all right until she went through my stuff, which felt like an absolute invasion of privacy, and then took all my money off me. And if that wasn't bad enough, she made me pee in a cup. She explained that this would become a normal part of being in rehab, which didn't make me feel any better. I thought these people would trust me. After all, I came here of my own volition. After this was done, she took me to meet my counsellor, who asked about my problem with alcohol and why I was there. The questions were stupid. I replied by telling her that I thought it was obvious why I was there. It felt humiliating.

After the session with the counsellor, I was taken into a room where a group of twenty people sat in a circle. It was not unlike the AA meetings, which felt comforting in a way, but even so, it was very nerve-racking walking into that room and facing a new set of people when I'd only really just got used to the group in Manchester. We went around and introduced ourselves, explaining how we felt. Most of the people there were drug addicts. That made me feel a bit out of place. Surely my drinking problem needed a different kind of treatment from someone addicted to cocaine or heroin? I couldn't quite get my head around that.

Back in my room alone, I'm questioning whether I've done the right thing coming here. Every bone in my body is telling me to get the hell out. Perhaps I am strong enough to beat this thing on my own and I don't need these people. But I'm here now so I'll try to make the best of it, because I can't get my money back.

28

The rumble of a wheelie bin being pulled past my bedroom window wakes me, putting the time at around 6.30 am. I wish there was another way for the rubbish to be collected on my street, but with it being a narrow cul-de-sac, the truck simply can't drive down the road.

I roll over and check my phone. No new dating matches to speak of, but plenty of news about what the media are now calling 'East London's modern-day Ripper'. One daily has coined it 'Date-a-death'. Another states, 'Quoting from a police source, these women were lured to their death by an online dating profile.'

By the time I'm dressed and up, it's half eight, a good time to catch Charlie for tea. I need to do stuff today that will stop me reaching for the bottle. I've taken some milk thistle, which helps rebuild the liver cells, and I'm feeling good, like this time I'm going to beat it. I am on a big story and I really can't afford another fuck-up. I'm a good reporter and I need to keep it that way. I bang on his door and he appears immediately.

'Morning. You not working today?'

'Gave me the morning off after the late night, unless anything new breaks.'

'Tea?'

'Ask a silly question.'

We head up to the kitchen in our usual fashion.

'How are you? Did you have a good night with your new lady?'

'I did, thanks. We had a wander around Brick Lane. Bought a few records at Rough Trade. I love that place.'

He makes the tea and I follow him into the lounge, where as usual he sits and rolls a ciggie.

'Want one?'

'No thanks. It'll kill you, that stuff.' I decide that today I'm going to try and stay off all vices.

'More chance of that happening via a dating site, according to the morning papers.'

'Yeah. It's pretty scary.'

'I don't think you should be going out on dates right now, Alex. Not with people you meet on that app, anyway. What's it called, COMEout?'

'I doubt anyone is going to kill me, a TV personality.'

'I'm serious.'

'So am I.'

'Don't be like that. I care about you.'

'Really? You don't act like it.'

'What? Don't be like that, Alex. We've had our moments, but you're not interested in me like that and you know it.'

I'm not going to answer that because actually I don't know how I feel at the moment. I'm all mixed up. I think that's another reason why I'm here, apart from starting detox. Charlie is the only thing that grounds me, because he puts up with my shit.

'So is this a new look then?' His flat is surprisingly tidy.

'What?'

'You've cleared up some of the crap.'

'Oh, that. Well, women don't like a guy who can't keep the place tidy, do they?' He's actually blushing.

'So you're serious then?'

'Not sure if I'd say that, but I like her, yeah.'

'Who is she? Where's she from?'

'She's from your part of the world, actually.'

'Manchester?'

'Somewhere up there, yeah.'

My hands are shaking. It's the withdrawal symptoms. It had to happen. I put the mug on the coffee table so he can't see it.

'You all right, Alex? You look knackered.'

'I am knackered, and I'm stressed. Mrs Wilcox, the woman we interviewed in Manchester, keeps calling me. It's like she's confessing to something she did to her daughter. Keeps saying it's all her fault. I spoke to her last night and she was an absolute mess. I've had five missed calls from her today already. Audrey, my producer is trying to track down Sarah's whereabouts so we can get her side of things. She's still very much a person of interest and no one seems to be able to find her, not even the police.'

I don't mention the conversation I had with the AA woman outside the church. That would involve getting into my past, and I need to let that lie today so I can start to detox. Need to keep my emotions on a level.

'Sounds like the woman might know something.'

'Like what?'

'I don't know. People aren't always forthcoming. Maybe she has something more to tell you, something that might help locate her daughter.'

'Maybe.'

As we sit there sipping our tea, I recall my stunt last night following Nigel, and shame washes over me. I really do need to get help. I wonder if Charlie is someone I can confide in, but I feel like an idiot. How am I going to tell him I followed Nigel down the street because I saw him with another woman? It makes me sound kind of bonkers. I don't even know why I did it now, but I was wasted. In the end, I do tell him, because that's what we do, we share our stupid shit.

'What the hell were you doing following him at that time of night? God, Alex, you need to get your impulse issues under control.'

'What do you mean?'

'You do impulsive things. It's like you have no control over yourself. You do know it's not safe around here at the moment, not to mention the fact that you would have come across as a crazy stalker if he'd seen you.'

'I wasn't following him, Charlie. I was on my way back from the shop. It's not like I planned it. It wasn't born out of impulse.'

'Women are being left for dead in parks, and you were wandering around on your own in the dark, pissed. You do stupid shit when you're drinking. I've witnessed it, you just don't remember.'

Silence falls on the room for a moment.

'Christ, Alex. None of this sounds good.'

Charlie's criticism comes at me like a slap in the face, and my usual affection for him wanes quickly.

'I've spent two days reporting on this story. I'm just knackered. Stop psychoanalysing me, for fuck's sake.'

'Never mind. I can see you're not ready to hear this yet.'

'Hear what?'

'Nothing.'

The atmosphere has changed. I no longer feel comfortable sitting on Charlie's worn-out carpet. It's time to leave. I don't need this shit on my morning off, especially after what I've just told him. I'm up before he can stop me.

'You haven't finished your tea. What's the matter?'

'I don't need you having a go at me.'

'I'm not having a go at you. I'm looking out for you because I care.'

I know he cares, but I have to go.

'Please, Alex, stay and finish your tea. I didn't mean to upset you.'

But I am already on my way to the front door.

'Alex, don't go off like this. I'm sorry—'

I leave, closing the door behind me, cutting him off mid-sentence.

–

Back home, and in need of a distraction, I launch the dating app to see if there are people still online looking for love. I'm my own worst enemy. I'm doing it to spite Charlie really. I just feel so shit today, like there isn't any good in me. The voice in my head is niggling, but I'm not going to let it win today. Almost immediately, a message pops up. The desire to date doesn't change. People in London are inevitably lonely, just like me.

> Scott sent you a message at 08:50

> **Hey there, Alex. How's it going? You look cute. What do you do?**

I'm in two minds whether to respond, but I'm also in desperate need of a distraction from the voice in my head.

> **Crime reporter! :-)**

> **Oh wow! I bet you're busy!**

> **Have been, yeah!**

> **Do you have any time to date? LOL!**

The world of online dating is good for some things at least: forgetting about real life and soothing my damaged ego. I'm playing with fire, but what the hell. Things really can't get any worse.

The conversation is boring and my body is starting to twitch, so I decide to go for a walk. The best thing to do when I feel like this is to get some air. It's sunny out and feels milder than the past few days, so I head towards the Fields, taking the road parallel to Navarino. I don't want to run into Mary from number three, not after last night. I'm now avoiding streets in my own neighbourhood. Great!

When I get to the park, I find my favourite bench at the lido café and plonk myself down with an espresso and a chocolate croissant. It's good to be out of the house. To get some air. The park is still quieter than usual. The dog walkers are back, but the play area is devoid of life. It's warm in the sunshine, which lifts my spirits after the spat with Charlie. He really upset me, but I'm not going to let it ruin my day.

My thoughts are interrupted by a call. It's DI Brook.

'Alex?'

'Speaking.'

'How's work going? Could we meet up when you're free?'

The call feels personal. I'm not sure how to play this.

'Is there a new development in the case?'

'I'd like to talk in person if that's all right.'

'Oh. Okay. Do you want to meet me at the news centre later?'

'It might be better if I come to your home.'

This takes me aback. 'Okay. Can I ask why?'

'It's just routine. Obviously we are following all leads. It's very important we piece together as much information as possible. I'm sure you can understand.'

'Yes, of course. If I can help in any way, I will.'

My flat is in a state that I wouldn't force my own worst enemy to see, so I offer to go to the police station instead, and he asks if I can come immediately. I really don't feel up to it, what with the withdrawal I'm currently dealing with, but then again, I rationalise that at least it will give me something to do, keep me busy. Anything that will help me abstain today is a good thing, even being called in to a police station. How messed up is that?

'Just tell the desk sergeant that I'm expecting you,' he says.

'Okay.'

Suddenly I have a craving for a shot of something stronger than caffeine.

29

September 2017

Dear Diary,

It's the end of the first week of rehab and I'm a train wreck. I thought this place was supposed to make me feel better, but it's having the opposite effect. I'm on drugs and my emotions are all over the place. The people are nice, but my nerves are shot and my head feels like jelly most days. I can't seem to get it together. I don't like the staff going through my stuff every day. It feels like being in prison. I also don't like having to pee in a cup daily. It feels like torture. It's not like I can buy alcohol in here – the place is in the middle of nowhere and I've got no money – so I don't know why they make us do it. It's very annoying and upsets me. Surely this should be about trust.

We're not allowed to use our phones. Not that I have anyone to call. The people I knew as a drinker don't fit with who I am any more, but still, taking my phone away makes me feel very cut off. I don't really know who I am. When I expressed this in the group session, I was told that those friends I used to go out with were outsiders, people who could never understand how I feel. I have been actively encouraged not to mix with them again, which feels a bit strange because the people here who are telling me this have never met my friends.

Tomorrow, I'm going to start one-on-one therapy, something I'm really not looking forward to. My therapist wants to talk to me about my childhood, a time in my life I don't have much recollection of really, which makes me think there must be a reason for it. I'm not sure what dragging up the past will do for my drinking and me. The food is good. though, that's one part of the programme I like. It feels healthy, which feels good. There is one guy here who says he's been in rehab six times now. Six times! It does make me wonder if it will help me and whether I have spent the money in the right way. It's all so confusing. I haven't really made any friends yet either. My sleep is messed up and I'm having nightmares. Last night I saw my mum sitting at a bus stop with Alex. They stood up together as if to board a bus that was driving towards me, but as the bus got closer, my mum pushed Alex into the road and she was killed instantly. It was terrible. My mother just stood at the side of the road laughing. Then I woke up.

30

The uniformed policeman on the desk told me to sit and wait, so that's what I'm doing. I'm feeling very restless; I wish I'd had a sip of something before I came here. Just a little something to calm me down a bit. I usually sip when I'm detoxing, which helps my body come down off the physical addiction, but today I'm going cold turkey. I'm not sure it'll work, because I'm feeling terrible. Absolutely awful. My mind feels really foggy for one.

Looking at the man behind the counter, who looks utterly bored and fed up, I thank my lucky stars that I really love my job at UKBC. It was a lucky break. I applied for it and within a matter of weeks they had hired me on the condition I move to London. After five years on the wireless, it was time to up my game or risk getting stuck where I was, so I moved. Took a risk. It was good timing. I had a clean break. Sometimes you need to do that. Sometimes you need to just move on. Forget what has been and turn over a new leaf. Staying in Manchester wouldn't have helped me do that. Just being back there this week brought up all those feelings again. The miscarriage; Greg. I needed to put that behind me and the new job really helped. It saved me in a way. Gave me focus at a time I needed it most.

The reception area in the police station is, as one would expect, mundane. Brown plastic chairs are lined up along the wall. There's a pathetic-looking plant in need of some care. It's no wonder no one wants to ever enter a police station. They could do with some magazines on the table, make it a bit more welcoming.

Bulletproof glass separates me from the super-humans beyond. I went on a date once with a police officer, shortly after I moved to London. He was nice but a bit OCD. He kept rearranging the items on the table and complaining about 'civilians'.

'Ms South?'

A round-faced man with an even rounder torso wearing a cheap polyester suit stands at a door to the side of the reception area. It amazes me how unfit police officers can be in comparison to other emergency services. He's smiling at me.

'Would you like to follow me, please?' He has the door pushed to, a gesture that directs me into a long corridor with strip lighting. The place smells of disinfectant.

'DI Brook will be with you shortly. He asked me to escort you to interview room two.'

'Interview room? Not his office?'

'Yes, interview room.'

'Oh, okay.'

I don't really know what else to say. The plump man shows me into a small room. It feels claustrophobic. I hope it doesn't take long, whatever this is. Then I wonder if DI Brook is pissed off about the interview we did with Mrs Wilcox and this is going to be a dressing-down type of exchange.

'Take a seat. He shouldn't be too long.'

The man shuts the door and leaves me to myself. The room is sparsely furnished. There are four chairs and a table, all fixed to the floor. The tiny window has bars on it. There's a lingering smell of body odour. I hope it doesn't belong to DI Brook. I don't know why, but I am starting to feel quite nervous. My hands are shaking and I'm not sure whether it's from the withdrawal or the situation I'm now in. Maybe Charlie is right. I really do get myself into some bother when I drink.

'Alex. Thanks for coming in.' DI Brook has entered the room and swoops down on the chair opposite me.

My heart is racing. I need to calm down.

He is just as I remember him: tall, well built. The body odour definitely isn't his. He smells like a pine forest. His suit is a smart dark blue, his shirt black and his tie grey, quite stylish for a copper. When he sits down, I notice his striking eyes – they are translucent, like the Northern Lights – and unlike most of the men who live in east London, he is clean-shaven.

'I appreciate you're busy with everything that's going on.'

'I've got the morning off. Not quite as busy as yesterday.' I smile, but he doesn't respond. I'm sweating. It's a cold sweat.

'So. You may or may not know why I've asked you to come in.' His manicured hands tap the file on the table in front of him.

'I guess it has something to do with the case.'

'Yes. Without going into too much detail, we looked at Sarah Wilcox's phone records, and one number came up repeatedly.'

'Okay. I'm still not sure what this has to do with me.'

'The number is registered to a Mr Greg Bailey.'

He lets this sink in before continuing.

'We did a search and found that the two of you used to occupy the same address in Manchester. In fact, you lived there for approximately six years.'

There's only one answer I can give, not that I really want to.

'Greg was my fiancé – now my ex-fiancé – and it was seven years.'

'Do you have any idea why Sarah Wilcox would be texting your ex-fiancé romantically?'

'Romantically?'

I don't know why I feel so sick hearing this. Mrs Wilcox did allude to it – not that I had any proof that it was my Greg she was talking about – but now that it's all out on the table, quite literally, in a file, there's absolutely no denying it. I'm feeling even more queasy than I did when I sat down. Looking at the file, I wonder: is it just the phone records in there? Or have the text messages been printed out? And I'm begging the universe not to show me that. I don't think I could take it. Not on today of all days.

He nods. 'Yes.'

'No idea. Why would I?'

'I can imagine this is hard to hear, but we really need to find him.'

'Well, I'm sorry, but I can't help you with that. I haven't seen him in at least nine months.' The Milk Tray comes to mind, but I say nothing of it.

'So you haven't been contacted by either of them since you moved to London?'

'Yes. I mean no. I mean…'

'Take your time Alex.'

I'm so confused by all the questioning, I just want to get out of here.

'I moved to London for work, Greg and I broke up, and there really is nothing more I can tell you.'

He stands up and readies to leave.

'Okay, well I won't keep you any longer. You are free to go now, but if you think of anything that might be of use, please call me.' He slides his business card across the table. 'My email has changed.'

I tuck the card in my jeans pocket and smile feebly. That's it. That's all he wanted to tell me. I need something more from this meeting. I need reassurance. I can't let him go like that, acting as if my Greg is a suspect.

'There is something.'

He's staring at me blankly, not saying a word, just listening.

'It's a bit embarrassing, to tell you the truth. You see, I met this guy in the pub the night Alice Fessy was killed. We met on COMEout and… well, I'm pretty sure he's a serial dater. I thought I should mention it.'

'It's not a crime to be a serial dater, sadly. In fact, there are plenty of men and women like that. The Internet makes it very easy.' His tone has softened. 'What would make you think he's a possible killer? Did he hurt you?'

I've already realised how stupid this sounds.

'Yes and no. Kind of. I mean, it's probably nothing. I shouldn't even have mentioned it. Really, please forget what I just said.'

'No. no. Look, if you have a concern then of course I will check it out. Is there a particular reason you think he might be dangerous?'

I really don't want to mention the sex part, but I've started this so now I have to finish it. Charlie is right. I do get myself into awkward situations when I've been on a binge. The voice in my head is there niggling at me, and I wonder if I'm not just being overly paranoid because of my withdrawal. Too late now. DI Brook is looking at me as if I have something really important to say. I need to win him over. I need to protect Greg.

'I'm a bit embarrassed to say it, but...'

'Anything you say will be treated in the utmost confidence. You can trust me, Alex.'

'Well, when we were making out, he had this obsession with my neck. I mean, I think he almost strangled me.'

'*Almost* strangled you?' I have his attention now.

'Well, I can't remember too well, but yes. He held my neck very tightly until I found it difficult to breathe.'

'Do you have a name?'

'Nigel.'

'A surname?'

'No.'

'A phone number?'

'Yes.'

He pulls his notebook from his inside pocket and holds his pen at the ready. I fiddle with my phone and dictate it to him, wondering whether I've done the right thing.

'When did this sexual encounter take place?'

'The morning that Alice was found.'

'Was he with you the night before?'

'Yes, we went for a drink and then he came back to mine.'

'If you were worried about him, why did you take him home with you?'

'I'd had quite a bit to drink.'

'Right. Well, what time did you meet?'

'Around nine o'clock.'

'Where?'

'At Pub on the Park.'

'Okay. Well thanks for this, Alex. That's very helpful.'

'Have you established Alice's time of death?'

'We think it could have been somewhere between eight and nine o'clock, so that would make it difficult for him to have done it, unless he killed her immediately before coming to meet you. How was he when he turned up? I mean, was he flustered?'

'Not really. I mean, he was a little out of breath, said he was running late, but not flustered. But then I don't really know him.'

'Okay. Well, thank you, Alex. We will follow it up. I appreciate your cooperation today.'

DI Brook walks me back the way I came in, smiles and shakes my hand before showing me through the door that connects to the reception area.

'We'll be in touch if there's anything else.'

'Anything else?'

'It's just routine.'

Within moments he has disappeared into the depths of the station. He looked quite smug as he did so, or is that my imagination playing tricks on me again?

31

September 2017

Dear Diary,

After the daily check when the staff go through my personal belongings to see if I'm hiding alcohol, I get to chill out for a bit in my room before the one-on-one session. Not that I'd really call it chilling out. I don't know how you can chill out in rehab. Everything seems so much more intense here. They have given me my phone back, which is good, even if I don't have anyone to call any more. I got a message from Greg asking where I was and if we could meet up. I didn't respond because I don't really know what to say. I don't want anyone to know I'm in here, only my dad. I guess my mum knows too. I'm sure he's told her where I've gone.

Talking to a therapist on my own was really difficult. It's so much easier to hide myself in a group setting, because when there are other people around, I don't need to talk too much. Tim, who is really good-looking, asked me to fill out a form with the following questions on it:

1. What is your earliest childhood memory?

2. Note down a happy memory from childhood.

3. Note down an unhappy memory from childhood.

4. Who are the family members who have the biggest influence on you?

5. *Do you have siblings? How many?*

6. *Are you close to your mother? Father? Siblings?*

He wanted me to write down my thoughts so that we could discuss them together in the next session. It didn't feel good. In fact, it felt terrible, because I couldn't really remember much about my childhood. Tim was very nice and said I could take as long as I needed, but after almost two hours the pages were still blank. I couldn't come up with anything. Nothing. It's as if my childhood never happened. I couldn't quite believe it. Tim said it's because I've blocked it out, but how can someone have absolutely no recollection of their childhood? It's just crazy. I've never thought about it before, but now that I have, I feel almost alien. I mean I don't know anyone who can't come up with something.

Tim told me not to worry, that it's not that uncommon, that I have suppressed things with drink, that together we will work to unblock the memories. He says I have to get to the bottom of what makes me drink so that I can stop. I need to know what my triggers are. For the first time in my life, I feel like I'm standing on the edge of a cliff about to free fall, not knowing how this will turn out.

32

When I leave the station, I receive a message from Nigel asking how I am. God, I feel terrible. I'm not sure if I've done the right thing. I mean, what do I know really? I don't reply and instead decide to ignore it. The police interview seems a bit unreal now. I'm not sure what my game was. Maybe I was upset after seeing Nigel with someone else, even though I had no right to be. I put it down to my brain being all out of sorts because I'm detoxing.

The weather has changed for the better; at least that's a positive. It feels much milder than it has for a while. Walking back across the Fields, I feel like the loneliest person in the world. I'm worried about Greg, but I'm angry too. What did DI Brook mean about him texting Sarah romantically? It's niggling at me. It really hurt to hear that even though I did a good job of pretending it didn't. I mean, who is this girl? I just met her a couple of times. What was Greg doing with her? And what was she doing with him? Perhaps it's time to contact him, to find out. But not today. Today is about detox.

The police cordons have gone now and the park looks and feels like it's getting back to normal. I plop myself down on one of the many benches at the north end of the Fields, wondering what I should do with myself. The sun is warming, but it's unable to melt my growing discomfort. I get a second message from Nigel, a link to a song. I don't reply. Not yet. I'll end up saying something I shouldn't because I'm all out of sorts today. I actually feel quite guilty about what I've just done. Fortunately my phone rings and I don't need to think any more of it. It's Annabel.

'Hey up, lass. How's things? Thought I'd call and see how your birthday turned out.'

'Hey. Not bad in the end, thanks. I had a drink with someone, nothing special, then ended up going to Manchester to interview the Wilcox family.'

'Yes. I saw. I also saw you weren't able to do a live report. What happened? It was a shame, as the interview was powerful stuff.'

'Thanks. Yeah, was a bit disappointing I didn't get on air from Manchester, but shit happens. Technology isn't foolproof.'

'True. So how was it going home?'

'Strange, but okay.'

'Listen, can we meet up? There's something I want to talk to you about and I'd rather do it in person.'

'When?'

'Are you free today?'

The only thing I want to do is go home and lie down, but it's best for me to keep busy. And it's best to be around people. Keeps me from hitting the off licence.

'Yeah. Well unless anything shifts on the story. They gave me the morning off.'

'Great. I'll come to you. Haven't been over that way for a while, and I hear the Fields are nice this time of year.'

I note the sarcasm in her voice.

'Safe as houses. I'm just doing a few errands around the neighbourhood.'

'Okay, so say in an hour? On the south side, towards Broadway? That way if we get too cold we can pop into a café and have tea or something.'

'Sounds good. See you soon.'

As soon as I hang up, I get another link from Nigel. Another song. I decide it's probably better to reply than ignore him because it doesn't seem like he's going to stop. Plus who knows what he was up to last night. Charlie was right. I'm good at reading stuff into situations I don't know enough about. It's the journalist in me, always looking for a story.

> Hi, Nigel. Good to hear from you. Bit busy today, but will be in touch. A x

Within moments, I get a text back.

> Okay. Let me know when you're free. Can't wait to see you. N xxxx

Two songs and four kisses. He's keen. I dig around in my bag and find some ibuprofen and neck a couple. I need to try and keep it together when I see Annabel.

—

An hour later, I'm waiting for her at the south end of the Fields, high on caffeine and painkillers. I seem to have spent my entire morning avoiding going home. I feel like death but she looks amazing. She was always slender and athletic but managed to gain quite a bit of weight during her pregnancy. Now, though, she has her head-turning body back. Baby Marlow is sleeping in a designer buggy.

'You look fantastic,' I say.

We hug it out for ages. It's been months since we've seen each other. I'm hanging on for dear life, not that she knows it. She's wearing a sporty parka with a duck-down hood. Black jeans and black Converse. Her hair is much longer than it used to be, and much redder. Marlow looks content wrapped in a fleecy alien-themed blanket. He's grown since she posted the last round of photos on Facebook. They change so much in the early days, don't they?

'Oh my God. He's so adorable, look at him.'

I'm being polite, but it's been quite hard to see her since Marlow arrived on the scene because it reminds me of what I don't have. A child.

'He can be. He can also be a royal pain in the arse. He's had colic so he cried a lot in the beginning. It was a real test of patience, let me tell you.'

I'm not going to buy into her feel-sorry-for-me line. She has a child. I don't.

'Well, you look great and so does he.'

'Thanks. I've been working out almost every other day. Did fitness in the park for a bit, and I've been swimming. I have this CD that I dance along to by Gwyneth Paltrow's trainer, it's fab. There's no way I'm going to let myself go just because I have a kid. Shall we walk and talk? It'll let him sleep a bit longer while we burn calories.'

'Sure.'

Our stroll takes us past the meadow, along a path beneath large oak trees. A number of cyclists whizz by in the adjoining lane.

'So what is it? Is it about work? Do you want to come back?'

'God, what I wouldn't do to come back to work, but no. It's too early still. Look, you know that girl who died? Maggie Horrocks.'

'The second victim? What about her?'

Marlow snuffles, then continues to purr.

'I think Charlie, your neighbour, knew her.'

I stop walking, and she does too.

'What do you mean, Charlie knew her?'

'Do you remember that swim club night we had? Where I got my certificate?'

'At King's Hall Leisure Centre?'

Annabel nods. We are standing in the middle of the Fields, where the path forks in two directions: to our left away from the cricket pitch, or to our right snaking along it.

'Is that where Alice Fessy was found?' She looks past the bushes and towards the play area at the north end, which is completely empty.

'Yes, in the wooded part next to the playground.' I gesture with a nod. A passing man looks at us; he knows what we're talking about, because everyone is talking about it. No one goes over there now.

'Bit morbid.'

'Just a bit, yeah.'

'Let's go this way instead.'

We turn left to cross the park, so we can loop back round to Broadway.

'I think you're mistaken about Charlie. He would have told me if he knew her.'

'Are you sure?'

'How long have you been thinking about this?'

'Since I heard about her death. I didn't want to get involved, but since the news about Alice Fessy broke, it's been on my mind.'

A chocolate cockapoo bounds across our path, almost colliding with the stroller.

'So you're telling me now?'

She shrugs her shoulders. 'I didn't want to upset you. I know you have a lot on your mind already.'

This annoys me, but I guess she means well.

'Don't you remember her being there that night?' she asks.

'Who, Maggie Horrocks? No. Should I?'

'You were smoking outside with Charlie.'

'I don't smoke Annabel, you know that.'

'Well, you're not a smoker. But you have the occasional one, don't you?'

'I have the occasional drink too, doesn't make me an alcoholic, does it?'

'Right.' She rolls her eyes at me, which I find a bit upsetting.

We turn left again and head back towards Broadway.

'Anyway, I saw him with her that night, smoking outside later on, and then again the next time I went to the club. In fact, I saw him with her a few times after that.'

'That doesn't mean he killed her.'

'No, but you know him well. Does he use dating apps?'

'Not that I'm aware of.' Although I do wonder how he met his latest squeeze. Maybe there's more to Charlie's dating life than he lets on.

Annabel is still pressing the subject. 'Well, do you think I should go to the police?'

'No. Let me handle it. There's no point in going to the police if there's a simple explanation. I'll talk to him first. Ask him if he knew her. See what he says.'

'Okay. I just feel bad about it. Knowing someone who was murdered, you know.'

I wonder if I should tell her about my morning at the police station, but before I have a chance, she bursts into tears.

'Oh my God, Alex, I'm such a mess.'

'It's okay. Come here.'

I put my arms around her and she holds on for a moment.

'It makes me really nervous, what's going on with these poor women.'

'Me too.'

'I didn't really know Maggie. She was just in my club, you know? But ever since Alice Fessy's body was discovered, I keep bursting into tears.'

'You're probably just tired.'

Marlow is stirring from his nap. What I wouldn't give to hold my own child in my arms. Annabel has it all. A proper family.

'I'm glad you came to me. A producer at work seems to think these women were gay. The drug that was used in the murders is common on the gay party scene.'

'Wow. Really?'

'Yes, really. I wouldn't worry about Charlie. I just don't see it.'

'Okay. God, I've been such an idiot, worrying myself sick. That's why I came to talk to you. You never overreact to anything. I love Marlow, but it's exhausting having a baby. I know it'll get easier, but I miss my job. I miss being out and about. Doing all the things I used to do. I miss my freedom.'

So that's what this is all about. I wish I had her problem, but then I need to get dry to have her problem, which reminds me: it's now almost twelve hours since I had a drink. Proof that I can control my drinking.

'I'm quite happy to babysit sometimes, if you want a break. You only have to ask.'

'Thanks, Alex. I really appreciate the offer.'

We hug it out some more.

'I'd better get going. I want to walk back to Dalston before it gets dark and before he needs feeding. Let's not leave it so long next time, yeah?'

'Absolutely.'

We have one last hug and she heads off down Broadway towards the canal.

On my way home, I try to recall seeing Maggie Horrocks at the swimming club that night, but I have no recollection of it. My memory is so shot these days. I do remember that her flatmate was interviewed by UKBC shortly after she was killed, though. I text Audrey and ask if she can get the woman's name and address. I need something to do other than go home. I'm pretty sure Charlie wasn't seeing Maggie like that, but if he was, I need to know.

Audrey is such a godsend. She replies within moments and signs off with a winky face. Google Mapping it says it'll take me twelve minutes to walk there. I'm not sure if it's such a great idea, but I really need to know now, and besides, my detox needs something to do. My mind is already made up. I hit 'route' on my screen and follow the blue dots.

33

Dear Diary,

Today's session was challenging. The therapist explained that I have created a false perception and image of who I really am. That was a head fuck. He also told me that my brain wouldn't be happy and healthy again for a while. That the alcohol I have been consuming for the best part of my life has warped the part that makes all my decisions and stunted my emotional growth. It has created a perception of the world that is misguided, and my moral compass is so out of whack it's amazing I have any empathy for anyone whatsoever. My years of alcohol abuse have created a monster that doesn't really know right from wrong any more. It's a physical thing apparently, and the only way to change that is to stay off the alcohol for at least six months. Only then will I really begin to understand the world around me properly and make sense of my own moral principles, transforming me into a much better person.

I've been dry now for a couple weeks and I do feel better. But there is a massive emotional void that I can't fill. The alcohol used to do that for me. The place is okay really. The rooms are nice, with a view of well-looked-after gardens. The beds are pretty comfy and I'm getting a good night's sleep, which is a real change. As a drinker, I hardly ever slept properly. I couldn't really call it *sleep. I used to nap between shifts at the pub and shifts on my park bench. I never found the time to properly discharge and allow my body to rejuvenate. I don't remember ever enjoying sleep until this week. My appetite is also coming back, day by day.*

There's such a mix of people here. I'm actually really surprised by it. I thought it would be low-lifes. People who were lost in the world, a bit like me. But there are some really successful types in here. Professional people like Alex. I wish she was here with me. We'd have a blast. It's not too bad, though. There's this one girl from Leeds, only nineteen. She's nice. She really didn't want to come but her family made an intervention. She's glad of it now. That's the thing about rehab rather than AA meetings. There are people here who really don't want to be here. People who have been forced to come by their loved ones. That makes me different, I suppose.

Tomorrow we start group therapy again while continuing with the one-on-one. I haven't spoken to my mum since I came here. She is an alcoholic too, I realise that now. I guess I'm slightly afraid of her opinion, which is something I discovered today in my one-on-one session. I feel embarrassed about it. I feel shame.

My therapist tells me I drink to hide a truth about something that happened to me, but I can't figure out what that is. I used to think that I drink because I like it, but maybe he is right. He says I'm blocking out the pain with the booze. Blocking out trauma because it's too disturbing. I hope this rehab thing can get to the bottom of why I drink, so that I can stop completely and have a normal life. I've started smoking. I need to stop that too. It's like replacing one addiction with another, although at least the cigarettes don't mess with your head the same way drink does.

I wonder if Alex has experienced the same breakdown in moral codes that my therapist was talking about, her being a

long-time drinker just like me. I consider writing to her and telling
her I'm in rehab, but then I think again.

34

Before long, I find myself outside Maggie Horrocks' house. It's a pretty house on a well-presented street. Two-storey semis line up neatly behind tidy front gardens. The thought that Charlie knew her has made me deeply troubled. If he becomes the story, I want to be ahead of it. Annabel is one of the only friends I have, and I trust her hunches.

Number 32A is a ground-floor flat. I can't see in because the windows have those French-style wooden shutters, which are not even half open. There's a selection of herbs growing in the garden: rosemary, mint and lavender. I wish my garden looked like this. It looks healthy.

I ring the doorbell a few times but no one answers. To the left of the front door is a path that tucks around the back of the property. The voice in my head is telling me to follow it, so I do and soon find myself in an equally well-kept back garden. There's a gravelled area with a table and two benches, lots of potted plants, and a greenhouse in which tomatoes are growing. There's a stack of cigarette butts piled up in a plant pot on the table. It looks quite normal. I don't know what I was expecting.

I knock on the French doors, a somewhat desperate act seeing as it's blatantly obvious that no one is in. My hand reaches for the handle, and before I know it, the door is sliding open and I'm standing in the lounge looking for anything that might provide me with a clue as to how Maggie Horrocks lived her life. There are some photos of her and her flatmate. They look happy. There's also a collection of alcohol on a shelf next to the photos. The voice in my head is telling me to take it, but I'm not going to. I'm not. My heart is racing: I don't know what I'm doing here. I leave the lounge and walk along the hallway, past a kitchen and a bathroom.

There's a faint smell of incense as I peer through an open doorway. I can see the bed from here; it's neatly made. I scan the room. There's no clutter, just a few pictures on the wall, a trunk with folded linens on top and a couple of floating bookshelves where a stack of magazines and design books are arranged with care. There's a bottle in my hand, so it looks like the voice in my head won and I swiped it. I don't even remember picking it up. I put it down. I'm not doing this. I've just decided to get the hell out when I see a pinboard behind the door.

There's a collection of bills on it, which on closer inspection reveal that I am definitely in Maggie's bedroom. I did wonder for a minute. I have got myself into several precarious situations while under the influence, but this really takes the biscuit. Perhaps I should be drinking. I make more sense when I do.

There's a photo of her with a guy. He looks like her brother. I'm surprised the police haven't taken it. They must have been here. There's not much else: a few take-away menus and some flyers advertising upcoming exhibitions.

Moments later, I hear the jangle of keys outside the window, and through the crack in the shutters I see a woman dressed in black plucking her keys from her shoulder bag before mounting the steps towards the house. Shit. I'm a first-class idiot. I could get arrested here.

I make for the lounge and slip back out through the French doors, tiptoeing around the side of the building with my heart beating in my throat. I leave through the front garden as quickly as I can and don't pause until I've reached the end of the street, at which point I stop and take stock. I am shocked at what I've just done. I really need to get properly sober. This is irrational behaviour of the worst kind. Since that bloody box of Milk Tray arrived, I've not been thinking straight. I need to get a grip, but I still need to find out if Charlie knew Maggie.

Standing in the cold, I weigh up my options. It's dark now and I really shouldn't be hanging around out here. I've made a complete pig's ear of it. I decide there's only one thing for it: go back and talk to Maggie's flatmate. Do what I came here to do, and see if I can find out if Maggie was having a relationship with Charlie.

I put my reporter's hat on and walk back towards the flat. Within minutes, I find myself outside the building again, staring at the front door, wondering what on earth has got into me. My pulse is racing, but I have to do this; I have to find out if what Annabel said has any legs to it. I ring the doorbell. When no one comes immediately, I feel relieved and almost walk away, but moments later, the door opens and the woman I saw jangling her keys stares blankly back at me. She looks like she's been crying. Her mascara has smudged and run down her right cheek.

'Anne Marie? Hi. I'm really sorry to bother you. My name is Alex South. I'm from UKBC. I wonder if you have a moment?'

'I know who you are. What do you want?'

'Could we talk for a minute?'

There's distrust in her eyes accompanied by a look of suspicion on her otherwise pretty face. Her hair is tied in a topknot.

'I'm really worried about what's going on. I want to help. I don't know if you knew this, but I met Maggie at the swimming club.'

She's weighing up my plea, which takes less than a minute.

'You'd better come in.'

I follow her through the hallway into the kitchen.

'Tea? Or something stronger?'

'Tea. Thanks.'

There's a breakfast bar in the kitchen. I haven't seen one of these since the eighties. I perch on a leather stool and lean up against it. I'm covered in a cold sweat. My hands are shaking but I'm holding it together as best as I can.

'So you knew Maggie?'

'Not very well, but I met her, yes, at King's Hall Leisure Centre, at the swim club.'

'She loved swimming.' Anne Marie has filled the kettle and switched it on. 'So, what do you want to know?'

'I'm not sure exactly. I'm just really worried about what's going on. I went to Manchester to interview Sarah Wilcox's mum and I felt really sad. I don't know, I feel like the police are missing something. Some vital clue. So I thought I'd come and see you. See if you felt the same.'

'What kind of clue?'

'I don't know. They're so focused on this online dating angle, I wonder if they're missing something. Maybe it's not about meeting people online at all, you know?'

'Yes, I know what you mean, but Maggie was going on casual dates with guys she met online, like most women in their thirties these days. I know because we had a drill. She would tell me where and when she was meeting them. She was very sensible. That's why it's so terrible what happened.'

The kettle has boiled and she grabs the milk from the fridge.

'Milk? Sugar?'

'Black is fine, thanks.'

Moments later, a mug of steaming tea in a 'Lionel Rich Tea' mug lands next to me on the breakfast bar, and Anne Marie sits down.

'And that night?'

'My phone was dead. I feel so bad about it.' She looks down into her cup, racked with guilt. 'She had texted me to say she was going out and that she'd be in touch, but my phone was dead and I never got the message.'

'Did she send you another text?'

'No.'

'Do the police know about this?'

'Yes, I told them everything.'

'Did she ever talk about anyone else? Someone she didn't meet online?'

'That DI Brook, he asked me about her personal life, but only about people she met online. Isn't that where the focus is?'

'Yes, that's what the police are looking at, but I'm wondering if she met anyone in her everyday life.'

She takes a sip from her *Back to the Future* mug.

'Do you use a dating app yourself, Alex?'

'Hasn't everyone? But I've always had good experiences... well, until recently.'

Her eyes widen and she puts her tea down. 'What do you mean?'

'It's nothing. Look, I don't know how to say this, but a friend of mine thinks Maggie was seeing a guy called Charlie. She thinks they met at the leisure centre in Hackney.'

'She never talked about a Charlie. Not that I can recall.' Her voice starts to wobble and she almost loses her composure, but pulls it back. Her expression returns to one of suspicion. 'Why are you interested in this Charlie? He mean something to you?'

'Look, I'm just trying to help. There has to be a better investigation, and if the police can't do it, we can. That's what I do, investigative reporting. I can pull all these strands together, but I need your help. We need to help each other so that the neighbourhood can be safe again.'

She says nothing, but her expression tells me she knows exactly what I'm talking about. I think I've struck a chord with her at last.

'I'm sorry. I don't mean to be rude, but I really don't know what's happening to me. I miss Maggie and I haven't had time to just sit and think about that yet.'

I reach over and squeeze her shoulder with my right hand.

'I can't imagine how that feels. It must be awful.'

'It is. All I want to do is shut the world out and deal with the fact that Maggie is...' Overcome with tears, she breaks down. I lean over and give her a proper hug.

'Look, there's a bastard out there and we need to stop him. Maggie needs justice for what happened to her, as do the other two victims, Alice Fessy and Jade Soron.'

She pulls away and wipes her face with a tea towel.

'I just can't get my head round what has happened. Maggie told me only the week before that she'd had enough of online dating for a while. That's why it's so unbelievable.'

'Is there anything here that might give us a clue as to who she was hanging out with?'

'I don't know. Maybe.'

'Shall we have a look?'

'But the police have been through everything.'

'They might have missed something.'

'Okay.' She has perked up a bit at my suggestion. 'Where shall we start?'

'The lounge?'

I follow her into the next room.

'How do you want to do this?' she asks.

She's looking to me for guidance, so I suggest she starts with the chest of drawers behind the sofa, and I'll sift through the post scattered on the coffee table.

'What are we looking for?'

'Anything that might help us figure out who she went out with that night.'

'Okay.'

Anne Marie gets on with rooting through the drawers while I tackle the post, which doesn't shed any light. It's just a bunch of bills and promotional crap. I don't really know what I'm doing here. I'm my own worst enemy when my head's not straight.

'I'm glad you're here. It's terrible coming home to an empty flat. Maggie was always here cooking, listening to music. I hate being alone.'

She starts to well up again. There's a box of tissues on the coffee table and I offer it to her. As I do, a beer mat falls to the floor. It must have been stuck to the bottom of the box.

'Thanks.'

Anne Marie carries on with her search. There's a phone number scrawled on the back of the beer mat. Looks like the kind of thing someone who wanted to keep in touch might do. I slide it into my pocket.

'So, what are you going to do, stay on here?'

'I don't know. Haven't thought about that yet.'

'It's a lovely flat.'

'It is, but it feels weird now, you know.'

'Yes. I guess it does.'

Just then my phone starts to buzz. Someone is calling me from an unknown number. It doesn't feel appropriate to pick up, so I don't, then moments later, I get a text message.

> Hi, Alex. I need to talk to you. I have something important to tell you. I know you are covering the story and I want to talk to you. I can give you a scoop if you want it, but first I'd like to talk to you. My mum's a liar. Please call me. Sarah x

The pit of my stomach feels it first. The adrenalin. I suddenly have a pressing need to leave. Can this really be happening? It's a mega lead. One I have to follow up even if it's a prankster.

'I'm really sorry, but I have to go. It's work. They need me.' I scribble down my number. 'If you find anything, give me a ring. Hell, give me a ring anyway. You're not alone, you know.'

'Okay. Thanks for coming, Alex. It's nice to have someone to talk to.'

We have a hug before I go. Once I'm outside, I receive another text from Sarah with an address and a simple sentence: *I NEED YOUR HELP*. The address is less than half a mile from where I am, which is unsettling. I'm in two minds about going there. I mean, it could be some crazy, trying to hurt me, you never know; but on the other hand, my career needs this. It would be an exclusive of epically career-making proportions, so I head off in that direction, bottle in hand. I must have swiped it on the way out.

35

Dear Diary,

Today I discovered something about myself that I am ashamed to write here. It hit me like a high-speed train, bulldozing my life into something resembling a broken pot that can never be put back into its original form. It happened in group therapy. I was listening to this woman talking about abuse she had suffered as a child, explaining how her uncle had touched her when she was seven years old. I mean, can you imagine. She said it out loud in the group meeting, I was shocked, but the emotions she exposed struck a chord with me, uncovering feelings that I had long buried, and in that moment I think I may have found the reason for my drinking.

Listening to someone else talk about it stirred a long-buried trauma, and now I don't know who I am any more. I'm lost. Completely lost. Everything I thought I knew about my life has changed, and not for the better. I wish I'd never come here. I wish I didn't have this feeling in the pit of my stomach. It's as if I've suddenly got this awareness about something that happened to me when I was a child.

After the session, a flash of memory from when I was four or five years old came back to me. I couldn't grasp it at first, but then another image appeared. An image so disgusting I didn't know what to make of it. I'm standing in the kitchen waiting for Mum to appear and give me some food, but she never materialises and instead a man stands in the doorway holding out some jelly babies. I am told to follow him to my room, where he promises to read me a story, but he doesn't read me a story. He tells me to lie down on the bed and take my clothes off. The memory is so disgusting I want to vomit. I want to cry, but I can't because I'm paralysed with fear. The fear that having uncovered this about myself, I will never be the same person again.

36

When I wake up, it's early morning. There's a load of missed calls from work, followed by an email asking if I'm okay. Shit. That email also says I was supposed to be at work last night. Fuck. As hard as I try, I can't remember how I got home. It's one big blank. I remember meeting Annabel in the park, then going to Maggie Horrocks' place, but after that, nothing. Absolutely nothing.

On the bed beside me is an empty wine bottle, and next to that, a bottle of vodka, half full. I have to stop doing this to myself, I really do. I must have blacked out. This is not good. If I don't get my shit together, I'm going to end up losing the one thing in the world that really matters. My job.

I check the headlines on my phone. Luckily there are no new developments in the case, so I probably got away with it this time, but I must detox today. I must. It will be tricky, because I'm working. I'm so pissed off with myself for caving in. I don't even remember buying the alcohol. I search my phone for any clues as to what I did, but there's nothing. I remember what Annabel said about Charlie, though. Shit.

First things first. I send an email to my editor explaining that I had low blood pressure yesterday, something I deal with every month around the time of my period. I apologise for not calling in, but say that as I hadn't heard from them, I assumed they didn't need me, and that I fell asleep. It's a lie, but it does the job.

Today's top story is the fallout from the Glasgow terror attack. They have arrested a guy, recently converted to Islam. It's such a cliché. Second story is about floods in the north of England. Cumbria has been hard hit and York is under two metres of water. I still can't believe I blacked out last night – I haven't done that for a while – but then I realise that yesterday was the anniversary of my miscarriage. It looks like Facebook reminded me last night with a happy photo taken just before it happened. It must have set me off. I'm filled with shame.

A knock on the door prevents me from spiralling into a black hole of shitness. It's Charlie. I don't know what to say to him yet about Maggie Horrocks and am unsure of whether to answer, but he's shouting at me to open up, saying it's important and he's not going away. I give in only after I've stashed the bottles under the bed. The last thing I need is another lecture from him.

'Alex. Thank God you're in. I've been feeling so bad since yesterday. I'm really sorry I had a go at you. Reading about these murders got me thinking.'

'Oh yeah?'

He follows me into the kitchen like a lost puppy.

'I really am sorry, Alex. I don't want to judge you. You know that, right? I'm just worried about you, that's all. You got home really late last night, didn't you?'

'Been long days. Don't worry about me. I'm fine.' I put the kettle on. 'Life really couldn't be better. I'm in an awesome place. Got a great job and over thirty thousand followers on Twitter.'

'Come here.' He stands up and puts his arms around me, which feels mildly patronising, but I let him do it because I know it'll get rid of him quicker. 'It's none of my business what you do or how you do it. I just care, that's all.'

'I get it, I really do, and I appreciate it, but honestly, there's no need for you to worry about me. I'm really great.'

'Okay.' He kisses my forehead tenderly. 'You mean a lot to me, Alex.'

'As much as your new girlfriend?'

I don't know why I said that. It sounds mean. Sometimes I just can't help myself when I've had a drink; it puts me in a defensive mood. Greg used to pull me up on it all the time. My head is thumping. I grab some aspirin from the drawer and knock back a glass of water. I've decided to leave the Maggie Horrocks thing until my head is clearer. The last thing I need is another argument with him.

'Look, Charlie, I don't mean to be rude, but I really need to get on.'

'Oh, sure. So we're good?'

'Yes, we're good.'

'I'm glad. Oh, by the way, I looked for your key, the one you gave me a while back, and couldn't find it. Did I give it back to you?'

'Oh. I don't think so.' He could well have done, not that I remember. 'Don't worry about it. I'll get a new one cut.'

'Up to you, just thought I'd mention it. Hey, what have you done to your wrist?'

I look down and see a series of grazes on the inside of my right arm. I must have got them when I blacked out. I don't remember. Shit.

'It's nothing. Must have happened when I was at work. Think we were trying to carry some heavy gear yesterday.'

'Do you want me to bandage you up?' He smiles.

'Don't be silly. It's just a couple of grazes, but thank you.' I give him a hug to compensate for my moody comments. We say goodbye and promise to catch up later.

It doesn't take me long to get ready, surprisingly, considering what kind of state I'm in. My brain is so foggy. I'm just about ready to leave the house, applying some red lipstick in the hallway mirror in an attempt to make myself look healthier, when there's a knock on the door. I assume it's Charlie back to tell me he's found the key, so I open the door completely unprepared for who I find on the other side.

'Hello, Alex. Mind if I come in for a moment?'

DI Brook looks as composed as he always does, although he's stooping, aware that he is taller than my door frame. I really don't want to see him the way I feel right now, or have his beady eyes darting around my home, but there's nothing I can do. He's already crossed the threshold.

'I'm getting ready for work,' I say, hoping to prevent him from entering further, but it's useless. He's already made up his mind that he's coming in.

'Just need to ask you a few questions. Routine stuff. In here?' He points ahead towards the open-plan living space at the end of the hallway.

The familiar whiff of pine forests tickles my nostrils as he glides past. I follow him into the kitchen.

'Do you mind?' He gestures to the chair where Charlie was sitting less than ten minutes ago.

'Be my guest. I really don't have long, though. I need to leave for work.'

I'm confused by the fact that he's here in my kitchen. I hope I didn't do something stupid last night.

'How can I help you, DI Brook?'

'It's about Alice Fessy, and more importantly, that fella you mentioned at the station yesterday. Nigel. Do you want to sit down?'

'I'm fine standing, thanks.' I'm not going to actively encourage him to stay.

'Okay. Well, we found CCTV footage of Alice exiting London Fields station around six o'clock on the night in question.'

'And?'

'Well, she was followed by a man. Possibly the man you mentioned.'

He pulls a file from under his coat and opens it, then spreads a collection of images captured from CCTV on the table.

'Do you recognise this man?'

The images are grainy and it's hard to tell who the man is. It's even hard to recognise Alice. I squint, but it doesn't help. Whoever he is, he's walking slightly behind her.

'Take your time. It's really important we identify this man.'

I stare at the grainy black and white image.

'I'm sorry, I just can't say for sure that it's him.'

I feel like my accusations have got slightly out of hand. I was only trying to protect Greg. But as DI Brook starts to put the pictures away, I notice that the man is wearing a pair of black and white stripy Converse, just like the ones Nigel put on in my bedroom the morning after he stayed. Shit. Now I can't not ID him, because if it is him, it's going to seem weird if I don't.

'I do recognise those shoes, though. Nigel has the same ones.'

DI Brook leans closer. 'Are you sure?'

'Yes. I'm quite sure. They're distinctive.'

He smiles. 'Well, thank you, Alex, that is very helpful. Very helpful indeed. Did you manage to find out his last name?'

'No. Haven't seen him again yet. I'm not sure I want to now either. Do you think he might have something to do with it?'

'We're following up all leads, as you can imagine. I tell you what, if you have his dating user profile handy, that would help.'

I really just want the detective out of my house, and if this helps get rid of him, so be it. I've gone and done the worst of it now anyway.

'Of course.'

I launch my dating app and show him the page with Nigel's details on it. I even send him a screen shot. I feel like a total cow doing it, but I have no option with DI Brook breathing down my neck.

'What about... my ex?' I can't bring myself to say Greg's name.

'We're still following leads. We haven't found him yet.'

After DI Brook has shown himself out, I sit and think. I don't know how I feel about what's just happened. Why come to my flat? Does he want to spare me the embarrassment of going to the station a second time? Was he in a rush to show me those images because they are about to make an arrest? I've just realised that I may become a key witness in a murder trial, if it gets that far. Perhaps that's why he came to my home address. It crosses my mind that I've never told him where I live.

37

Dear Diary,

I have another week left in rehab. I want to call my dad and tell him to come and get me, but then I think better of it. What would I tell him? Does he even know? I really, really, really want a drink. I need to blot this out. We talked about it in my one-on-one session, which was really difficult because I don't want to share this with anyone, let alone a good-looking man, but Tim was really understanding. He said it wasn't my fault. I don't think I've ever felt this bad. I want to die. I just don't want to be here any more. Knowing what I know now, I don't think anyone will ever love me. How could they? A victim of childhood abuse. I hate Alex for setting me on this course. And I hate my mum for allowing that man to do such a thing.

My family life has been completely destroyed with this one memory. I don't think I'll ever be able to look at my mother again. And my dad, how did he let this happen to me? I wish I had never listened to Alex or the people at AA. What do they know about childhood abuse? I just want to be back on my park bench with my bottle of gin. Back to who I was four months ago. Anything would be better than this. They say ignorance is bliss, don't they; now I really understand what that means. I couldn't even cry today. It was such a shock. I just felt dirty. I'm not sure

I'll ever forgive Alex for this. I'm not sure I'll ever forgive any of them.

197

38

It's eleven o'clock by the time I get to work. Philippa, the editor on shift, sees me arrive.

'You okay, Alex?'

'Much better, thanks. Sorry for not coming in yesterday. I thought someone would call me if I was needed. I tried to get in to see the doctor, but I couldn't get an appointment. I really need to do that when the story dies down.'

She grins at the pun. 'Are you well enough to work? We don't want you collapsing on air.' She's trying to look concerned, but really she's more worried about her bulletin. I don't have the best track record.

'I'll be fine. Don't worry.'

'Good.' She turns on her heel and struts off across the newsroom.

Audrey is logged on to one of the hundreds of computers dotted about the place, so I find a spot next to her and sit down.

'Hey, Alex. How you doing? Missed you yesterday.'

'Took a rest day. Felt a bit under the weather.'

'Oh, sorry to hear that. Hope you're feeling better.'

'Much better, thanks.'

'I've been trying to locate Sarah Wilcox. There have been plenty of sightings of her around London Fields. I've been talking to a few people on Twitter, trying to piece together a map that might tell us about her habits and where we might find her. Weird that the police can't just locate her from her phone or address. You'd think they could do that easily. I mean, no one just disappears any more, do they? I was thinking about calling her mum and talking to her, but I wanted to run that by you first.'

'Yeah, maybe, but she's unstable.'

My two screens spring to life just as a collective 'Shit!' sounds around the newsroom.

'Oh God, no.' Audrey turns to me, fear in her eyes.

'What is it?'

'They've found another one, Alex. They've found another fucking woman.'

Philippa has appeared as if by magic. 'It's London Fields again.'

I feel queasy. The water bottle in my bag is filled with vodka, and all I can think about is how much I need a swig, but Philippa is talking to us so I need to pay attention. Keep it together a bit longer.

'Alex, we need you down at the scene right away. Audrey, you'll go with her. I'll find you a cameraman and he'll meet you there. We need you live on the one o'clock bulletin.'

My head is in a spin. While Audrey organises a couple of things, I sneak off to the toilet and feed my shakes with a shot. Next thing I know, we're in a taxi. Audrey won't stop talking, but I don't engage. I'm exhausted both mentally and physically. I need all my strength just to get me through the next few hours. I'm pissed off that I wasn't able to detox yesterday. It sucks, actually.

The taxi drops us at the north entrance of the park and we walk the rest of the way. The familiar white forensics tent comes into view. Uniformed police are combing the area. DI Brook is standing outside the tent, hands in pockets. This time he looks in my direction and nods. There are plenty of people milling about. Laura MacColl is there, looking sparkly, and Jack has just arrived. Audrey goes to help him.

'Miss South, we meet again.' DI Brook is suddenly standing in front of me.

'Sadly.' I manage a feeble smile. 'So, can you give us a good clean quote on camera that you believe unequivocally that it is a serial killer? Is four women enough?'

'We need to go through the same rigorous process of investigation before I can do that.'

He is fudging it again. In his hand is a clear plastic bag, which he shows me. 'We found this at the scene.'

'What is it?'

'A key.'

'Do you think it belongs to the suspect?'

'Possibly.'

'Why would anyone leave that behind? It seems careless, doesn't it?'

'Maybe they were high and didn't notice they'd dropped it. It's dark out here at midnight.'

'That's the time of death, is it?'

'In a window either side of that, yes.'

'How was she killed?'

'Drugged and strangled like the others.'

'Do we know who she is?'

'We're working on it. I can't imagine it will take too long.'

He leaves me with that thought and heads back towards the tent.

Jack and Audrey have set up with the tent behind us. It's a good shot for the bulletin.

'What did he have to say?' Jack nods in Brook's direction. 'Still none the wiser, I bet.'

'Well, he still won't give a good clean sound bite about a serial killer.'

Jack is angry. 'That's ridiculous. East London has a modern-day Jack the Ripper on its hands and the DI in charge of the case can't just say it as it is. The whole investigation is a bloody joke.' He's shaking his head. 'They need to find this guy and they need to do it quickly.'

'It's shocking the way they're dealing with it.' Audrey finds herself agreeing with Jack. 'They should be suspending the dating app for a start. Incidentally, I tried to get an interview with the site yesterday, but they won't talk to us.'

My phone is buzzing. It's Nigel. I resign myself to answering.

'Hi, Alex, how are you? I just heard the news. Terrible. Really terrible. Are you okay?'

'Hey. Thanks for calling. Yes, we just got to London Fields. It's not great.'

'So that's where they found her?'

'Yes.'

It might be time I asked Nigel his whereabouts on the days of the murders.

'Good God. The police really need to get their shit together. That's four women now.'

Although he doesn't sound like a serial killer, but what does one sound like anyway?

'They do.' I walk away from Jack and Audrey, who are chatting passionately with each other. 'I'm really sorry I didn't get back to you, but work has been crazy.'

'I bet. It's totally understandable. You must be exhausted, you poor thing.'

'I am.'

The body bag is being moved from the tent. I take a swig from my water bottle.

'Listen, I'm around all week, so just give me a call when you're free, if you like.'

'Okay. Hey, can I ask you something?'

'Anything you like.'

'Are you dating other women?'

There's a pause in the conversation.

'I'm not fussed if you are. I'd just like to know where I stand.'

'Interesting. I got the impression that you didn't want anything serious, so forgive me if I ask why you want to know.'

'I just wondered, that's all.'

'You're a beautiful woman, Alex, and I'd like to see you again. Does that make things clearer?'

I blush at the comment, which is stupid considering I'm not planning on sleeping with him again. I'm really not sure how to play this now.

'I genuinely do want to see you again, Alex.'

'Okay. Well, I will try to find some time, I promise. I'm not very good at this, as you might have noticed.'

'Don't worry. I like you and I think we had a good time. I'll wait for your call, then, shall I?'

'Yes. That sounds like the best plan.'

We say goodbye and hang up. I take small relief in the fact that the police haven't questioned him yet. I wonder why not, though. Perhaps they have alternative evidence. I'm so tired today. I check Greg's Facebook page to see if there are any clues to his movements, but I'm still blocked, even after the Milk Tray. Anyway, it's time to get cabled up and ready to report. As I make my way back to Audrey and Jack, my phone buzzes again. It's Mrs Wilcox this time. I take the call.

'Alex. I should never have done that interview. I want you to remove it from the website.' Her voice is cold and clear.

'Okay, but can I ask why?'

'I want it removed from the website and I want that to happen today. I trust you'll sort it.' She hangs up.

Audrey sees the look on my face.

'You okay?'

'That was Mrs Wilcox. She wants us to pull the interview.'

'Why?'

'I don't know. She wouldn't say. Only that she wants it taken down from the website.'

'Shit.'

'Can she do that after it's been published?' Jack pipes up.

'Why don't you call her back and try to reason with her?' Audrey says.

'Honestly, Audrey, I'm not feeling great. Do you want to do it? I'm happy to hand the baton to my ambitious young producer in this instance.'

'Really? Are you sure? But do you think she'll talk to me? I mean, her point of contact has been you.'

'I think you're quite persuasive when you want to be, probably more so than me, the mood I'm in.'

'Okay. Send me her number. Thanks, Alex. You can trust me. I'll do my best.'

'I know you will. If she's adamant, can you also get on the phone to Philippa and explain what happened.'

'Of course.'

At least I don't have to have that conversation.

Jack sighs. 'Let's get you cabled up, Alex.'

The park is buzzing with activity, and a small crowd has gathered close by. Since the news got out that a fourth woman has been found dead, people have come to see what's going on.

Jack has his hand held high and is counting down on his fingers. I can hear the presenter on the line. And then suddenly we're live on air.

'And in breaking news, police are investigating a suspicious death after a body was found in an east London park this morning. This is the second body discovered in the space of a week, and the fourth in two months, sparking fears that there could be a serial killer on the prowl in east London. For more on this story, we cross live to Alex South, our crime reporter, who is at the scene.'

'Thank you, Jane. That's right, police are now investigating the second suspicious death in east London this week. A woman's body was found by a runner this morning in London Fields, just a few metres from where I'm standing, and not far from where Alice Fessy was found last week. It is believed the woman died around midnight last night and in similar circumstances to those of Miss Fessy, as well as Maggie Horrocks and Jade Soron. There are no more details at this stage. As you can imagine, police are still searching the area for any clues that might lead them to who brought this woman out here late at night to kill her.'

'This is the fourth suspicious death in a month. How are people feeling over there today?'

'People here are on edge. The three previous victims were all using online dating sites, which is one theory as to how they may have met their killer. It's extremely worrying, because millions of men and women in the UK use dating apps, many of them in London. We have one of the highest rates of Internet dating in Europe and the industry is worth billions. So yes, people are scared. The dating site under scrutiny is the popular app COMEout, which locates a potential match by using your phone's GPS. Police have warned women to be very cautious of using the site at this time. We asked COMEout what they thought of the situation, but they have declined to comment.'

'Alex South, thank you.'

The bulletin moves on to the next item.

'That's a wrap.' Jack turns the camera off.

'Brilliant!' Audrey looks pleased with herself. 'You're so good at this, Alex.'

'Thanks. We should package for the evening bulletin. Jack, can you shoot some images of the crime scene, and the two of you get a few sound bites from people. Then we'll do a piece to camera.'

'Sounds like a good plan.' Audrey has the mic in her hand.

'Okay. I'm just going to sit down for a minute.'

'I've got it covered, Alex, don't worry.'

I walk away from the scene to find a quieter spot. I'm truly exhausted; all I want to do is sit on a bench away from everyone. At least my shakes and sweats are being kept at bay by the vodka disguised as water in my bag. My phone buzzes; it's a message from my fertility app telling me I'm now out of my fertile window and it's countdown to pregnancy. I rub my tummy, wondering if it's my lucky month, not that I could cope with raising a child at the moment. Everything seems to be crashing down on me.

I launch my meditation app and do a few deep-breathing exercises to calm me down. Just as I find some solace, Laura MacColl walks towards me lighting a cigarette. She's also escaping the circus for a minute, but in a cosy down jacket, unlike me. It is cold out here today, but somehow the chill is keeping my head straight.

'Hey, Alex. How you doing? You look like you could do with one of these.' She's waving her cigarette at me.

'I'm okay, thanks. I didn't know you smoked?'

'I keep it quiet, you know.' She smiles warmly. 'It's a bit grim, this, isn't it?'

'Another woman dead, yes it is.'

'Just heard about the key. Not that it means anything without an address.'

She's sitting next to me now as if we are mates.

'So, did you know Sarah Wilcox personally?'

The question throws me.

'What do you mean?'

'I went to that yoga place under the arches yesterday and the instructor – what's his name, Jimmy? – he said you used to go there and so did she.'

'A lot of people go there.'

'Yes, I suppose so, but you're both from Manchester, right? Do you think you're potentially at risk?'

'From what?'

She exhales a plume of smoke. 'Well, you live around here.'

'So do thousands of other women.'

'I guess so. I didn't mean to offend you, Alex.'

'No offence taken.'

I can feel myself getting annoyed with her, and given the fact that I'm trying to detox on the job, I think it's best to leave her to it. I know myself, and I don't want to get into an unnecessary argument.

'I've really got to get back to my crew, Laura, sorry.'

'Oh, okay.'

As I walk away, Laura's question swirls around in my head. Did I know Sarah Wilcox personally because I went to the same yoga place? Maybe that's why DI Brook has suddenly taken an interest in me. Maybe he thinks I know something. I only wish I did.

39

September 2017

Dear Diary,

I feel like I'm about to burst out screaming at the next person who tells me time will heal me. I wish I'd never trusted Alex with my secrets. I don't know why I ever became her friend. I'm angry with myself for holding her in such high esteem, giving her way too much credit. How could I have been so stupid? She thinks she's clever, with her big words and her fancy job, but she lied to me. She told me she wanted me to get better, but she was only ever interested in herself. She doesn't think about anyone else. She's selfish and messed up. The fact that she ran away after the miscarriage proves it.

Greg told me everything. That she lost the baby and then just left without telling him where she was going. She didn't think about me or him, or anyone for that matter. She just left us all behind. And now here I am in this fucked-up place in the middle of nowhere, because she put me here. If it weren't for her, I'd still be sitting on my park bench. I was okay then. My life was simple. Now I have to empty my bag every day while a stranger goes through my stuff.

I'm herded around from room to room being told that my life is about to get so much better now that I've discovered why I drink, but it's all bullshit. My life isn't about to get better, because I wish I didn't know what I know now. I wish I'd never found out why I drink. Not everyone needs to know, you know.

My therapists say that until I can learn to love that part of me, I will never stop drinking, but how can I learn to love that part of me? I threw up in the therapy room. What the hell is that? It was as if my body rejected that memory, like it just wanted to get rid of it.

Since that happened, I feel like I've been walking on shaky ground. I couldn't eat tonight. The people in the centre have been really nice. Really sweet. I can see it in their eyes that some of them have been through the same kind of realisation, but it doesn't make it easier. I just want to shut off the reality and go back to how things used to be before I met Alex. This has ruined my life. I will never be the same person. I don't think I will ever love that part of me, which means I will probably never stop drinking, so this whole thing was a complete waste of time and money.

40

Audrey and Jack are busy gathering interviews for the report. DI Brook seems to have fucked off. I guess he's keen to get to the lab and find out what Forensics know so he can draw some conclusions about whether all four deaths are connected. London hasn't been threatened by a serial killer for decades, and the thought is a terrifying one.

I've gained over four thousand followers on Twitter since my lunchtime report, which brings the grand total up to around forty-five thousand. I'm fast becoming a household name thanks to this story. I just wish I could get dry at the same time. I will. I know I will.

Daylight is starting to fade and with it the temperature is plummeting further. I'm not sure what the plan is yet other than to file something for the evening bulletin. The editors will probably want me live again from the scene to top-and-tail the report: to introduce it and then give a few more details at the end; some insight that wasn't in the report itself.

My water bottle is empty now. I've done really well today, sipping slowly to keep me afloat. I need a refill, though, so I wander off with the excuse that I want to warm up for a bit. There's a café opposite the park on the main road with an off licence next door, so I head there.

After I've emptied a couple of shot bottles into my water bottle in the ladies' toilets, I find a table and order a coffee with notes of ginger, hoping that it might save me from feeling worse than I already do. I feel like hell, I really do. I'm detoxing by cutting down slowly this time. The all-out abstention didn't work, so this is phase two.

I take a seat by the window, where there's an unob-structed view of the park. I know Audrey will call if she needs me. She's confident enough to ask the right questions. It's reassuring to have her producing, especially when I feel like this.

Holding onto the warm coffee mug as if my life depends on it is helping me feel almost normal. As normal as one can be when in the midst of a detox. The aroma is comforting. I get my notebook out and start to think about what I might say in the report. As I'm staring out of the window, mulling over the first line, my eye catches a man walking along the perimeter of the park, looking around as if he's lost, and for a moment I swear it could be Greg. My mind must be playing tricks on me.

Moments later, I've left the warm confines of the café and am standing outside, unsure of which way to go. I am trying to find the man I'm convinced is Greg. There was just something about him that felt so familiar. Did he go into the park? Or just walk past it? I decide to walk in the direction he was headed.

I reach a crossroads and there's no one around. I don't know what I'm doing. I should be concentrating on my reporting; this is a wild goose chase if ever there was one, and my mind is all over the place. Perhaps I was just hallucinating. Worse things have happened. I sip from my water bottle as if that will help me decide which way to go.

I'm still standing on the edge of the park, watching the traffic lights change, when I receive a call. 'Newsroom' flashes on the screen, but I can't pick up. I'm paralysed with fear and yet I don't know why. I'm a mess. A real mess. Moments after the newsroom call, 'Audrey' flashes on my screen. Something must have happened, so this time I pick up.

'Have you seen the latest, Alex?'

'What's happened?'

'They've arrested someone for the murder of Maggie Horrocks.'

'Shit.'

'What do you think we should do? Abandon what we're doing and get over to the police station? They're going to hold a press conference within the hour.'

There's a knot in the pit of my stomach.

'Call the newsroom and tell them we're heading over to the station. I'll meet you by the gate on the south side of the park.'

'Okay. Should I bring Jack?'

'Yes, bring Jack. The channel will want to carry the press conference live.'

'Okay.'

I really hope it's not Nigel or Greg. I wonder if I should get on the phone to Anne Marie. Maybe she can be in our news package. I'll deal with that after the presser.

By the time we get to the police station, Audrey has read almost everything there is to read on Twitter about who the potential suspect could be, which is very little. There's no hint of a name or where he's from.

'I hope he fucking rots in hell!' Jack is happy about this development and not holding back from expressing it. 'They should cut his balls off and feed them to the dogs.'

'Not very fair on the doggies.' Audrey is teasing him.

There's already a herd of cameramen jostling for a good spot, which all changes when a uniformed police officer appears.

'Ladies and gents, we will be holding a press conference inside in about one hour. If you want to follow me, I will take you to the room so you can set up your cameras and get seated.'

There's a mad scramble to follow the officer back into the building and Jack disappears in the scrum. Audrey and I hang back. She's trying to talk to Philippa and find out if they can carry the announcement live, while I don't want to run into DI Brook before the press conference.

I spot a shop across the street and gesture towards it. Audrey nods and turns away; she's too busy to worry about what I'm up to. I need something to put in my mouth, chewing gum or boiled sweets.

'So they've caught the guy, have they?' the young Turkish cashier asks me.

'We're waiting to find out.'

'Awful story. But then people don't know who they are meeting these days online. Whatever happened to meeting in a pub or at a party?'

When I get my wallet out of my bag, I see a beer mat with a number on it. I vaguely recall having picked it up while talking to Anne Marie. When I come out of the shop, Audrey isn't there – she must have gone inside to talk to Jack – so I find a public payphone close to the station and dial the number scribbled on the mat. The line rings until a voicemail picks up. The message is short and pretty standard, but the male voice is unmistakable. It's Charlie. And I've never known him not to answer his phone. I try his home phone from my mobile, but again, no answer. Maybe the journalist in Annabel was right. Shit.

41

October 2017

Dear Diary,

It's time to go home. I've been in rehab a total of three weeks and the experience has changed me forever, changed my life. I will never be able to go home again. Never. Never be able to return to what I left. I'm sitting in the train station in Wilmslow wondering what to do, where to go. I haven't called my dad to tell him I'm on my way back. I haven't called my mum, not that she would even care. I don't think I will ever be able to speak to her again, not after what I discovered about her. It is her fault that I drink. My own mother. She left me to be abused for years. My father didn't protect me from any of it.

The clinic has given me the name of a drop-in clinic in Manchester that I can visit. They have advised me to seek out some private therapy to help with the emotional trauma I'm trying to come to terms with, but I don't have any money. I think my dad should probably fund it, so that's one thing I might put in action. Make him pay for his part in it, financially speaking. He has plenty of money. Always working. They told me to go and see my GP; that he might be able to help me get therapy on the NHS, but that would mean talking openly about what happened, and he's a friend of the family so that's never going to work. I really don't know what to do with myself, so I buy a bumper packet of peanut M&Ms from the kiosk and munch my way through the bag. While in the shop, I see a selection of white wine. This is my first encounter with alcohol since I went into rehab. It looks so tempting. I'm not sure how I feel about this. I don't have enough money to buy a bottle even if I wanted to, though, which is a very good thing.

The therapist in rehab told me that drinking wouldn't block out the reason why I started in the first place, so it won't help me now. Tim said that once the genie is out of the bottle, so to speak, it's almost impossible to put it back in. I need to be sober anyway if I am going to make something of myself. Three trains to Manchester come and go, but I don't get on any of them. I feel paralysed by indecision, so I just sit on the platform watching and waiting. For what, I don't know.

It's dark by the time I decide what to do, which is to call Greg and see if I can stay there. He says yes, although I'm not sure he really wants to. I tell him I have nowhere else to go, that I can't go home, and that if I do, I might do something stupid. He doesn't want me to do that, so he agrees, albeit reluctantly. I explain that I've come out of rehab and am sober; I guess that's why he says it's okay. He wants to help an alcoholic stay sober. So I board the last train to Manchester and the next phase of my life begins.

I feel uncertain of what will happen next, but I'm hoping I will get back on my feet. I text my dad to tell him I have left rehab and am staying with a friend. He texts back to say he is sorry. I guess he knows what I know about my mum. And maybe he knows a bit more.

By the time I arrive back in Manchester it's very late, and when I ring Greg's doorbell it's gone midnight. He lets me in and then goes back to bed. The sofa is made up. I hate my life. I hate how I've ended up here.

42

'Good afternoon. Let me start by thanking you all for coming.'

DI Brook has put on a black tie since I saw him last. Makes him look more authoritative on camera, I suppose. I'm boiling in my coat, for a change, but there's hardly enough room to make notes comfortably, let alone take it off.

'Early this morning, the Metropolitan Police made an arrest in connection with the murder of Maggie Horrocks.' DI Brook has the perfect poker face, near impossible to read. 'We currently have a man in custody and are in the process of questioning him over his relationship with Miss Horrocks. He has not been formally charged, and at this stage, I'd like to repeat that we are only questioning him. We believe he may have vital information on her death.'

John from the *Evening Standard* pipes up. 'How old is he? Where's he from?'

DI Brook clears his throat and leans forward on his elbows, his hands crossed.

'He is forty-two. We arrested him locally.'

Well, that's Greg out of the picture, thank God. He turns forty later this year. We'd planned a whole list of things to do for his fortieth, a list that was discarded after

I walked out. I don't know how old Nigel is; he could be forty-two, I suppose. And Charlie? I saw him this morning, didn't I? Although I also saw DI Brook at my flat.

Audrey pipes up and poses a tough question, a good question. 'Is he your main suspect, and do you think he's connected to the other women?'

'As I said, we are currently questioning him in connection to Maggie Horrocks, but the investigation is ongoing and we will release more details when we feel it's relevant.'

'Does he use the COMEout dating app?' Audrey is still pushing for answers; good for her, someone should, and I'm in no state to do it, sipping from my water bottle. 'And do you have a name for the woman found today in London Fields?'

'As I said, the investigation is ongoing. You can rest assured that we will release more details when and as we get them.'

DI Brook tugs on his tie as he gets up, but before he leaves the room, he gives me a serious look. Fortunately, it goes unnoticed by Audrey, who is pissed off with the charade of the press conference.

'That's it? That's all they're going to tell us? What a joke.'

My phone is buzzing and the name Anne Marie flashes on the screen.

'I need to take this, Audrey. I'll just be outside.'

'Don't go far, we need to do a live report on this. Jack will set up. Live in about twenty-five minutes.'

'Okay.'

I answer the call as I enter the corridor, where a ray of sunlight blinds me for a moment.

'Hello.'

'Alex, is that you?'

'It is. Anne Marie?' I'm trying to sound casual, but I know what she's about to say. I look for a moment of privacy, which I find in the toilets.

'Yes. I saw the news and I just wanted to say thanks.'

'Thanks for what?'

'For coming here last night. I don't know what you did, but if they've got him, I'll be forever grateful.'

I'm staring at myself in the large mirror. There's a crack from left to right, the whole thing hanging on by a couple of very fragile-looking supports. A bit like my sanity.

'Well, let's see, shall we. The police haven't said who is in custody yet, but if I send you a photo of a guy, would you be able to tell me if you recognise him?'

'Sure.'

'Right, hold on.'

I launch Facebook and take a screen shot of Charlie's photo, then text it to her.

'Just sent it to you.'

'Okay. One sec.'

I can hear her fiddling with her phone. Then a long silence before she eventually speaks.

'Oh my God, Alex. Yes, I do recognise him. Maggie knew him.'

'How? How did she know him? Was she dating him?'

'No. I don't think so. I'm not sure.'

'Think, Anne Marie, it's really important.'

'I think she might have worked for him.'

'Worked for him?'

'Yes, she helped design his website if I'm not wrong.'

I don't really know what this means, but I feel relieved. At least Charlie's connection isn't romantic, so even if he is the man in custody, which I sincerely hope he isn't, it's unlikely they'll charge him with murder. Holy shit. This can't be happening. Why didn't he just tell me he knew her? That hurts.

'Are you sure about that, Anne Marie?'

'Yes. I'm sure.'

'Okay.'

'Alex, will you keep me in the loop if the police say anything else? I mean if they identify the man in custody?'

'Sure. I'm sorry, I have to go. Got to get ready for a report.'

'Of course. Thanks again.'

Audrey has already texted me to ask where I am. I check my make-up in the cracked mirror before leaving the loo and head outside to the live position. The report goes fine, considering how little I know. The news centre gives us a clear and tells us to wrap for now, so we split up and go our separate ways.

As I'm leaving the station, I receive a text from Nigel to see if I fancy a quick pint at Pub on the Park. Relieved that the police have yet to question him, I agree to meet. Might as well. It'll keep me distracted from myself, which is not to be underestimated. He's already there when I arrive and stands up to greet me with a light kiss on the cheek.

'Hi, Alex. Glad you came.'

He's already got the drinks in, so I sit down and sip from the glass of white wine on the table.

'Listen, I'm sorry about the other night. I didn't handle it very well.'

'That's okay.' I've done much worse since then, effectively shopping him to the police over his online dating habits mainly because I was feeling insecure. Booze can make you do really unforgivable things.

'So here we are.'

'Yes, here we are.'

'So you've been busy?'

'Yes, it's been hectic. I can't quite believe what's going on.'

'What have the police said?'

We swap stories about our days. Sitting opposite his warm smile, I realise I've got him all wrong and feel incredibly guilty about what I've done, so I decide to confess, hoping he'll appreciate my honesty.

'I need to tell you something, but you have to promise me you won't freak out.'

'Sounds intriguing, Alex.'

'I'm serious.'

My stomach is churning. I take a much larger sip of wine, a swig really, though I'm just going to have the one glass.

'The police showed me a CCTV image from outside the station the night Alice Fessy was killed. The image is of you.'

His face changes instantaneously, like he's just had some terrible news, which of course he has.

'What do you mean, it's of me?'

'It shows you leaving London Fields station in the same frame as Alice, walking just behind her.'

He looks confused. As if I've just asked him something in a foreign language and he can't understand me.

'What? So they've decided I'm involved because I happened to get off the same train as her. I live here. What the fuck?' He looks genuinely shocked. I wish I hadn't said anything now.

'Hang on a minute. Why would they show it to you?'

'I'm friends with the DI running the case. He knows I live around here so asked if I recognised the man in the image.'

'Bloody hell, Alex. What did you say?'

His reaction makes me withdraw from telling him the whole truth.

'I didn't say anything. Only that it didn't look like you were together. I guess you just left the station at the same time.'

'But I don't understand why the police would show you an image of me on CCTV footage in the first place.'

He won't let that part of it go. Shit. I can feel the blood rushing to my face.

'Like I said, I know the DI. We've worked together on other cases. I'm a crime reporter, you know. We develop a relationship with our sources. I'm telling you to help you.'

He scratches his stubble with his right hand.

'Yes, of course. I appreciate you giving me the heads-up, but if they question me, we were together that night. Did you tell this DI that?'

'Kind of.'

'What do you mean, kind of?'

'I don't like talking about my personal life in detail with the police.'

'Well, you're effectively my alibi.'

It occurs to me that maybe he set our date up for exactly that reason. I don't know why I'm feeling so bad about it.

'Anyway, you're my alibi too.'

I'm trying to make light of the situation, but he's not buying into that. Instead he stares into his pint, looking increasingly worried.

'Look, don't worry about it. It's just an image that means nothing, and as I said, it really doesn't prove anything. You're not holding hands with her or anything.' I reach out and touch his arm.

'Right.'

'I wish I'd never told you now.'

'No. You did the right thing. Thank you.' He reciprocates my touch with a hand on mine, but it's half-hearted. 'I'm sorry, I'm not good company. I've had a really long day today. We're working on this TV series at the moment, trying to find a woman who can play the lead. Funnily enough, we're looking for someone who looks a bit like you. My sister is also in town.'

I smile softly, but feel really awful about putting his life under surveillance the way I have.

'Listen, I need to get going, but I'm happy to meet up again, if you want to?'

He's making excuses to leave; I don't blame him.

'Okay.'

We say our goodbyes, and just like that, the night comes to an end. I feel terrible about what I've done, but not surprised that I've managed to push away a good man. I've got form for doing that. On my way home, I get a text from Audrey. She's forwarded me a link. It's a report

223

by our competitor, Laura MacColl. Mrs Wilcox has been talking to her; it's not good.

43

Dear Diary,

I stayed at Greg's for a few nights before I realised I had no business being there. The world looks so different now that I'm a self-confessed victim of childhood abuse and sober. I used to think everyone knew the difference between right and wrong, but they don't. People are messed up just like me. I asked the AA group if anyone needed a lodger. Jamala said I could stay with her for a while so that I could figure out what to do next. She has been so supportive. She hasn't had a drink in five years and she knows how lost I feel at the moment. It is good staying with her because she doesn't have alcohol in the house, which has helped me stay off it. I know that I have to completely change my environment if I want to stay sober; the only problem is, I'm not sure if I really want to. Everyone tells me it's the best thing to do, but is it? I still can't shake the shame in the pit of my stomach and the feelings of disgust at what happened to me.

I'm attending AA meetings regularly again. The people I meet there have been amazing. They are the only people I can really connect with now because they are simply there for me. They listen without judgement. They listen to my fears and they smile and nod then thank me for sharing. It's a comfort because since becoming sober I've started having some very dark thoughts.

Thoughts that I've never had before. For example, yesterday I saw an injured mouse while walking in the park, picked it up and crushed it with my bare hands. I mean I clenched my fist and squashed it until it was barely recognisable. The worrying bit is that I found it mildly amusing. Who does that? One of the people at AA said they felt anger towards their father, who is also an alcoholic. I thought perhaps the squashing of the mouse was the same sort of anger, which has possibly been building inside me all this time. And now that I'm sober, those feelings are coming to the fore. More childhood memories have started to reappear. Memories that catalogue repeated abuse over a period of years, and not only by the men in my mother's life while my dad was MIA, but also by my mother herself. She was cruel to me from an early age. She didn't nurture me; in fact, she used to lock me in my room for hours on end. I remember her calling me evil. I don't remember her ever saying anything else really.

I met with my dad in a neutral place. I needed money, so I had to. He put his arms around me and cried for what felt like forever. I've never seen him cry before, ever. It unnerved me. All he could say was sorry, over and over. I didn't tell him about the memories and how his absence from our lives had allowed her drinking to rob me of my childhood. I'm envious of Jamala in a way because she started drinking in her early twenties just because she liked the taste of it, which became dysfunctional later in life. She says she inherited the disease from her family. There was no painful reason to drink; she was merely predisposed to it.

I now see that I may have also inherited it from my mother, but the trauma of abuse led me to pick up the bottle at a really early age; put that with a predisposition and the rest is history. I told Jamala about the abuse. I'm not sure why, but I felt like I could confide in her. She said it wasn't my fault, and I know that, but there is something deep inside me that can't help feeling

226

responsible for what happened to me. I mean, why would my mother lock me in my room and call me evil? None of it makes any sense, but then abuse doesn't, does it?

There are so many unanswered questions swirling around in my head. Jamala says it will get easier with time, that time heals all wounds. I'm not sure if that's true. I didn't tell my dad the whole story when we met because I don't think he would ever be able to look at me the same way again. I know I wouldn't be able to look at him the same way. I could see the pain in his eyes when he talked about Mum's drinking; also because she's still at it. He feels he failed in some way. That he was unable to reach her like he did me. Although it was Alex that reached me, not him, but I let him pay for rehab, which has been healing for him, I think. He told me that my grandmother was also a drinker, which confirms what I thought. It is a family disease. He explained that he left when I was very young because of Mum's drinking, but then he came back. He came back for me. Little does he know that by then it was too late.

I had my first drink when I was nine. I just hid it from the outside world really well, like my mother did. He had no idea that I started that young and he never will. I now know that I drank to numb the shame from the abuse. It was the easy thing to do. That's how my relationship with alcohol began. I never drank to the point of getting completely wasted. I just did it so I could suppress my emotions. So I could forget. By the age of ten, I was addicted. I spent my teenage years drinking with friends. Everyone was trying it, experimenting, so no one noticed my drinking was habitual. Plus there was so much booze at home it was really easy to get my hands on it.

I would pour vodka into my water bottle and put it in my school bag. I don't remember much after that. Much of my teenage years was spent trying to forget what happened to me while my dad wasn't there. His guilt plays out in his inability to take time off from work. I guess he felt he needed to make up for it somehow, so he became a high earner, hoping that wealth would ease our pain. It didn't.

In a way, it might have been better if Mum was broke, then at least she wouldn't have been able to buy alcohol. Dad offered to put some money in my bank account, and I said yes. In fact, I think he's going to make it a regular thing so I can make a fresh start, a new life away from all this. It's the guilt, you see. He has plenty of that. He wants to somehow make up for those years when he left us. I may as well let him, because I need the money for where I'm going. London. I saw Alex drunk on the evening news. She needs help.

44

There's a loud bang in the hallway of the building, which wakes me up. It's gone two o'clock in the morning when I open the door to find Charlie slumped by his mountain bike in the dark, clutching a bottle of wine in his right hand.

'Alex, gorgeous Alex. There you are.'

He's blind drunk. I have only seen him this wasted once before, and that was when he broke up with his ex, about a month after I moved in. That's when we first slept together.

'Women can be so heartless…'

'Yes, I know. That they can. That they can.'

He tries to stand up but slides back down the wall. The bottle slips from his hand, creating a torrent of red on the carpet. This isn't exactly how I envisioned seeing him after I discovered he knew Maggie Horrocks.

'Let's get you inside, shall we?'

It's quite awkward given the narrowness of the hallway, but although he's much bigger than me and is now crushing my shoulder, I manage to get my arm around his back and help him up. I'm not cleaning up his mess, though. He can do that himself.

'Where's your key?'

'In my pocket.' He's slurring his words. 'You're such a darling, Alex. You really are a darling.'

I search his pockets but can't find the key. God, I really don't need this. Not today. Not on a day I'm detoxing. I'm going to have to bring him into mine or leave him to sleep in the red puddle. I'd prefer not to have to make either of these choices, but I'm stuck with them. Physically it would be impossible to get him up a steep flight of stairs on my own anyway. He's a big guy and it's proving difficult to move him. Christ, there's a wet patch on his jeans, which is now touching my leg. Ugh. Luckily I'm wearing my black leggings, but if I don't get these wine-soaked jeans off him, it'll end up all over my flat. What a fucking mess.

I deposit Charlie in the bedroom undressed and resign myself to a night on the sofa. He's out within moments of hitting the pillow. What a day. My body feels like crap, but I suppose this drama brings it all home; it's a good reminder of what I have to do. Alcohol is destructive. I have to stop drinking. I'm awake now, so I make a cuppa and read Laura MacColl's piece on Mrs Wilcox. I wanted to read it before I went to sleep but was too drained.

The interview isn't on camera, which means it's not quite as powerful as it could have been, thankfully. They are leading with her anger at the police for not informing her of what is happening with the investigation, especially in light of the arrest this afternoon. She also criticises our report, and me in particular. I don't know why she has taken such a beef with me. I mean, she agreed to our interview and was friendly when I met her. I assume she's distraught, as any mother would be, and experiencing extreme mood swings.

Laura's report also suggests that the gym card found by the body was dropped weeks before the death of Alice Fessy and was a false flag in the investigation. I expect DI Brook won't be happy with this development, because it's moments like this that can hinder an investigation.

Over fifteen hundred people have liked the page and at least three hundred have commented on it, mostly readers expressing their anger at the police and sympathy for Mrs Wilcox. She's becoming a bit of a media darling by all accounts. I recall Dutch's words. He didn't like her one bit. He had a sense that something was up with her. Viewed her as an attention-seeker. Thinking of Dutch reminds me of our night together. I launch my fertility app, which tells me there's three days until I can take a pregnancy test. I live in hope.

The temperature has dropped tonight. There aren't nearly enough extra covers in the flat to stay warm on the sofa, and I don't fancy sleeping under a pile of towels. I decide that it's too cold to give up my bed while detoxing. Charlie will just have to deal with that. He's out for the count and doesn't notice when I climb in beside him. Thankfully he's not snoring, which would have just topped it all off. Shortly afterwards, I drift off into a well-needed deep slumber.

—

When I wake up, there's a bad energy in me. I've had a nightmare. They happen when I detox. Greg featured in it, which hasn't happened for a while. We were at a function, an outdoor event. It was summer, a time of fun and relaxing, but it was anything but relaxing. He was flirting with a woman; I don't know who she was. From behind she looked a lot like Sarah Wilcox. I was sober, but he was plastered. There was a deep feeling of betrayal in me. I took myself out of the situation by walking away and leaving the function, and ended up in a huge house where a party was going on. Everyone was having a good time, but I didn't care about that because I was searching for someone, although I don't know who. Then I woke up.

Daylight is creeping into the room because the blinds are only half closed. Charlie rolls over and wraps his arm around me, nestling his face into the back of my neck like a cat in need of affection. Moments later, he runs his finger down my arm to my thigh, though he still hasn't said a word. I'm not sure what to do, so I do nothing and say nothing. It's awkward but electrifying at the same time. I pretend I'm still sleeping, but I'm sure he knows I'm not.

It doesn't take long before he's kissing the back of my neck, then my shoulder, then brushing my lower stomach, and I begin to feel aroused. He's not quitting and I don't want him to because I need this too. I want to feel loved after that terrible dream. I want to feel needed, if only for a moment. I lean into his body, wrapping my arm around his back, giving him a sign that I consent to his moves. That I won't push him away.

Charlie is a good lover. He has such a light touch it would be difficult to push him away even if I wanted to, and before long our bodies are entwined until we've exhausted our desires. It's about finding solace in someone else: me from my fucked-up life, him from what I suspect is another break-up with someone he quite liked.

'Good morning, gorgeous.' Charlie has a cheeky smile and ruddy cheeks.

'Hello, you old fool.'

'Well, that's charming, isn't it?'

'A bit like you last night! There's a bottle of red wine all over the hallway carpet, which you'd better clean up before the landlady sees it. I'm not taking the rap for that.'

'Don't worry, I'll take care of it. It's not like you haven't benefited from it this morning.'

'Yeah, right. Just what I needed, a drunken person in my hallway in the middle of the night.' As I say it, I have a mild case of déjà vu. Greg used to say this to me all the time. I feel pleasantly exhausted, though.

He's sitting up now, his well-built chest on show. He's quite enjoying himself. I've got my T-shirt back on and am looking for something to cover up my bottom half.

'You were in a right state last night. What happened?'

'I had a right to be. The fucking police picked me up yesterday and took me in for questioning over Maggie bloody Horrocks.'

'They did what?' I'm still annoyed that he didn't mention he knew her, but then I'm not doing any better given that I've just slept with another potential suspect.

'They had me in a bloody cell until one o'clock this morning. Just because I knew her and apparently I have a dating profile on that site.'

'Oh, it's all coming out now. Now that you're in trouble. Yeah, come and dump your shit on me, why don't you.'

'Don't be like that, Alex. You're the one person I can talk to, always have been. The one person who doesn't read into things. You like facts. It's who you are.'

'It's not one of my finer qualities.'

233

Not that I even know what those are these days. I'm starting to feel the need for an alcoholic beverage, and it's early. My life is becoming one big shit storm. How did this happen? I moved here to get away from drama and now I seem to be in the middle of it.

'For the record, the dating profile they showed me was created by someone else. Not me. A case of stolen identity. Can you believe it?'

'What?'

'Yeah, right. Mental. Look, I think you're adorable, Alex. You took me in last night, not many women would do that.'

'What else could I have done?'

Looking into his laser-blue eyes, I wonder if I should open up to him and tell him what's been going on since DI Brook hauled me in too. Be honest about my life for a change, like he is being with me. Just let it all out. Admit I'm an alcoholic in need of help. But I can't. Not while I'm on the story.

'Do they think you're a suspect? Are you?'

'Noooo, of course not. That's why they let me go. I just knew her, that's all.'

'Fuck, Charlie.'

'Yes please. Let's make love again, my sweet Alex.'

'Would love to, but work calls.'

I wink at him and make for the bedroom door, hoping to find some dregs of something somewhere in the flat. I'm desperately in need of alcohol this morning, just to get going. There's a can of cider in my bag, which helps

When I return to the bedroom with tea, Charlie is dressed and holding a piece of jewellery in his hands.

'This from someone special?'

'That? Old junk is what it is.'

I hand him the tea, forcing him to put it down. It's a piece I haven't worn for a while.

'Doesn't look like old junk. It has your initial on it entwined with… what's that? An S?'

'An ex gave it to me a long time ago.'

It's a lie, but easier than explaining that I don't know. I can't believe I've still got that thing. It was a gift for my birthday last year that arrived with a note from 'Sarah'. I didn't make the connection at the time but wonder now if it could have been Sarah Wilcox. I meant to try to find out, but shortly after that my life turned to utter shit. These reminders of my past creeping into my life in London are doing my head in. I wish I'd never called in to the newsroom now. Wish I had never taken on this bloody story.

'So the S was your ex?'

'Yes. No one special.'

He knows I'm lying. He knows me too well, but I'm not going to change my story if that's what he wants.

'But you've held onto it?'

'I thought I'd thrown it away, but I suppose it got mixed up with other stuff when I moved.'

'Jesus, Alex. What have you done to your leg?'

He's pointing at my thigh, and when I look down, I see a huge bruise.

'I don't know, probably knocked into something. It's not a big deal.'

'I hope I didn't do that to you when you picked me up off the floor last night.'

'I'm pretty sure you didn't, don't worry.'

He's right, it is quite a bruise, but then I find them all the time after being on a binge. The things I walk into are unclear while under the influence. And the blackout is probably the culprit. I could have done anything that night, really anything.

I have Charlie's spare key in my hand, having found it in the kitchen drawer.

'Here, take your key. You can bring the mug back later. I'm sorry, but I really need to get on. Another long day ahead, most likely.'

'So that's it, you're kicking me out. Charming.'

'Yes, I suppose I am.'

'Guess I touched a nerve, did I?'

Moments later, Charlie is gone and I'm left staring at the bracelet, a bracelet I'd completely forgotten about, but which I should probably get rid of, give to charity or something. I should have prodded Charlie about the police interrogation further. It's my job to uncover all the facts. My head really isn't thinking straight. He's probably dead to the world now, though. I put the bracelet in my bag and promise myself to get rid of it today.

45

November 2017

Dear Diary,

So here I am, living in London. I made it to the capital. It's much bigger than Manchester and I find myself getting easily lost. I can't get my bearings at all. Jamala's friend Suzy rented her spare room to me in Fulham. It's a nice area. Feels very much like Didsbury in a way, village-like, although of course there are a lot more people from other countries living here. It's very international. Suzy is also an alcoholic, so it's easy to be around her because we can talk openly about it. We go to AA meetings together. The group numbers about eight on a slow day and up to twenty when it's busy. They are nice people. It helps to keep me sober. I mean, it's my sobriety that has got me this far, isn't it? To move to another city, to start again. Something that didn't seem possible only a year ago. I'm finally achieving something in my life.

At the AA meetings, I find it difficult to share with the group, although I was never really any good at that in Manchester either. Rehab forced me to because I was made to open up by the programme. So I attend the meetings in silence, listening to what everyone else has to say and hoping to identify with them, which is part of recovery. I can see myself in others, I mean in their actions, but I'm way ahead of them emotionally. They say they feel guilty for having hurt people with their drinking, but I don't see why I should be made to feel guilty for something that wasn't my fault.

I haven't touched alcohol since I left rehab — well, only once, but I decided not to do that again because I risk ruining everything I have worked for. I feel so much more together these days. I think it's the first time in my life I've felt genuinely excited about the future.

My dad sends money every month. He pays my rent and gives me an allowance to live. He thinks I'm using part of it for therapy, but after my rehab experience, I decided to knock therapy on the head. Don't see the point in it now that I've made a new start for myself. I do need to see Alex, though, talk to her. I think it would be good for me. Just to settle things in my mind. Oh, and Suzy also has a cat called Womble. It's fat and waddles around, hence the name. She overfeeds it, spoils it actually. Womble is a cute cat but can also be a bit annoying. He constantly rubs up against my leg when I'm eating. Suzy says he's just looking for affection, but I had this urge yesterday to hurt him. I have these sudden urges now to hurt living things, bugs and animals.

46

December 2017

Dear Diary,

It's almost Christmas and Suzy has kicked me out after I almost killed Womble. She came back from work and found me sticking pins in him. She thought I had gone mad. I'll admit it was a pretty strange thing to do, but I'm not sure what came over me. I just had this urge to hurt him after he wouldn't leave me alone. Anyway, it's probably a good thing that it happened, because I've finally moved into my own space, which is tiny but it's mine. It's not how I thought it would be. Living on your own can be quite lonely, especially at Christmas. But I need to find my independence if it's the last thing I do. It's the only way I'm really ever going to sort my life out. My mum always told me I couldn't stand on my own two feet, so I am doing it and at a time of year when it's not easy to be alone. Although in a way, as an alcoholic it is easier, because everyone is drinking at this time of year. Life kind of revolves around it.

I've spoken to my dad a few times on the phone since I left, but I haven't spoken to my mum because I really needed to cut her off. She's a trigger for me now, and so I have to keep away from her. All she does is put me down and make me feel terrible about myself. I don't need that in my life. I'm trying to start something new. Start afresh. I need to stay focused on being sober. I'm thinking about doing some online dating, but I'm not sure where to start with that really. There are so many websites, it feels quite daunting. I signed up to one yesterday called COMEout. It's advertised on the Underground and is promoted as a place online where women can meet both men and women, and vice versa. It looks fun but I'm nervous about meeting new people because I have to come clean with them about my drinking, which is really hard. And actually the thought of talking about myself generally is quite frightening.

There's one reason I'm in London really and that's Alex. I owe her in a way. She saved me from myself. I was rotting away in my mother's house but now here I am living independently in the capital. Who would have thought that a year ago? I think Alex needs my help. In fact, I'm sure of it since I witnessed the episode on TV. The whole country saw it. Since then I haven't seen her on telly at all. I see her name on bylines on their website, but it doesn't seem like she's getting on air. I'm guessing it's her drinking issue. I know I can help her like she helped me. I wonder what she's doing for Christmas. Maybe I should send her a card.

47

It's day five since Alice Fessy was found dead in London Fields. A day since another woman was found dead there too. It's been just over a month since the first victim was found. Britain's newspapers are demanding the police use the term 'serial killer' which they are still loathe to do. They keep skirting around it by saying the murders are connected. The public is largely fuelling these demands on social media. As one daily put it, 'Police fail to connect the dots', a reference to child's play.

Mark Cohen, the CEO of the dating site COMEout, has been talking to our tech correspondent, voicing his opinion on the investigation too. He told UKBC: 'We have been fully cooperating with the police as public safety is our number one concern.' It's sounds a bit like lip service if you ask me. The story is on our website today and is getting a lot of attention as Londoners work out whether to take their dating offline. I wonder if we should really be giving him an avenue to lie like this to the public, but such is the business I work in these days.

My work status is 'on call'. Our hours this week have been flexible, and they told me to take a rest unless anything breaks on the story. So I'm back to seeing if I can get to grips with my detox, because I need to sort it out. I don't know what I'd do if I lost it, actually. Probably drink myself to death. I've been sipping the can of cider since Charlie left, pacing myself, hoping that after this can is done I'll just stay off it for the rest of the day.

Sober days are much harder than drinking days, contrary to popular belief, because I have to face myself. Face up to what I'm doing with my life. The fact that I'm still single and childless at thirty-nine. It is the reality of the choices I have made.

I've made myself a proper breakfast for a change, scrambled eggs with salmon and fresh carrot juice with ginger. I've also put away all my laundry, which feels good. It's not like I'm a lazy person, but when I'm drinking, the days just roll into one and before I know it a whole month can go by and the pile of washing is still on the table, the out-of-date milk is exactly where it has always been in the fridge, and the bills don't get paid on time. One thing at a time, though. I have to wean myself off the booze today while the story has died down, so that by evening I'll be dry again. That's my most important task.

The kettle boils and I make my fourth cup of tea in the space of an hour. I need to drink something. I might even do a crossword. I love word conundrums. They keep my mind busy, for one. I've checked my Facebook page and responded to some of the birthday wishes; another thing I wouldn't do if I were drinking. It's good to reply to people, to connect. I need to make more of an effort to do that so I don't feel so lonely. Dutch has messaged to ask how I'm getting on and expressed concern about the news of another victim. He says he might be in London next month and that he'd like to meet, if I'm up for it.

My body is still playing up; it doesn't feel completely straightened out yet. My mind isn't fucking with me as it was, although I don't feel fully composed. I have managed to stay off the dating apps, including COMEout, which feels good. It's quite hard when I'm at home because it can be lonely.

A few messages come back from those I've responded to on Facebook saying it's good to hear from me, a novelty in some cases. I sent Annabel a couple of texts and a message on Facebook an hour ago asking her to get in touch so I can update her about Charlie, but she hasn't read them yet. As I'm about to make my fifth – or is it sixth? – cup of tea, a message alert appears on my phone. It's from an unknown number. I swipe right and a name comes into focus. It's a text from him, from Greg. Shit.

It starts in my shoulders and ends in my toes, the nervousness that is sweeping through my being, and not in an excited-can't-wait-to-see-how-this-turns-out way, but rather in a dreadful-what-happens-next way. My mind is telling me to calm down, but my body is doing the opposite. It is freaking out. Is it really him? Is it really? It is, it's Greg and he wants to meet up. He's seen the news about Sarah Wilcox and he wants to talk. Shit. There's a half-bottle of wine in the fridge and I'm tempted, I'm really tempted.

48

Greg is standing by the information desk at Liverpool Street station when I arrive. He has a rucksack on his back and is the spitting image of the photo I saw on the dating app in Manchester. His hair is really short. It suits him. He looks younger. I wonder who took those photos.

'Alex. Babe. Come here.' He hugs me for eternity. His nose touching my forehead the way it always did, he takes a long breath in. I do the same. He smells exactly the same. Not that he has a signature fragrance; it's just Greg. I have always loved his scent. It's comforting. Standing here with my face buried in his chest brings it all back. It's like we've never been apart. Call it biology, call it what you will. I called it love. He was my rock, but I chipped away at it until the fragments were too jagged. That's what I did. Luckily today my detox is going okay, so although the voice in my head is still there telling me to have a drink, and my body is craving it, I think I might just make it through the day without having to sneak off for a shot of something, which is good because Greg can spot that a mile off.

When we finally separate, he stands back and takes a look at me, still holding on to my hand. I don't want to get emotional but I can't help it. I can feel the tears starting to form and I need to keep that in check. I can't cry in public, not the first time he sees me in ages. Keep it together, Alex. Keep it together. I can't let him have that part of me.

'My God, Alex, you look great. TV really suits you.'

His smile dazzles me. I realise I've missed his voice the most.

'Shall we get a coffee?'

'Sure.' I can't think of anything interesting to say, but at least he thinks I look great.

We leave the station and walk over to Spitalfields Market. He talks and I listen. He's genuinely pleased to see me. I don't know why I'm so surprised really; we were tight at one time until I left. I imagined he'd still be angry with me for leaving, but he isn't. He seems healed. I wish I was, but I'm trying, I'm really trying. I'm better than I have been for a long time. Today is not a drink day and the alcoholic in me is safely tucked away. He hasn't asked me about that yet, but he will. He always does.

We find a café inside the market and order coffee. I still can't quite believe we are here sharing a joke and a hot beverage. I always secretly hoped he'd come and find me. Told myself it was all behind me, but really who was I kidding? I'm so happy that he's here.

'I've been following you in the news, you know. It's hard not to.'

'Yes, I suppose it is.'

'I saw you went back to Manchester to interview Mrs Wilcox.'

'I did.'

'Is she okay?'

The question takes me aback. I'm not sure why. Greg always did care about others more than himself; it's why he put up with me for as long as he did. I'm not sure how to answer, so I go for the vague generic response.

'As well as any mother can be given the circumstances.'

'Of course. Of course.'

It's annoying, if I'm honest, that he cares about others before himself. It was frustrating living with that, I remember that now. When his mum called him with a complaint, he would run to solve it for her, even if it was at the expense of our relationship.

An awkward silence opens up between us, and as I sip my coffee, I feel every part of me is being observed, scrutinised. It's probably not what's happening. Bouts of paranoia come with the drinking. I need to keep that in check, not give him a hard time. It'll prove that I'm doing so much better than I was.

'You must have good connections with the Met through your job?'

'I have a few, yes. Although I'm not sure half the time if they are feeding me intel to help their own investigation.'

'Yeah, right. Part of the job, I expect.'

'Indeed.'

'So, Sarah Wilcox, they still don't know where she is? You see the thing is Alex… I knew her.'

He looks wounded, but then so am I. DI Brook's questions about the phone calls and texts between Greg and Sarah come to mind, and then I have the most hurtful thought. Perhaps Greg isn't here for me at all. He did say he wanted to talk about Sarah, but what about us? My stomach feels tight and I want to bolt. I wonder if I've done the right thing meeting him like this, because it is stirring emotions in me that I find difficult to face, but watching him across the table from me, smiling while sipping his coffee, I realise I have missed him more than I would ever care to admit, even to myself. I rub my tummy, wondering if I'm pregnant, knowing that it'll never feel like it did with him.

He lets out a huge sigh and looks at me with those dreamy dark brown eyes. Maybe I should say sorry for what happened. For what I did, abandoning him after the miscarriage. I wonder if now is the time to mention the Milk Tray, ask him why he sent them, or just say thanks, but then I change my mind because he's still banging on about Sarah.

'I just can't believe it, you know.'

'I know. It's difficult to process.'

'I'm not sure you really understand, Alex. I saw her the day before she went missing.'

I hear the words and it sends my head into a spin. I can feel my body physically recoil.

'Alex? Are you okay? You look a bit pale.'

'I'm tired, just tired.'

He can sense a change in me, because he has suddenly tensed up. There must be more to this than I first thought. It was stupid of me to come here, pathetic, in fact. The Milk Tray was more likely born out of guilt than a desire to reunite. People do that all the time, don't they, play out their own issues without thinking about their real intentions.

'Look, Alex. There's something I need to tell you.'

We are in a crowded coffee shop, but it feels like we are the only two people here. I want the floor to swallow me up, because I think I know what's coming.

'Sarah and I, we were… well, we were, you know…'
He rests his head in his right hand. 'I don't really know how to say this.'

'What? You were what?'

'You know I still love you. I never stopped loving you.'

An unpleasant feeling is bubbling in the pit of my stomach, and all I want right now is something to numb the pain I feel in every part of me.

'God, Alex, it's such a mess. Why did you go off and leave me like that?'

I have no response. I really have nothing to say, because I didn't prepare for this. For what he is saying or trying to tell me. So I ask a question, because it's the one thing I know how to do.

'What were you doing with her here in London?'

He's shaking his head. He looks broken.

'You need to tell me.'

'I slept with her, Alex. God, I feel terrible saying that to you.'

The words cut through me as much as my leaving must have cut through him, and I don't feel quite so bad about the fact that she's missing. Good riddance, is all I can think.

49

Dear Diary,

It's a new year. I feel like a completely different person compared to this time last year. Much more in control of my life. I've embraced the dark thoughts and am starting to enjoy them in an oddly ironic way. I got through Christmas sober, on my own. It wasn't so bad in the end. Much easier than having to constantly explain to people that I didn't want a drink. Dad sent me some extra money, so I bought some new clothes and went on a few online dates. The website COMEout is pretty fun and easy to meet people on. It connects people who know each other on Facebook and also friends of their friends, which is good because you can get an idea of whether you have things in common. It also locates people by GPS so you can meet someone within walking distance at any time of day. I don't want to meet someone who lives on the other side of London, which makes it an attractive app to use. I changed my profile to 'woman seeking woman', to see if I could make some new friends, and came across a few profiles of women with Facebook connections to Alex. First- and second-degree connections. I spent a while browsing through these. Pretty women, in their thirties, local, creative. That was intriguing, even though I'm not entirely sure why.

50

After I left Greg at Liverpool Street station, I went on a bender for the rest of the day. Or I suspect that's what happened, because I'm lying on my bed fully clothed and it is now the next morning. I don't remember how I got home. My head hurts like no one's business. I was supposed to be at work this morning, but I'm already two hours late for my shift, which is terrible.

Work has been trying to get hold of me. There are a number of missed calls on my phone. Audrey has texted to say she's aware that my neighbour Charlie was questioned over Maggie Horrocks and thinks we should interview him. She's still come up with nothing as to the whereabouts of Sarah Wilcox and is looking for a new line on the story. She's like a dog with a bone. Anything to keep it up there in the headlines. She's ambitious, I'll give her that. I need to talk to Charlie. It didn't happen yesterday because I met Greg. Talking of whom… He's texted me three times. He wants to meet up again, but I'm not sure that's a good idea. Seeing him triggered a huge drinking session while I was trying to detox. I feel like a complete loser and am worried about my job. I climb out of bed and take three painkillers instead of the recommended two. It's official. I'm a mess. Again.

In the kitchen, I switch the kettle and TV on. On the bottom of the screen a breaking news strapline flashes: Police name fourth victim in east London murders. I go back to my phone and double-check my messages. Audrey sent me a text at six o'clock telling me this fact. Shit. Now I know why work has been trying to get hold of me, and Greg for that matter. I really need to get my shit together.

From what I can see on my work email account, the news broke around two o'clock this morning. The Met put out a statement and Audrey has been trying to get hold of me since just after that. Double and triple shit. Just shit. My phone rings again, but this time it's Mrs Wilcox. I'm not going to answer it.

My head feels like it's about to explode. I don't want to go anywhere, I really don't, but I have to. I have to face work. Face the unanswered calls. The questions. It's a top story, and although yesterday was a rest day, I was still on call, which means being available when something breaks. I'm going to need a bloody good reason for my disappearing act this time. Still, I reason, it's only nine o'clock and the news broke at two. As long as I call in soon, it'll be fine.

Charlie is home. I can hear movement upstairs. Perhaps I should talk to him. I need to find out what the police said to him, whether they asked about me or Greg, but I haven't seen him since he stayed here and I don't think I'm ready for that. I text Audrey to say I'll call her shortly. She texts back immediately: *Everything okay?* To which I respond: *With me, yes, my neighbour not so good*. I've decided to blame my absence on someone else. That person being Charlie, seeing as she now knows about him. She must be cultivating her own source at the Met.

I take a shower, having not fully worked out my story for work yet. The hot water helps moderately. After that, I make a strong cup of coffee. My phone buzzes, and I assume it's work. Deciding on an accident and emergency story, I pick up.

'Hey, babe. It's me. I stayed at a mate's in London last night because I'd really like to talk more, in person. Please? Sarah Wilcox is dead and I need to talk about it. Can we?'

It's Greg. I'm so unprepared for this conversation that I'm not sure which way to play it. I feel like everything is coming at me from all angles and I can't think straight. The one thing I know is that if Greg sees me like this, bent out of shape, he'll know I'm still drinking, and that's one thing I can't afford to happen.

'I don't know. I'm really busy with work today.'

'I've thought about it a lot, seeing you yesterday, and I know it must have been a surprise to hear what I said, but I'd really like you to hear me out. I feel I have some explaining to do.'

A silence follows. A silence I break with one word.

'Okay.'

And just like that, I agree to meet up with him again, to 'hear him out', whatever that means. I never have been able to say no to Greg; it's why I left, walked out without a word, because I knew he'd try to stop me and I knew I'd cave in. I don't offer him a time or a place, because I have to work and I don't know when I'll be done. He accepts this and says he'll wait to hear from me. I still really need to talk to Charlie, but I don't have time right now.

Surprisingly, at work, Marysia is glad to see me, which is a relief. I thought I'd get a bollocking after my late start, but luck is on my side. She seems to be super-relaxed, which I soon learn is because her husband bought her a big fat diamond for their wedding anniversary, putting her in the best of moods.

'Thank God you're here, Alex. We had to put Naomi on the story overnight but she's made a bit of a hash of it – doesn't understand legal. I heard your neighbour had a bit of a fright. Is he okay?'

I'm not sure if she's referring to the police questioning him or to my made-up tale about his accident, which saw me take him to A&E early this morning.

'Yes, fortunately I have spare keys to his place so I was able to rescue him. They sewed his finger back on.'

'Christ. I hope it heals well. So, you're here now. The police have named the fourth victim as Sarah Wilcox, the missing woman. The news broke in the middle of the night, so anything you can get from your sources at the Met would be very useful. They still haven't officially connected all four deaths. Do you think you could push on that side of things? Also, what about following up with Mrs Wilcox, Sarah's mum? I'm sure she has something to say now.'

'Sure. I'll get on it.'

'Keep me in the loop.'

Marysia walks away, clearly having complete confidence in me to deliver, which is a relief because I'm not sure I do. My water bottle is in my bag filled with a stash of vodka, ready to pick up the slack should I need it.

Audrey is plugged into a computer and headphones, which she removes on seeing me.

'Hey. Your neighbour okay? Hope he doesn't lose his finger.'

'Me too. I think he should be good. We got to the hospital soon enough, apparently.' I raise my eyebrows for added impact.

'Oh, good.' Audrey seems even less concerned with Charlie's welfare than Marysia. 'So we know who the latest victim is now. Can you believe it? Sarah bloody Wilcox. And wait for it, she was also a member of COMEout, even though the CEO is adamant that the app has nothing to do with it. The police still seem to think that's important. This morning they issued another warning to women using dating apps in east London. I wish they'd just put a ban on it. This shit is frightening. Marysia says she wants to keep the story going and do a spot on the evening bulletin. So we need to see if we can find a new line. I still think we should interview your neighbour. He's the closest we've got to someone affected by the investigation. Maybe he can tell us just how shit the police are being about it. I'm sure he's got an opinion on it.'

Fuck. We can't go anywhere near Charlie, because then she'll uncover my lie about being late.

'He's resting after his accident. I'm not sure he'd agree to it.'

'Well, yeah, but it's just his hand, right? We don't need to have that in the shot.'

'He's on super-heavyweight painkillers. I'm not sure he'd make much sense.'

'Why did the police pull him in?'

'He knew Maggie Horrocks. She did some work for him. Found the job on a local noticeboard. It's not all that exciting.'

'Yeah, but still. He must have something to say about what's going on. Being picked up by the police can't have been much fun. Is he on COMEout?'

'I don't know, Audrey. I don't think we should bother him today.'

She's realised this train of thought is going nowhere.

'Why don't we do a report looking into how many people use dating apps? Might be good to get DI Brook to respond to the COMEout statement about how the app has nothing to do with it. I mean, come on. People weren't born yesterday and the police really need to step up here before someone else dies.'

It's better than chasing Charlie, so I agree. 'Sounds like a good idea. Do you want to organise a camera while I call DI Brook?'

'Perfect.' Audrey wanders off with purpose towards the crew desk, which is situated on the second floor.

I'm reluctant to call DI Brook, but we need a story and one that doesn't involve my neighbour. To my surprise, he agrees to it, and within the hour we are back at Hackney police station waiting for him to appear.

'Alex. Hi. Sorry to keep you. It's been one hell of a morning, as you can imagine.'

'Hi. Sure. No problem.'

He makes no attempt to ask me anything remotely personal about Greg or Nigel and instead concentrates on the interview. Jack tells us we're rolling.

'Thanks for talking to UKBC, DI Brook. So firstly, can you confirm the name of the fourth victim?'

'Yes, it's Sarah Wilcox. Once we had talked to the family, we were able to release her name. It is our belief now that all four women were drugged, most likely while out on a date. All four had a profile on COMEout. We are still investigating leads from their conversations online. Although there is one difference with Sarah Wilcox, she was drugged but not strangled, which raises questions about whether they were killed by the same man.'

'You say all four women met their end in the same circumstances, but you are still reluctant to use the term serial killer, aren't you?'

DI Brook wipes the bottom half of his face with his right hand and scratches his chin before answering this one.

'And that's why. We still don't have conclusive proof that all four murders were carried out by the same killer, as I said Sarah Wilcox casts a new light on it.'

'But you said they were connected?'

'We said there were similarities in the method.'

'But you are saying that all four women were members of the dating app COMEout and most likely met their killer online? You used the word man, does that mean you've got a suspect in your sights? You arrested someone over the weekend. Did that bring any new information to light?'

'To answer your questions in order – yes, all the women were members of the dating app COMEout. Our advice is for the women of east London to refrain from using online dating apps because we want to keep them safe. We're not clear yet whether the killer was male. The weekend arrest resolved one line of enquiry. It didn't present a new one.'

'So it could be a woman? Why would a woman do this?'

'We aren't ruling out any possibilities. My job is to protect the public from potential risks, and we believe at this time that there is a high risk from this app and others. The freedoms of online dating are enjoyable for most, but they do pose a risk because they leave people, men and women, vulnerable. Offenders can take advantage of this. Male or female.'

I wrap up the interview shortly afterwards.

'Why didn't you push him on the serial killer line?' Audrey looks frustrated.

'I did.'

She looks pissed off. 'Well, there's probably something we can use.'

Jack nods, as if he knows anything.

My phone buzzes telling me my Twitter following has just reached eighty thousand. That's real firepower in our business. A measure of my success. This story has been the making of my career.

'We need some online daters too,' Audrey says. 'Maybe Jack and I can do that and meet you back in the newsroom. I spoke to a couple of people earlier. They have agreed to talk on camera.'

'Very good.'

I've texted Greg back to tell him where to meet me: a coffee shop close to work. He's wearing the same clothes as yesterday, not that it matters. I'd fancy him if he wore the same clothes for a week. There are some people who just have that hold on you.

'Thanks for coming, Alex, I really appreciate it. I know you're super-busy.'

I nod because I don't really know what to say. I notice that my water bottle is half empty. Christ. My heart is racing and I'm doing my best to just keep it together.

'Look, I feel I owe you an explanation about Sarah.'

'Why? We weren't together. You can do what you want.'

'I still want to explain.'

'Okay.'

I want to hear this, but at the same time I don't, because I'm starting to properly lose it, and I can't, not now, not while my career is on the up. Greg already has a coffee. He keeps fiddling with the teaspoon, but I don't bother ordering a drink. I sip from my water bottle instead. I'm past caring. Underneath his good looks, he is just as nervous as me.

'I'm not sure where to start really.'

'How about the part where you shagged her? Don't you think you should talk to the police?' I don't mean to be defensive, but I can't help it. I want to tell him about the need to come forward, that the police have his name as a person of interest, but I can't. I don't know how to do that.

'I'm sorry, Alex. I'm really sorry. I need you to understand what happened.'

'Go on.'

'After you left, I was a complete mess. Things got really dark for me for a while. I was in total denial about the fact that you'd gone, so when she turned up on my doorstep, I turned to her for some comfort.' His eyes tell of the pain I imposed on him by walking out the way I did.

'She turned up on your doorstep? How did she know where you lived?'

'She worked in our local pub. You didn't know that, I guess?'

'She went to those AA meetings you forced me to go to. That's how I knew her, but when she got a little obsessed with me, I stopped talking to her.'

'Well, I'm not proud of the fact that I slept with her. You have to understand. She was together at a time when I wasn't. And she picked me up. She understood what I'd gone through, the drinking. She put me back on the right path. I didn't sleep with her then, but it left an impression in my mind, you know, so when she contacted me to say she had moved to London and she wanted to see me, I agreed. I was flying out of London for a stag do. Figured it would be a place to crash. I suppose it was also a way of feeling close to you again. She said she'd been in touch with you and wanted to tell me how you were doing, and I believed her.'

Just then, my phone buzzes. It's Nigel calling. Perfect fucking timing.

'I didn't have any intention of sleeping with her,' Greg continues. 'You have to believe me. It just happened.'

I don't pick up, but Nigel calls back. He's not giving up.

'I'm sorry, Greg, but I really need to make a call. It's work-related.'

'Oh, okay.'

'I don't know how long it's going to take. Can you wait?'

He nods, but looks hurt. I leave him still playing with the teaspoon and step outside for a moment.

'Alex. What the fuck is going on? Another woman is dead. Do you think the police are going to arrest me? That image they have, the one you told me about, I'm worried.'

259

'Should you be worried?'

'What are you talking about? If they arrest me, I'm going to tell them I was with you the night Alice Fessy was killed. You're my alibi.'

And with that he hangs up. My head is spinning.

It's weirdly comforting to know that Nigel's life isn't picture perfect, but I'm nervous about him being picked up by the police now. I don't need to become a witness in this case. That would finish my career. You don't recover from things like that. I take a swig from my water bottle to calm myself down and return to Greg, who picks up where he left off.

'The next day I left for Spain thinking I wouldn't see her again, and now she's dead.'

'Yes. I know the DI on the case. Maybe you should contact him if you're worried.'

'Christ. Why would I do that?'

'They will have checked her phone records.'

I let that linger between us. He rests his face in his hands.

'I swear to you, Alex, I wasn't seeing her like that. I slept with her once. It was really just a place to crash that got out of hand.'

'So you stayed at her place?'

'Yes.'

'Jesus, Greg. Do you have the address?'

'No. I met her at King's Cross and we got on a bus. It was late. I don't remember where it was. London streets all look the same to me.'

What a mess, I think.

'Can I ask you something, Alex? Are you seeing anyone?'

It's not a question I was expecting. It's a perfectly normal thing to ask, I suppose, but the timing feels off. I don't want to give him the satisfaction of knowing that my personal life hasn't recovered from our break-up, so I interrogate him about his instead.

'I saw your photo on COMEout when I was in Manchester. Are you online dating?'

'What the hell is COMEout?'

'It's a dating site. God, Greg, which century do you live in? And don't you read the news?'

'Sometimes. It's all so dull and depressing. My mate set up a dating profile, but I've never even logged on.'

'You do know that COMEout is the dating app the police are looking at as a potential way that the killer found his victims, which might make you a suspect.'

'I told you, I don't use it.'

'Tell the police that.'

He looks afraid. The last time I saw this expression was when we lost the baby. He knew then he'd lost me too.

'Do you think I should?'

'No. I'm joking.'

'How can you joke about something like that? Four women are dead, Alex.'

'Oh, so you do read the news.'

'No. I watch you on TV.'

'I wasn't fucking joking. I think you should contact them before they contact you.'

This isn't going well. Then it starts to get worse. He looks at my water bottle, then back at me.

'Are you still drinking?'

'Why do you always have to bring that up?'

'Because I care about you.'

'It's like torture listening to you talk about it.'

'Are you in a recovery programme, Alex?'

'I'm in a good place right now. I don't need this. My career is doing really well.'

'I'm not asking you about your career. I'm asking you about your recovery.'

'I'm doing fine.'

I look at my phone as if receiving a text. I need to get out of here.

'I've got to get back to work, Greg.'

He wants to say something but doesn't. He just shakes his head and stares into his coffee cup. The disappointment is written all over his face. It hurts me, but I'm bored of this record. I've heard it too many times before. I didn't invite him back into my life to hear it again. I'm doing really well and I deserve some recognition, and if he doesn't get that, he can just get lost.

51

Dear Diary,

I've stopped going to AA meetings because I can't face seeing my old flatmate after the cat incident. Searching for Alex's connections on COMEout has become something of an obsession. It's fascinating to see the links between people. It's truly amazing to think just how connected we all are. The Internet is great for this.

It's probably time that I started looking for a job, but tracking Alex's career and her thousands of friends on Facebook is so time-consuming, plus Dad is sending me money so I'm financially okay. I've had some really dark dreams lately where I want to hurt my parents, hurt Alex. Hurt myself. It's like this urge just comes over me. I think it's all part of recovery. I remember my therapist in rehab telling me that I would need to practically reinvent myself. I considered doing some more private therapy, but then it just seems to take me over the past again, and that's a place I don't want to visit. It's far too painful and it messes with my head.

52

After the evening bulletin has finished, I get the all-clear to go home. I don't hang around as my body is in so much pain. I need to lie down and sleep for the next twelve hours. But when I exit the building, Greg is standing outside in the cold waiting for me. There's no way I can avoid him, so I cross the road towards him. It's really chilly now and he's not wearing a jacket, which makes me want to get him in out of the cold. Even though he's upset me again, I still love him.

'I'm sorry, Alex. Can we please not fight? It's too painful.'

'Then stop giving me a hard time. I'm doing really well at the moment.' I hand him my scarf, which he takes gladly. 'I've just done a report on the evening news bulletin where I was on set being interviewed. You should be proud of that, not going on at me about the past.'

'Yes, you're right. I just worry about you, you know.'

He wraps the scarf around his neck and tucks it into his woolly jumper, which has holes in the sleeves. It's one of the things I love about him. His unapologetic scruffiness.

'That's very sweet of you, but there's really no need. I'm fine, really.'

'Great. So, can I take you out for dinner?' He's smiling now, a sparkle in his eye. It's tempting, so tempting.

'Where to?'

'Anywhere. The world is our oyster.'

He's making me smile too.

'The night is young.'

'I wish it was. I have to be up again at seven to work this story.'

'We can go wherever you want, Alex, just steer the way.'

I know I really shouldn't, as I'm in such a mess, but before long we're in an Uber heading back to my neighbourhood, to a Thai restaurant on Hackney Road. Greg orders a beer, but I don't. He doesn't say anything about my drinking, but stares at my water bottle, the one I've been carrying around all day that has a smidgen of clear liquid still in it.

Dinner is nice. He tells me about the stag do he went on, which sounds like an absolute disaster. We have a good time in each other's company. It's like we've never been apart, like we just picked up from where we left off. It's wonderful, actually, and I wonder why I walked away. Greg and I fit like a pair of skinny jeans, moulding to each other's curves. It was like this from the day we met, playing Whitesnake on YouTube in a hotel lobby. We just knew that we were meant to be together.

In the days that followed, we exchanged over three hundred songs via text message. Songs that we both loved. Not everyone experiences that, finding someone with exactly the same taste in music. I know my friends haven't. Annabel chose Chris because he was sorted, together, he could provide for her if she had a baby, but she hates his music and hobbies. Greg and I were glued together by more than a sensible choice. We were glued together by music, culture and jokes. The stuff that happens every minute of every day.

He pays the bill, which is nice of him considering I'm the one earning the London salary.

'So, where are you staying, then?'

'I'm kind of homeless at the moment; been living with a mate in Leicester for the past six months.'

'Leicester? What are you doing there?'

'Trying to start my own business. Production. Been doing freelance gigs all over the country.'

'Okay. But what about tonight?'

'Thought you could show me where you live, seeing as you forced me to come to your neighbourhood.' He's grinning like the Cheshire cat.

The moment I've been waiting for has suddenly arrived, and all I can think about is whether there are any bottles lurking in places he might find them.

'That depends on how nice you are to me.'

'Oh, I'll be nice. I'll be very nice. Don't you worry about that.'

And there it is: a simple sentence laced with a smile is all it takes for me to let him back in, a promise that he'll be nice to me. It won't last, it never does once he discovers I'm still drinking, but for now I'm living the illusion, because deep down I still desperately love him and I need this. I need some comfort. Something familiar. Something I can hold onto.

On our way back to mine, we pass through the Fields and I give Greg a run-down of where Alice Fessy was found. How I picked up the story and how my editors are really pleased with the work I'm doing. I don't mention

Sarah Wilcox and neither does he until we hit Navarino Road.

'Jesus, Alex. I think this is where Sarah lived.' He's pointing at the red mansion block opposite Mary's house. 'In fact I'm sure it is.'

He's already through the gate and walking up to the front of the block, so I follow.

'I don't think you can just go snooping around like this so late at night, especially with what's going on. People are nervous.'

But as he mounts the steps, I have a sudden momentary déjà vu. I was here. Recently. But why? I can't remember. Shit. My head is spinning, and I have an immediate urge to turn around and walk back down the path, away from this building.

'Hang on.'

He's looking through the front door. I'm waiting at the bottom of the steps, wondering where this is going. Annoyed again with his obsession with Sarah. But within moments, his posture has relaxed and he's coming back down the steps.

'I must have been mistaken. One street does look like another at night.'

'Can we go now?' I don't want to linger any longer than I need to. It's cold and I'm also feeling a bit paranoid about running into Nigel. Especially after his angry call earlier. I haven't told anyone about that. I suppose Charlie is the only person I can talk to about it, but I don't want to see him either.

Walking away from the mansion block, I have a deeply haunting feeling that there may be something in what Greg said about Sarah living here, but my memory is so bad. I've had two blackouts this week already. I wish I knew what I did that night after I left Anne Marie's house, but I really can't remember. I know there was a reason I left, but where I went is one big blank. Standing outside that building, though, something in me stirred; what and why I'm not sure, but I have a feeling it had something to with Sarah Wilcox.

As we turn the corner to my street, Greg takes my hand and my heart starts to race. The pulse in my wrist is having spasms. It's a hand I held for seven years. A warm, familiar hand even in this freezing temperature. I'm unsure of what to do because the chemistry is still there even after all this time.

Once over the threshold, I know there is no way back, but I'm not sure how I feel about it. I'm afraid of what it means. It's all I've wanted to do for a year, since I lost our baby – have him hold me and tell me everything is going to be all right – but now that the moment is here, I'm afraid he'll discover my old habits again.

In the kitchen, he sits down while I put the kettle on. He's scanning the room with interest. I'm just praying that I've not left a trail of bottles all over the place. It could happen.

'Nice place, Alex.'

'Thanks.'

'It's good to see you've done so well for yourself. Maybe leaving Manchester was the best thing you ever did. Maybe it all happened for a reason, you know.'

'I don't know if I'd go that far, but thank you.'

Before I have time to protest, he's standing behind me, wrapping his arms around my waist.

'I've missed you. I've missed us. I know we lost something, but maybe we can find it again.' He brushes the back of my neck with his hand, and my entire body tingles. 'I don't care about what happened in the past. There's only ever been one woman for me, you know. I'm lost without you. I'm sorry I didn't trust you to beat this thing.'

He turns me around and cups my face with his firm hands.

'How did we let it get to the point of no return?' His eyes sparkle in the dim light. 'I need you in my life.'

I don't know what to say. I wasn't expecting this.

'Are you okay? You seem a little edgy?'

'That's because I am edgy.' I make a rock-and-roll symbol with my right hand and wink while doing it. He laughs.

'I'm serious. You seem nervy. Is everything okay?'

It's the drink, but I can't tell him that.

'I'm fine. Just tired. It's been a long day, emotionally and physically.'

He's still holding my face in his hands. 'I've really missed this,' he whispers.

'Me too.'

We kiss on the lips for the first time in a year, but it feels so natural.

'You know, it was really sweet of you to send me Milk Tray for my birthday.'

'What are you on about?'

'The birthday gift.'

'It wasn't me, Alex. I didn't send you any Milk Tray.'

'Oh. I got a box on my birthday. I thought you'd sent it.'

'No, sorry. Not me.'

He's so close that I can feel his breath on my skin, but the moment is disrupted by the sound of my very loud electronic doorbell.

'Are you expecting someone? A lover you haven't mentioned? The sender of Milk Tray?'

There's a loud bang on the door. I would have chosen to ignore it, but Greg steps back and the intimacy drains away.

As soon as I open the door, I regret it. Facing me is DI Brook with two uniformed police officers.

'Hello, Alex. We know he's here. I'm afraid we're going to have to bring him in for questioning.'

They push past me before I have a chance to speak. The crackle of a police radio resonates from inside the flat, and moments later Greg is being escorted out into the street.

'Alex, what is going on?'

I want to tell him I didn't do anything, that this has nothing to do with me, but I can't because I can't physically get the words out. The shock of what is happening has stunned me into silence. DI Brook must have had me under surveillance to know Greg was here. Suddenly a cold breeze blows through the house, and I have a strong sense that the police have been in my flat while I wasn't home, searching for I–don't–know–what.

One of the uniformed officers warns me not to go anywhere. 'We will be in touch, Ms South.'

I can hear Greg calling my name as they walk him down the street, directing him to a police car. I'm so confused by what's just gone down that I can't do anything. I notice Charlie watching from the upstairs window as I go back inside. His face is devoid of emotion. I think he's upset with me, but I'm not sure why.

After the police have gone, I find the vodka bottle. I don't even bother with a glass. My head is spinning. I can't put it all together. I need to confide in someone, but who? I need to talk through what is happening, because my life is truly falling apart again. Once the news gets out that the police have arrested another man in connection to the murders, there'll be another wave of interest from the media. If they discover Greg's identity, and who he is to me, I'm utterly screwed.

I can't handle what's just happened. I can't be home alone or I'll just drink myself into another blackout, which would be one too many this week. I make a decision and head off towards number three Navarino Road.

53

It's gone midnight when I find myself standing outside Mary's house, hoping to find some wisdom from the glamorous elderly dog walker. I climb the steps and lift the solid brass knocker. It takes some effort. Moments later, the door opens and the grandmotherly figure welcomes me with her kind smile. Without warning, I break down in tears right there on her doorstep. I don't know what has come over me.

'Come in, dear. Come in.'

She ushers me in and wraps her arms around me like a cuddly blanket. After a good old hug, she shows me through to the garden, where a gas heater is fired up next to a table underneath a jungle of ivy and rose bushes.

'I know it's a cold night, but the sky is so clear you can see the stars, not a common occurrence in London, so I thought I'd enjoy it. Look, can you see the Plough?'

She's pointing skywards. I look up. It is just as she described it. A crystal-clear night sky with thousands of bright stars sparkling above us, and I can, I can see the Plough. There's something quite special about that, especially in London.

'Shall we have tea?'

I nod; it's all I can manage. The garden contains an abundance of wildlife. I feel safe here, yet I don't know why. Maybe it's because it's a complete escape from my life. From what I have become. From all of it.

She leaves me to star-gaze and returns with the trolley, which she parks inside the back door. She hands me a box of lavender-scented tissues.

'You've got yourself into quite a state, haven't you? Do you want to tell me all about it?'

'I don't really know where to start.'

'Why not at the beginning?'

'My fiancé — well, actually he's my ex — has just been arrested as part of the murder investigation.'

'Oh.' It's meant to sound like surprise, but it doesn't. 'I can see why that might be quite stressful. You did the right thing coming here. No good being on your own at a time like this. Would you be so kind as to serve?'

'Of course.'

I pour the tea and we sit in silence listening to the breeze brush against the ivy.

'Why did they arrest him?'

'He knew Sarah Wilcox, one of the victims. But he knew her because of me. I feel so bad about that now. It's my fault. It's all my fault.'

'Do you think he did it?'

'No.' My body shakes at the thought of it. 'He's not a murderer. They have no real leads so they're tapping the weakest one. I saw him today. It was the first time I've seen him for a long time. We were having a really nice evening, but when we got home, the police turned up and took him away. What if he thinks I turned him in because of what he told me about Sarah?'

'What *did* he tell you?'

'That he'd slept with her.'

'Oh my dear Alex. You poor thing. That must have been extremely painful.'

I decide that now is the time for me to offload. To confide in someone before it eats me up inside. I'm running out of options. I need to talk before I go mad or have another blackout.

'I left Manchester a year ago after having a miscarriage. It was tough, but I buried the pain and left. Ran away, if you will. Shut out Greg, my ex. Disappeared without a forwarding address. I needed to regroup. To protect myself. Things were getting a bit messy. We'd lived together for seven years and were planning to get married, but the miscarriage changed everything. I lost my baby. Our baby.'

She looks thoughtful. I feel oddly unburdened saying this out loud. I've never told anyone before about what happened. No one. I just bottled it up. Held it all in. Buried it in alcohol, the root cause of my miscarriage and my break-up with Greg. The root cause of everything that is wrong with my life, if I'm honest about it. Yet still I can't stop myself.

'It's normal to react like that. You're only human, Alex, but you can't keep running from yourself. It won't help you achieve a happy life and it definitely won't help you prolong it. You can't keep going the way you're going.'

Her tone has changed and I'm not sure I like it. I don't need a lecture. That's not why I came here. I need someone to listen. To understand the emotional pressure I'm under. I haven't finished my tea yet, but I think it's time to leave.

'I should get going. I have some work to do.'

'At this time of night?'

'Yes.'

'You're only going to hurt yourself, you know, Alex. You can't go on like this, toing and froing the way you are. You need to make a decision and stick to it. You should tell the police.'

'Tell them what?'

'That's for you to work out. I just think your soul will be at peace if you confess.'

'Confess to what? What are you talking about?'

'I can see you want to speak to someone, but you're not sure how to start that conversation. We've all had our moments, Alex. It's how you deal with them that matters. It's how you find forgiveness for yourself.'

I don't even say goodbye. Just get up and go. I don't need someone lecturing me about how to live my life. I'm doing really well at the moment. Every day I gain thousands more followers on Twitter; that's the measure of my success.

On my way home, I stuff the lemon ginger snaps I took from her kitchen in my mouth. How dare she tell me to sort myself out? I am sorted. I've been a lead story for the better part of a week. That's the proof right there.

54

Dear Diary,

I sent Alex a message via Twitter today. Told her I'd moved to London. That she could confide in me. She always did find it hard to talk about her addiction, which is weird because she had no problem talking about mine. She must know by now that she has a serious drinking issue. I want to help her because she helped me. I feel like I owe her something. Like I should return the favour, you know. Call it karma.

I know she's still drinking because I've seen her buying booze from the shop around the corner. You see, I moved to London Fields after I figured out where she lived. It wasn't that hard. She tweets about her life and posts photos on social media. All I had to do was hang out in the park for a month until I saw her crossing from one side to the other, a bit like how we met really. From there, I was able to follow her. I know where she lives. I know she has a neighbour called Charlie. He's quite good-looking, too. In fact, I borrowed his photo and set up a profile using his name on COMEout. It's been quite fun, if truth be told.

I haven't heard back from Alex, but I also wrote to Greg to tell him that I'd been in touch with her. He replied almost immediately. Wanted to know how she was. I invited him to *come and see for himself. To come to London. He said he might just do that.*

55

I wake up to a million news alerts informing me that the Met has another man in custody, this time in connection with the death of Sarah Wilcox. I'm guessing one of my competitors has a source inside the station, and has managed to get a sliver of intel to this effect. Amidst the news alerts, Audrey's name flashes on my screen. The time is 8.35 am. I've slept in by an hour.

'Morning, Audrey.'

'You heard the latest?'

'Hard not to. My phone is going bonkers.'

I'm not in a good mood this morning. In fact, I'm worried sick about the fact that my ex-fiancé is now in police custody. I fell asleep fully clothed for the third night in a row – marvellous. There's an empty vodka bottle on the pillow next to me.

'We need to get down to the station in case they release any information on who this man is.'

'Yes, you're right. Shall I meet you there?'

'I'll be there in twenty minutes with Jack. I've already spoken to the on-duty editor. It's Mike today.'

'Okay, good.' I don't know Mike, but I'm sure he knows me. 'See you there.'

Charlie is banging on my door. 'Alex, let me in. I need to talk to you.'

It's just what I don't need, but he's not going away.

'I know you're in there.'

I can't be bothered to put up any resistance this morning, so I unlatch the door and let him in.

'I really need to get ready for work, Charlie.'

'I've seen the news. Who was that man last night? Was it Nigel, the guy you met on the dating site? Is that who the police have in custody? Oh Alex, what's going on?'

'First of all, I haven't got time for this right now. Secondly, I'm okay, thanks for asking. And thirdly, I'm pissed off that the police seemingly thought it was okay to come into my flat and arrest someone.'

'Aren't you glad about it? They could have saved your life.'

I'm not sure which way to play this. My head hurts.

'I'm sorry, Charlie but I really need to get on.'

'I'm here for you if you need to talk.'

'Thanks, but right now I have to get down to the police station. Oh, and Charlie, I really need you to promise that you won't tell anyone what you saw last night.'

He's looking at me curiously.

'Promise me. Please. I don't need to get caught up in this story. Not in that way. It will seriously affect my career. It could be the end of it, in fact.'

'Don't be ridiculous.'

'I'm not being ridiculous. You have no idea.'

'Don't they say all publicity is good publicity?' He's grinning with excitement. This must be the highlight of his week.

'For fuck's sake, Charlie, this isn't funny. I'm the reporter, not the story. So no, it isn't. Not in this instance.'

My face is deadly serious, and his smile fades.

'Okay. I promise. I won't say anything and I won't talk to the press; they've been on my case since I got hauled in.'

'Who has been on your case?'

'That Laura MacColl.'

'Are you fucking kidding me. Don't talk to her, especially her. I'm going to have to ask you to go. I need to take a shower. I'm supposed to meet my producer in twenty minutes.'

'Right, of course. Wow, how exciting.'

'No, it's not. Four women are dead. It's really not.'

He leaves, shutting the door behind him. At least I have his assurance that he won't speak to anyone about last night, or being picked up by the police. I think I can trust him. He may be a bit of a panic artist, but he's loyal to the core. I down a couple of painkillers and get myself together.

–

Audrey and Jack are outside the station along with the rest of the vultures when I arrive. The voice in my head is already at it, telling me I need a fix.

'Alex, thank God. Can you work your source and find out what's going on?'

'I'll do my best. Give me five.'

I walk away from the group to find a quieter spot, then take my phone out of my pocket and pretend to dial. I can't call DI Brook. I can't. What am I going to ask him? I'm still angry about what he did. They must have had me or Greg under surveillance. It's one big fucking mess, just like my life. The only thing that seems simple is how much I need to detox.

After a few minutes, I stroll back towards the group.

'He's not picking up. No surprises there.'

'Damn. We need to find out who this guy is.' Audrey is desperate to get the story, and I don't blame her, but the only thing I can do is stand by and see what happens, and get ready for the worst.

Three hours later, we are still there and the police have told us fuck all. I've been sipping from my faithful water bottle just to get me through the morning. Surprisingly, I'm feeling much better than I did when I woke up. The media entourage is getting weary. Some have sloped off for lunch, while others stand guard. My stomach is tied in knots imagining all kinds of worst-case scenarios. I know Greg's not guilty, but if it comes out that he is in any way connected to the case, well that's just not worth thinking about, because it'll link me too. Greg knew Sarah because of me. And I knew Sarah because of AA. And that part of the story will finish my career. I don't need my competitors asking me about Greg, trying to catch me off guard, because that's exactly what will happen if it gets out. Laura McColl will have a field day.

After another couple of hours, DI Brook emerges from inside the station without warning, looking like he's had a very long night. The pack of media professionals all scramble to get a good position. I'm trying to keep a low profile and remain at the back while Audrey gets upfront. Just as Brook stops on the steps, obviously preparing to say something, my phone starts buzzing. It's a NO CALLER ID number. I walk away from the melee to take the call. It's Greg.

'What's going on?' I ask.

'I'm not mad at you. I want you to know that.'

'Okay, understood, but what's happening?'

'They've been tapping my phone to try and find me and well, waited until I was somewhere they knew I couldn't run from. As if I would. But you know, I guess they wanted to be sure.'

'Okay. And?'

'And nothing. They're quizzing me about my relationship with Sarah Wilcox.'

I don't know what to say to that. So I decide to tell him the truth for a change. Mary was right. I can't go on like this.

'Greg, I need to tell you something. I need to tell you how I met Sarah.'

'I know how you two met, it was at AA.'

'Not exactly.'

'What do you mean, not exactly?'

'I met her on a park bench. I was messed up. You were putting so much pressure on me and I had no one to talk to, so I spoke to a stranger in the park.'

'You did what?'

'She used to sit in the park drinking, and I met her there. After that, she came to AA with me. I was too scared to go on my own, unable to admit my problem, so I took her with me. I needed an excuse to go and she was it. I'm not sure how mentally stable she was when we met, to be honest. I didn't think anything more of it until I heard she was missing, and then when I met her mum there was something off about her. Like she was hiding something.'

'Hiding what?'

'I don't know. A secret. Maybe about Sarah's past. I'm so sorry, Greg. I never meant for you to get caught up in this.'

'Hey, don't worry. I'm a big boy. They're just checking out my Spain story. They'll have to let me go when they realise I wasn't in the country when she was killed.'

'What about the other women? Are they questioning you about them?'

'Yeah, but it's not going to go anywhere. They can't prove anything on that score. I want to work things out with you, Alex. It's why I came to meet Sarah. I know I did something stupid, but that's why I came to London. It was for you.'

Crunch time. I have to choose whether I get involved deeper or walk away. If any of this gets connected back to me, I'll be up shit creek professionally speaking and I can't risk that. Not even for Greg. It's the one thing I can rely on, my work. I can't give him the guarantee he wants, I just can't, so I deflect because it's easier.

'I'm sorry, but I have to go. I'm working, trying to behave like I don't know who the police have in custody. You're causing quite a media storm.'

'Where are you?'

'Outside the station.'

'Shit. Sorry, Alex. I'm so sorry.'

'It's okay, but I really have to go.'

'Okay. And Alex?'

'Yes?'

'I love you.'

The words go straight for the jugular and my heart feels a jolt of electricity through it. I hang up, unable to say anything in response. I walked away from him because I couldn't stop drinking, and here I am, still drinking. Nothing has changed. In fact, that's not true. Everything has changed. I have an epic number of followers on Twitter. I've become a household name in the news business. The public trust me. And that is a success story. That's not what an alcoholic does.

As I get back to the group, I catch the back of DI Brook re-entering the station.

'What happened?'

'You missed the press conference, that's what happened.' Audrey doesn't look too pleased with me. There's discontent in her eyes today. She thinks she's doing all the work and I'm getting the glory. I've seen it before in producers and I'll see it again. I feel for her, because in a way she's right, but it's how it works. We all have to pay our dues.

'Don't look at me like that. I had to take the call. It was a family emergency.'

She doesn't appear convinced, but fills me in on the presser anyway.

'He didn't say much really. Just that they had been questioning a man since last night over information they believed could prove helpful to the investigation. Same old shit as last time. I'm not sure they're any further along in their investigation. East London doesn't feel much safer than it did yesterday, if you ask me.'

'Okay. So we do a live report? Not much to package.'

Audrey talks to the news centre, who agree to live reports throughout the day.

–

By the time I get home, it's gone seven o'clock. My water bottle is empty and I am physically exhausted. It's an effort just to put one foot in front of the other. Even my breathing feels laboured. As I turn onto my street, I notice someone perched on the wall outside my flat. I initially think it's Charlie, having lost his key again, but soon realise it's Nigel, and he looks riled up. My nerves take another nosedive. I deliberate whether I should just turn around and leave, but it's not going to go away, this mess, as Mary said, so I take a deep breath and walk towards him.

56

Dear Diary,

I've had that dream again where I'm suffocating my mother. It was incredibly violent. She seemed so insignificant. So easy to break.

I felt bad the last time I had that dream. But not this time. This time I enjoyed it.

57

Nigel stands as I approach. I feel his height towering above me.

'Why are you not answering my messages?'

'Nice to see you too. What's up?' I make a point of greeting him, because we are not lovers; we had a one-night stand and this kind of shit is not okay.

'Why did you tell the police you were concerned about my online dating habits?'

'I didn't.' I'm just going to outright lie, because I owe him nothing and he's standing between me and my next vodka.

'They came to my workplace yesterday afternoon and questioned me about the night we met.'

'I told you they had an image of you on CCTV walking behind Alice Fessy. I didn't have to tell you that, you know. Count yourself lucky you had a heads-up.'

He doesn't care about that. I guess he didn't really believe they'd ever question him.

'They also said you had expressed concerns about me being a potential serial dater. Why would you do that?'

'I don't know what you're talking about. I said I'd seen you leaving the pub with another woman, who I guessed you'd met online.'

'When?'

'I don't know, last week, the night after I got back from Manchester, I guess.'

'You have no right to say anything about me to the police. I could say shit about you. I'm sure other media outlets would love to know your dating habits.'

'That will just make you look bitter or even defensive, so if they do think you're a potential suspect, it might give credence to the idea. I'd watch that if I were you.'

I'm in no mood to be nice.

'I'll scream if you don't piss off. You shouldn't be here. This is harassment.'

'What the fuck, Alex? What planet are you on? You fucking shopped me to the police, gave them my number.'

He's grabbed my wrist and it hurts. Perhaps I need to tone it down, but I can't because I'm fucked off. Really fucked off, and when my emotions get the better of me, I'm screwed.

'I'm not the one who has an ex pouring drinks over me. You've got issues.'

'That's below the belt and you know it.' His grip is getting tighter.

'You need to take your hands off me.'

'Or what? You'll shop me to the police? You've already done that. If they believe it's me, perhaps I should really give them something to think about.'

The angle he has my wrist at has brought me to my knees, and a sharp pain is penetrating my arm.

'I'm friends with the DI on the case and I'll have no qualms about talking to him about this little visit.'

'It won't matter if you're in no state to talk to him, will it?'

His eyes are full of rage, and for a split second I wonder if he is capable of murder, but moments later he lets go and I collapse on the ground.

'I won't let this go if you take it further, you know,' he hisses.

Relief from the pain that infused my arm washes over me, and still I can't keep my mouth shut.

'Is that a threat?'

'It's a promise.'

He turns and takes off down the street. My eyes follow him to make sure he's gone, and just as he turns on to the main road, I spot Charlie passing him within arm's reach, heading my way. I need to calm down. I wait for Charlie to reach me before entering the house.

'Alex? You okay? You look worried about something.'

'That's because I am, Charlie. I am worried about something.'

In the hallway, I burst into tears.

'Hey, hey. Don't cry. Why don't you put your bag away and come upstairs for a cup of my finest brew?'

He touches my shoulder like a concerned big brother, then unlocks his door and heads upstairs. I drop my bag inside my flat and follow him.

There's something reassuring about being in Charlie's kitchen. He never judges me, but then he doesn't know anything about my past. Maybe now is the time to tell him. The kettle rumbles to the boil and he makes the tea.

'Biscuits?'

I nod and smile, then follow him into the lounge, where we take up our positions.

'What's going on, Alex?'

'The man the police took away last night. That's Greg. My ex-fiancé.'

'What? I didn't know you were engaged.'

'I was, in Manchester. In fact, that's why I left.'

Charlie is rolling a ciggie. 'Want one?'

I say nothing, but nod. He reaches out and hands me the rollie.

'So why did the police take him away?'

'They've arrested him in connection with the investigation. He knew Sarah Wilcox.'

'Shit. Been there, done that.'

'It's not funny, Charlie. He's being questioned over a murder.'

'God, Alex, I know your memory is shot, but really? They pulled the same stunt with me, remember? They went through all my phone messages, my emails. It was really invasive. They even said I had a profile on COMEout, which isn't true.'

'What?'

'I mentioned this to you already, don't you remember? Get your shit together, seriously. I've never used that app in my life, but they showed me a profile with my picture on it. It was kind of mental. That's why they picked me up, because I had connections to all the women via that app. Not that I'd ever logged in from my phone. Fortunately I have a lawyer because of my business, and together we provided alibis for the dates of all three murders, so they had to let me go.'

'Fuck, Charlie, I had no idea.'

'Well you might have done if you got your head out of a bottle of vodka for a minute.'

That cuts deep. I stub the cigarette out and prepare to leave.

'Don't fucking leave, Alex. That's what you always do. You just run from any kind of criticism. And I'm only saying this for your own good, because I actually fucking care. You need to get sober.'

He's right, of course, on both fronts. That's what I do. I run. I run from anything and everything that might make me uncomfortable, because I can't take it. I've not developed the resilience. And that is because of my drinking.

'I know I have a problem, all right. But I'm in control of it.'

'Are you? Because your ex-fiancé is now in police custody being questioned about the murder of Sarah Wilcox, and you put him there.'

'I beg your pardon?'

'Okay, I might be pushing it a bit there, but you knew her, Alex. I saw the way you reacted that day when her photo flashed up on the television. I don't know how you knew her, but you did. I've known you for the best part of a year now. I know you think I'm stupid, but I can tell when you're lying. I also know she lived around here, because I ran into her a few times at the lido. I told you that too, not that you remember.'

I want to get up and run, but I can't. There's something liberating about Charlie speaking his mind like this.

'How did you know her, and what does it have to do with your ex-fiancé?'

'He slept with her. He put himself in police custody, not me.' As I say it, the tears tumble down my cheeks.

'Shit, Alex. I didn't know.'

'That's just it, Charlie, you don't know. No one knows. Only Greg knows how much pain I'm in. I lost my baby and I don't think I'll ever have the chance to have another one. That's why I moved to London, to get away from the pain, but look at me now. The past has caught up with me and I just want it to stop.'

I'm practically sobbing now. My head is about to explode. Charlie knows I'm deeply disturbed, because I've never lost my composure this badly in his company before.

'I'm a friend, Alex. You can trust me with anything.'

His eyes are kind and I know he means well, but I'm having a really hard time with this.

'Do you have anything stronger than tea?'

Charlie returns from the kitchen with a bottle of tequila and joins me in having a shot.

'Greg met Sarah after I left Manchester. She muscled her way into his life. That's all I know. He says he came to London to see her so that he could find me, because she'd told him she knew where I was. That's all I know. I didn't really know her. She was just someone I met briefly in Manchester while out for a walk one day.'

I can't tell him about the blackouts. I can't tell anyone about those, because that would be admitting to the extent of my problem out loud, and I don't have that kind of problem. I can control my drinking. I'll get dry in a couple of days. I just need one day to start my detox. A day off from everything.

'Shit, Alex. This doesn't sound good. Do you think he killed her? Maybe they had a fight or something and it got out of hand. Maybe Sarah's death isn't linked to the other three. The police are saying that the others were strangled but she wasn't, right?'

This time, I do stand up and prepare to leave.

'Greg's not a killer. He's not. He's a good man. I'm the mess in all of this.'

'Hey, calm down. I'm just playing devil's advocate.'

'Well, don't.'

With that, I'm striding across the room towards the door. I can hear him shouting after me as I head downstairs, but I don't look back. There's only one place I'm going, and that's my kitchen, where I know there's a bottle waiting for me. That's my only real friend.

58

Dear Diary,

I got Alex's email address and wrote to her again. I figured she probably doesn't check her messages on Twitter, because if she did, she would have definitely got back to me. I told her about rehab and explained that I have been sober now for going on four months. That I don't know what would have happened if she hadn't come along that day and sat on my park bench. I told her that she saved me. That she has had a profound impact on my life and I will be forever grateful.

59

I wake up to the sound of my phone ringing. It's Anne Marie, Maggie Horrocks' flatmate. I pick up. She tells me she's found something that might be of interest. We agree to meet in a café on Broadway Market within the hour. It's around ten o'clock in the morning and nothing has shifted on the story. The police still have a man in custody. That's all the channels are reporting. I suppose at some point I am going to have to talk to DI Brook, just to find out what the hell is going on. When they picked Charlie up, they released him pretty quickly, so I wonder what the hold-up is with Greg. Then I remember what Charlie said about it, that Sarah's death isn't linked to the others and perhaps Greg just lost it and killed her by accident. I don't want to even imagine that scenario could be true, so I busy myself getting dressed and heading out to meet Anne Marie.

She's already there when I arrive. And when I sit down, she hands me a small grey leather-bound notebook.

'It was Maggie's. I found it when I was packing up. The police must have missed it when they searched the flat. It has her online dating info in it.' She reaches across and points to a pocket on the inside of the back cover. 'I wouldn't usually do this, but I want the bastard caught, and the police are useless.' She nods at a newspaper being read by the woman at the next table. The headline reads:

KILLER STILL FREE. 'I believe you have a genuine interest in finding out who killed these women.'

'Thank you for saying that. Do you want me to send the notebook back to you?'

'No. I have no use for it. If it provides any clues to what happened, I'll be glad.'

'Okay. Thank you.'

'I hope you figure it out.'

Her eyes display a mixture of grief and expectation. She talks about her former flatmate with such fondness, it's very sad.

We finish our coffees and have a long hug before going our separate ways. I head back towards the Fields, hoping that the lush greenery in the park will lift my spirits. There's a knot in the pit of my stomach. It's been there since Greg was taken into custody. My heart is aching the way it did after I left Manchester. I feel like I've sunk right back into those feelings. I finally admit to myself that I really do miss him, but there's also nothing I can do. It's too late for that. I can't tell him that I still love him, because I'm still drinking and he won't accept that. But what he fails to realise is that I'm not a drunk like Sarah was. I used to see her knocking back booze on her own in the park every day when I went to work at the radio station. I've never been like that. Drinking tinnies in the park with other drunks.

Audrey has emailed me to ask if I'll write something for the website. The notebook in my bag might hold something newsworthy, so I reply positively, hoping that by agreeing to do it we will be on better terms. She was really pissed off with me by the end of yesterday and I need to smooth things over. She deserves some recognition for how much she's contributed to the story. So much so that I wonder if she might want to write something instead of me. I shoot her a text in that vein and she jumps on it.

I am walking at a snail's pace towards home. Mostly because I'm actually finding it quite hard to walk this morning. My body is in desperate need of some respite from the drink. I promise myself that today, if it's the only thing I do, I will detox.

The Fields is quite busy, in contrast to a week ago. People are taking advantage of the mild and sunny weather. It's as if the murders never really happened. We all carry on, I suppose, pick up our lives and try to move forward. Passing under the large oak trees that must have stood here for centuries, I make a deal with myself to just get on with it. Not look back in anger. Celebrate my new-found success at work. It's quite something having been on the teatime bulletin almost every day for a week. I wish Greg could see that.

Back home, I make a cup of tea, put my phone on silent and open Maggie's notebook. Inside, there are notes and sketches, ideas she had during moments of inspiration. It's very poignant looking through the pages filled with doodles and portraits of people she knew. I find the pocket Anne Marie showed me. Inside is a small piece of folded paper, and on it, a user name and password.

I log out of my own COMEout account and log into hers. She was popular, by the looks of it. There are roughly twenty conversations, all of which stopped on the day she was reported dead. I scroll through the windows, looking for a glimmer of something, anything, to shed light on who she met in the weeks before her death.

It's what one would expect on a dating app, a collection of good-looking men. There's Kieron, 42, a creative director with full arm tattoos. He is quite witty and clearly charmed by Maggie's replies. They discussed meeting up, but it doesn't look like anything came of it. Not that I can really ever know. They may have swapped phone numbers and continued the conversation on What'sApp. That happens a lot with dating online.

I sift through more conversations and profiles. It's a window into the most intimate part of her life. Reading these conversations makes me feel incredibly sad. Maggie was very sharp-minded. Funny and intelligent. Such a waste of a life. The whole thing makes me think of Greg again. I don't know what to say to him. I want to admit my drink problem. To possibly try again. I was so happy when I was carrying his baby, so why couldn't I stop myself drinking? I've been so cowardly about the whole thing, but I just wish he'd stop judging me. See my success. Why doesn't he get that?

The words in the notebook look all jumbled up, like the words in my head. I can't seem to find anything of interest. I don't really know what I'm looking for. I return to her dating profile. There is a conversation between her and Charlie, or the fake Charlie, so he claims. I read the messages and I have to say I agree; it doesn't sound like him at all. The whole thing sheds no light on what happened to her, though. All it does do is highlight the fact that she was looking for real love. A deep connection that might fulfil something in her. That's what we all want, isn't it? It's all Sarah Wilcox wanted, I suppose. To be loved. To be truly loved.

I feel bad about what happened to Sarah now. And about talking to her in Manchester last year. I also wonder what might have happened if I hadn't. She might still be alive and Greg might be at home with me and not in police custody. Shit. It's been almost twenty-four hours now and they still haven't released him. This isn't looking good.

60

Dear Diary,

Some days I feel on top of the world, and others I feel dreadful. Truly dreadful. Like I'm another person. I do things I'm not proud of. I have violent thoughts that come out in fits of uncontrollable anger. I just explode. I thought being sober would give me my life back, and while it has in a way, the sobriety has allowed another part of me to emerge. It's a part I truly don't understand. Some days I have really, really dark thoughts. I'm wondering if I should go back to one-on-one therapy, because something is not right. But then I'm scared of what more I might discover.

I wrote to Alex again. I explained to her that I need her. That I think I really need to find my way back into a programme to deal with who I am now, before I do something stupid, but as usual, she didn't respond. She behaves like I don't exist. I decided that perhaps she wasn't seeing my messages, so I managed to get her mobile phone number from her place of work. Pretended I had a scoop that I would only share with her. It was quite easy to get it, believe it or not.

I called, but she didn't answer, so then I texted and she finally agreed to meet up. I can't actually believe it. At last we're going to meet. I sent her my address and she's coming over. I'm so happy,

I can't describe how I feel. It's what I've been waiting for all this time. I'm going to tell her I can help her and I think she can help me too, like she did before. If it's the last thing I do, I will help her admit to her problem and I will admit mine too. We can help each other and everything will be better. I want to be better. I really do.

61

Mr Wilcox called to tell me he is in London and wants to see me. I'm not entirely sure why, but I agreed to meet him, because maybe it'll shed some light on what went on between Sarah and Greg, and maybe that'll help get Greg out of police custody.

We agreed to meet at a hotel in Old Street. He is in the lobby when I arrive, sitting in a high-backed leather chair. I recognise him from the photos I saw when I interviewed his wife. Although he looks much frailer in person. When he realises I'm standing next to him, he gets up and extends his hand to greet me. A smile softens his face and he looks younger for a brief moment.

'Alex. Thank you so much for coming. I didn't really know who else to call.'

We sit down. He rests his clasped hands on the table between us. There's no wedding ring on his finger.

'I've ordered a coffee. Would you like something?'

'I'm fine, thanks.'

Just then a waitress approaches and deposits a mug of coffee on the table before leaving us alone. He stirs in one sugar, then leans back and clasps his hands again.

'I'm not really sure where to start.' He's looking up to the ceiling, as if searching for some guidance from above.

'At the beginning?' It's a cliché, but I'm not really sure what else to say.

The hotel lobby is quiet. There's a couple checking in, but other than that, we have the place to ourselves.

He leans forward, his hands still clasped, and looks me straight in the eye.

'My wife has been hospitalised. Been up to her old tricks.'

I remember the marks on her wrists and hope that's not it.

'Sarah had a lot of problems. A lot of problems, not unlike her mother.'

The coffee is now in his hands and he takes a tiny sip.

'I found her, you know. My wife. She was sitting in bed. She'd had too much to drink, as always. But this time it wasn't the same. She didn't look the same. When you're married to an alcoholic, life is messy.'

I'm not sure where this is going, so I say nothing but try to look attentive. The painkillers I necked just before I got here are kicking in, and my body has a reprieve from the aches and pains of the abuse I've inflicted on myself this past week.

'My wife drinks too much. Always drinking. I tried to help her stop many times, but she didn't want to, you see. On this occasion, her liver just decided to give up. She won't last long. It was only ever a matter of time. She's lucky she even got this far really.'

The sound of cutlery being put away ripples through the lobby. There's a dining room to our right with a bar.

'Sarah drank as well, and that is because of her mum, but then you knew that, didn't you?'

The comment takes me aback, but I do my best not to react. Instead I focus on the steam rising from his cup, which is being blown sideways as he talks.

'Unlike her mother, Sarah did go to rehab. She did try to get better and that's partly because of you. She told me about how you met, in the park last year. That you changed her life when you took her to AA. I want to thank you for that.'

'But I didn't do anything. I really didn't. I met her a few times. Hardly knew her.'

'You changed her life. You set her on the path to recovery. Sometimes all it takes is a nudge in the right direction by a stranger. Often those around you are too close to the issue, you know.'

I wish I had something to drink. I find some gum in my bag and shove it in my mouth.

'I'm sorry, Mr Wilcox, but I think you're mistaken. I really didn't know Sarah that well.'

He's not listening to me. He's talking as if no one ever listens to him.

'All the experts say you need to get to the bottom of why you drink to stop drinking. But the reason for Sarah was complex.' He puts his head in his hands. 'She drank because of the pain, but then neither of us tried to stop her because of the pain. If I hadn't left when she was young, her life probably would have turned out very differently. I don't think I'll ever forgive myself for that, for abandoning her. Leaving her with her mother, who couldn't provide the nurture a child needs to become a secure, loving individual.'

'But you're here now. You care. I don't really follow.'

'When Sarah was a baby, I left her with her mother for a number of years. It was during those years that the damage was done. I couldn't stand the drinking, you see. I was in no state to take Sarah with me, and it would have become a legal battle. I wasn't really sure what I wanted. I just knew that I couldn't be around the drinking. I couldn't enable my wife.'

This is actually a very brave confession by an emotionally tortured man. It moves me, and for a passing moment I understand how it must feel to be in Greg's shoes.

'By the time I came back, Sarah was a different person. She had started having dark thoughts. Very dark thoughts. It was the lack of love in her that caused it. I know that now.'

His hands are shaking, not unlike mine but for different reasons, so he puts the coffee down on the table and wipes both hands over his face, an act that gives him a moment to think.

'Do you mind me asking?' I say. 'What do you mean by dark thoughts?'

'By the age of eight, she was having episodes, and she needed treatment, but by then it was too late.'

'Too late for what?'

'To change what had happened to her.'

He rests his hands on the table and leans forward, his head dropping. When he eventually looks up, the overwhelming emotion on his face is shame. I know what shame looks like. I've lived with it all my life.

'I'm not sure why I'm telling you this.'

'Because I'm a journalist and you want the truth?'

He ignores me and continues.

305

'I don't suppose it matters anyway. It will all come out in the end. You see, as hard as this is to admit, I think Sarah's sobriety may have had a profound effect on her, and maybe she got involved in something that wasn't quite right.'

'What exactly do you mean?'

'I spoke to Tim her therapist at rehab. I think that was his name. Anyway, he explained that she had serious trauma that had created neurological issues.'

He opens a notebook that was on the table and reads from it.

'He said that those traumatic feelings had become unconscious memories hidden in her deepest, darkest vaults. That the lights connecting to the neurological pathway had gone out so she was able to move her life forward temporarily. But the sobriety lit up this pathway, which he believes could have thrust her backwards to relive that trauma. The results, he said, could be very dangerous. She could have violent episodes, triggered by the memories that had started to come back. I'm wondering if this might be partly responsible for what's happened here.'

'What are you saying, Mr Wilcox? That your daughter was capable of murder?'

'I suppose I am.'

His head drops again, but my story just took a turn in an award-winning direction. I wonder if DI Brook is aware of this aspect of Sarah's personality. I need to tell him. Maybe it will help Greg's case.

'I truly believe that my wife is in hospital because of her guilt. I think she knows something important, but she's in no state to talk yet. She's unconscious, you see. This time she almost finished herself off.'

'I see.'

'The police say they still haven't located the flat where Sarah was living in London, but that's because she rented it in a different name. She didn't want her mother to find her at any cost.'

'Do you know what name she used?'

He looks very serious.

'She rented a place in your name, Alex. I told the police this morning.'

62

I call DI Brook from the hotel lobby and question him about the fake profile set up in Charlie's name, but he offers no explanation and sticks to the official line that they are investigating all leads. It's infuriating, to say the least. I also tell him I'm aware of the fact that Sarah was a violent individual who was renting a flat in my name, but all he does is thank me for my concerns and hang up.

Mr Wilcox has agreed to do an interview, given that his wife is now in hospital and his daughter is dead. He wants to open up about Sarah's mental health and her alcoholism, believing that it might have some bearing on the case. The news centre is unsure what to make of my latest scoop, but they agree to it for lack of knowing what else to do with the story. They need a new line to keep it going, as the police haven't said anything since yesterday. I'm hoping it might keep the focus off the man in custody too, buy some time on that side of things. So Mr Wilcox and I take a cab to HQ.

The interview is raw, emotional and passionate. He's a broken man, confessing his darkest secrets for the country to judge. He admits he is guilty of not addressing Sarah's drinking when it started because he was in denial, as he had been about his wife for most of his married life. He urges people to take alcoholism seriously. For the government to recognise it as an inherent disease in order to make diagnosis easier and treatment cheaper. He believes this would help families own up to it rather than pretend it isn't happening. Talking to us is part of that denial finally being lifted, I suppose. He feels that the police have made a hash of things and he is angry that it has resulted in his wife being in hospital.

The lawyers are going to have to look at it to ensure we can't be sued by the Met for influencing the investigation, but this is the stuff TV is made for. We are about to link it to the bigger picture, using the string of murders to open up a real debate about how the country is dealing with alcoholism. It is an incredibly moving interview. A grown man admitting he failed his daughter – well, it doesn't get much stronger than that.

Within an hour of the interview going live, it has received upwards of one million hits.

Audrey is elated. 'I'm going to get a promotion on the back of this, and you'll probably end up with something too. How lucky is that, I mean, that we got the interview. I'm sorry if I've been a bit grouchy lately, I'm just tired and I think the case was getting to me.'

'That's okay. Sometimes things just work out another way. Enjoy this moment, Audrey.'

'I've got almost twenty thousand Twitter followers now – that's power in our game.'

'It is,' I agree.

'You've gone over a hundred thousand followers, Alex, you're like the Twitter queen of the channel. It's not been a bad week, has it?'

'Not at all. This has launched your career, and cemented mine.'

'Which is great, isn't it? But there's a killer still out there. That hasn't changed.'

'Not for much longer, I hope. I have a feeling that it might soon be over. I'm going to get a coffee,' I tell her. 'Want one?'

'No, thanks.'

Walking out of the news centre, a real sense of achievement fills me for the very first time in my career. Now the editors will have to take me seriously. The story is a national obsession. #SarahWilcoxRIP is trending on Twitter since Mr Wilcox spoke out about the results of his denial.

I find a spot on the terrace outside with my coffee to soak it all up. I hope it won't be long before they release Greg now so we can talk things through properly. There's no way he's involved with any of this, I'm sure of it. Mr Wilcox practically told me his daughter was capable of killing. The police must be putting that all together. They must. I've made a resolution to tell Greg exactly what's going on with me. To be honest and see what he says.

The air this evening is warmer than it has been for a while, and with it comes a softening of my fears. Just one week ago I was working on the desk, a job I'd been sidelined into. My career was starting to falter, but this story has changed all of that. It has secured my position in the natural pecking order. I'm a well-respected reporter now. It has saved me in a way. I can't remember how many painkillers I have taken today, but I feel quite light-headed. That's another thing I need to cut out, and I will. I'm going to get better.

I get a call from the on-shift editor to thank me for the interview and to tell me to go home. Nothing is moving on this story, and if it does, they have someone who can pick up the slack. I think I've paid my dues and finally feel I can relax about my job security for a change.

I feel mildly optimistic about the future for the first time in a while, so when I spot DI Brook striding towards me flanked by two uniformed officers, it's a bit of a surprise.

'Hello, Inspector. Did you see the interview?'

'I did, strong stuff, but that's not why I'm here.'

'Are you going to let Greg go now? I'm sure he's filled you in on how he knew Sarah. He's no killer. In fact, she's the one with a violent past.'

'Yes, we know. And that's actually why I'm here, because our investigation has uncovered new information. Alex South, I'm arresting you in connection with the murder of Sarah Wilcox. I have to caution you that anything you say may be used against you in a court of law.'

'What? What are you talking about?'

'Don't make this difficult on yourself, Ms South. I need you to come with me.'

63

They cuff me and put me in a police car before driving me away. Thankfully it is getting on for nine o'clock, so the dayside teams have gone home and the terrace is quiet, although Ayla is having a fag by the main doors. I'm not sure whether she sees me, but it won't take long to filter through if she did. Fucking hell, how did I end up in a police car with cuffs on? I wish I'd never bloody met the Wilcox family.

I am deposited at the police station and put in a cell like a real criminal. I don't get the interview room this time. The room where DI Brook first questioned me about my relationship with Sarah Wilcox. He thinks I killed Sarah or in some way was involved in her death. It's absurd.

They leave me in the cell overnight, and after a bowl of what can only be described as the worst porridge I've ever tasted, they take me to the interview room. Without a drink to prop me up, my body has started to enter total withdrawal and is collapsing into an unrecognisably broken state. I barely slept at all last night, instead experiencing cold sweats that have left my clothes more than a bit damp. It's fair to say I've never felt this bad in my entire life. Not even when I lost my unborn child. That was dreadful, but there was a numbness to it all. Plus there was Greg supporting me. And there were parameters to measure it by. This, however, is the unknown, so physically gruelling I feel like I could die.

DI Brook appears after a little while, a file in his hand. He looks like a man about to crack the case wide open. Energised. He swoops down on the seat opposite me, and a woman I've never seen before follows him into the room. He doesn't spend time dilly-dallying and cuts straight to the chase.

'For the tape. Interview with Alex South of Navarino Grove, London Fields, in connection with the death of Sarah Wilcox of Navarino Mansions, London Fields. Ms South, we know you visited Sarah Wilcox at her London flat even though you said you barely knew her. We also know that you received a call from her number, and a text message, shortly before you were seen entering her home on the night before her body was found. We have an eyewitness.'

Sarah lived in the block Greg recognised the other evening, the one opposite Mary's place. I'm assuming Mary is the witness. I'm angry that she didn't just come out and ask me about that night. The night I had my blackout. That's obviously what they're getting at, because yes, I now remember that I did receive a text from Sarah, I just don't remember what happened next. This is turning into my worst nightmare. DI Brook clears his throat before opening the file in front of him.

'This is an image from a CCTV camera on the corner of the road where Sarah Wilcox rented a flat in your name. It shows you pushing a wheelie bin away from the mansions in the direction of the park around the time of her death. Do you want to tell us what you were doing there? What were you doing with a wheelie bin outside Sarah's flat the night she died?'

That's when I start to hyperventilate. I can't quite take it all in.

DI Brook pushes the image across the table so it is under my nose. When I look down, I recognise myself. I can't remember any of it, though. I was drunk to the point of blackout. I've done some really crazy things while blacked out, but this? This takes the prize, an award-winning fuck-up.

'Now is the time to talk, Ms South.'

But I can't. I can't talk, because the events of that night are so unclear. Fortunately, a knock on the door stops the interrogation and offers me a reprieve. DI Brook disappears, leaving me with his colleague. She just sits there in silence, watching every twitch I make, which is a lot of twitches because my body is in free fall and desperate for a drink. It's been over twelve hours since they brought me in. Over twelve hours since I've had a drink. My body is going cold turkey, and not out of choice. This is dangerous territory for an alcoholic.

'Alex, If you tell us the truth about what you did, it will help, you know.'

'I can't.'

'Yes you can.'

'I'm…'

I know what I need to say, but everything in me is resisting.

'Go on. You can talk to me, Alex.'

Her eyes are softer now. Either that or I'm hallucinating. I'm seeing all kinds of things actually. Namely Sarah standing in the corner of the room. I shake my head as if that will help clear my brain. I have to tell someone. I have to say it, because I have to survive.

'I'm… I'm a…'

'I'm listening.'

'I'm an alcoholic and I need a drink or you could end up questioning me in hospital.'

'What?' I can see she isn't expecting that.

'I'm an alcoholic. I'm not proud of it, but I am, and I haven't had a drink now for probably fourteen hours and I'm starting to get the shakes. It's quite dangerous to just stop; it can kill a person, you know.'

At this, she almost chokes, then stands up and leaves me alone in the room.

When DI Brook returns, which isn't for quite a while, he has a doctor with him, who agrees that I need a drink or they could be dealing with another dead person, this time one in their custody. We make a deal: a glass of vodka for everything I know about Sarah Wilcox.

I tell them about the emails and the messages I've received on social media recently, and how I ignored them thinking it was just someone being a bit of a weirdo. I get plenty of crappy emails in my line of work. I answered her text because it was a good lead and I was desperate to impress my editors. I must have gone there that night to hear her out, but I honestly can't remember what happened because I blacked out. The doctor confirms this is a real possibility, not that it helps my case, because that's when they charge me with the murder. The admission that I went there is enough, apparently. I should have asked for a lawyer, but I'm not in the right frame of mind. The doctor understands it, but the police don't.

They think I'm just some drunk making excuses for bad behaviour.

They say they have forensic evidence that I was in Sarah's flat, and that I used the wheelie bin to dump her body in the park. I have no comeback to that, because I can't prove otherwise. The grazes on my wrist and bruise on my leg don't look good. They are clear signs of a struggle, which in their minds means I killed her. They say it is only a matter of time before they connect the other murders to me.

They have released Greg. He left me a note that they allow me to read. I kind of wish they hadn't, because it just smashes my heart into a million pieces all over again.

> Dear Alex.
>
> It was genuinely lovely to see you and to see that you're doing so well. I want you to know that I will always love you, but I can't go back to being in a relationship with an active drinker who is not yet in a recovery programme. Alcohol by the looks of it is still your first love, and I can't compete with that. You probably don't remember sending them, but I did receive some messages from you over the past year. They were aggressive and defensive at the same time. I put it down to the drink, but hoped with your new job you'd managed to face the fact that you have a problem. Given what the police have told me, though, I see that everything is not quite what it seems on the surface. I urge you to go back to AA so that you can beat

this thing. You have a disease that is going to destroy your life unless you ask for proper help. You need a professional to guide you into recovery. You need to face up to things before it's too late, if you do want to be a mum.

I can't enable you any more, I'm sorry. I just wish you'd sort yourself out, because you can be such a lovely person, but the alcoholism needs treatment before it ruins your life, and it will, it always does one way or the other. You need to stop lying to yourself and face the music.

I wish I'd sent the Milk Tray, but it wasn't me.

Take care of yourself.

Greg

Everything I've worked so hard to achieve is over now, as is my relationship with alcohol. I suppose that is the only shining light amidst this darkness. I don't know how I ended up here. Whether I'm a victim or a killer. I can't remember what happened that night. That's the absolute worst of it, because I don't know if I'm innocent or guilty. The booze drove me to that place. A place of no defence. I suppose this is what they call rock bottom.

Epilogue

July 2018

Dear Diary,

I'm an alcoholic and I am powerless over alcohol.

I admitted this for the first time in my life while in police custody. I have now been dry for one hundred and sixteen days.

The murder charge against me was changed after a discovery was made in Sarah's flat. I may never know what happened that night, or whether I killed her. It's quite hard to live with that, but I simply can't remember. The coroner believes she died from a fatal dose of GHB mixed with alcohol, which she probably ingested before I got there, rather than the knock on the head that likely occurred in a fight we must have had. That was the logical explanation given the marks on my body.

The key found on her body unlocked a cupboard that held stocks of GHB as well as photos of Jade Soron, Maggie Horrocks, Alice Fessy – and me. The police also discovered a diary containing a suicide note. The note was Sarah's way of helping me in her last moments, I suppose, because without it I could have been convicted of murder. It's not a done deal yet, though, as my defence has to prove beyond reasonable doubt that I didn't do it, and that's quite difficult in such circumstances, so I'm told. There's a lot of evidence against me, but then there's a lot of evidence against her too. Charlie's identity was stolen and I believe that she used it to attract the girls she killed.

The most likely reason why I put her body in a wheelie bin and took it out to the park is that I thought I'd killed her during a fight. In my panic, I tried to cover up the accident and thought the police would see her death as part of their ongoing investigations. This is all supposition, of course, as I can't remember what I did. I definitely had no idea at the time of receiving the text from Sarah that she had killed Jade, Maggie and Alice. The message she sent was deleted from my phone. I must have done that too. The police are working on trying to get it back. That should help my defence.

Sarah's therapist supports the suicide theory. He told the police that after rehab she must have been overwhelmed with an intense sense of hopelessness when she realised what she'd done as a sober person. Put that with being unable to help me and it had created the kind of despair that saw her take her own life.

The police couldn't put the other murders together at first because it really had nothing to do with online dating and everything to do with me. I was the connection. All three women were linked to me or friends of mine on Facebook. Sarah simply used the dating app with a false identity to start a conversation with them. She was never after a sexual relationship; she just wanted to get them alone in a bar so she could drug them which allowed her to strangle them.

Her motivation could have been as fundamental as seeking attention from me, but the sad reality is that I'd only met Maggie Horrocks once, and the other two were just friends of friends, people I'd never met. The Milk Tray had been sent by Sarah too, in a bid to make me think of the past and what I'd lost. She had become a woman obsessed with fixing me instead of fixing herself, and had externalised the process after being left to her own devices without the proper follow-on care. I might have been able to help her if I'd responded to her messages, but we'll never know now.

The police had the diary analysed by a string of professionals, who all said the same thing. That Sarah Wilcox showed signs of obsessive behaviour towards me. The fact that she had moved to within half a mile of where I lived and rented a flat in my name had sealed that theory for them. After that, they spoke to Mr Wilcox and discovered that she had seen a child psychologist when she was eight, but denial in the family had prevented further sessions that could have turned her life around.

It was noted in her file from that time that Sarah had displayed psychopathic tendencies, expressing a desire to kill her mother. Her parents knew she was only nine years old when she started drinking, but they didn't stop it because it had ironically turned her into a better person by suppressing those evil thoughts.

I'm an alcoholic and I have no control over alcohol. I wish I had been able to say that a year ago, because if I had, none of this would have happened and four bright, amazing women might not have died. It's hard to know what might have happened to Sarah had she had the proper care she needed post-rehab; I like to think she could have made a full recovery. My therapist told me that she was thrown into sobriety too quickly without a loving, nurturing carer to help her face her past in a safe environment, which had left her fractured mind extremely vulnerable to the past traumas she had started to recall.

I'm an alcoholic and powerless over alcohol. I can say that now, but it took me being arrested for murder to admit it to myself. The police agreed to change the charges to disposal of a corpse with intent to obstruct or prevent a coroner's inquest, which can carry a heavy sentence, but I might get away with a fine because of the suicide theory.

The irony is that I now have upwards of two million Twitter followers, having embraced my alcoholism and told my story, a number that will surely only grow because I am going to write a book about my addiction and where it got me. Greg has been in touch to tell me how proud he is of me and that he hopes the trial goes well. Who knows what the future holds on that score. I'm trying to stay in the present and take it one day at a time, something Sarah was unable to do because her fractured mind pushed her between two worlds, past traumas and present frustrations.

I'm an alcoholic whose deep denial caused the deaths of four women, and for that I am eternally sorry and promise never to drink again.

Who are you?

Acknowledgements

I'd like to say a massive thank you to Steph, Laura, Rod, Rob, Seun, Jamie and David Y, who in the early days gave me critical feedback and support to get this book off the ground. To Pete for brainstorming with me over many many cups of tea. To Ivan who believed in it from its conception. To Cathal. To Sara who pushed me onwards with her genuine enthusiasm and Donna who got me closer to the finish line. To Tricia and Danielle who spurred me on when I lost the plot. To Russell. To Nigel who helped me through an incredibly tough time. To my brother Adam and his crew. To Marie. To David L. To Fatih for being a friend for life. To Nadene. To Alex who has supported my writing with conviction. To the CWA. To my colleagues in BBC Newsgathering who have always shown enthusiasm for my writing endeavours. To George. To Sinead. To Alan. To Caroline. To Guney. To the Al-Anon family. To everyone at Canelo for being so supportive and excited at the prospect of bringing this story to light. And lastly but not least, to Amber and crew, who continue to inspire me and make me believe that the future is brighter.

About the Author

Jody Sabral is based between the South Coast and London, where she works as a Foreign Desk editor and video producer at the BBC. She is a graduate of the MA in Crime Fiction at City University, London. Jody worked as a journalist in Turkey for ten years, covering the region for various international broadcasters. She self-published her first book Changing Borders in 2012 and won the CWA Debut Dagger in 2014 for her second novel The Movement. In addition to working for the BBC, Jody also writes for the Huffington Post, Al–Monitor and Brics Post.